MONTANA WEDDINGS

*Three sensational stories,
three exceptional women,
three marriages of convenience,
and three wild, sexy men on their
way to wedded bliss in Whitehorn!*

Suzanna Brennan: With a baby on the way, it seemed rather too late for Suzanna to wish for her hasty groom-to-be's heart. But once she's sharing her bed with her new husband, she can't help wishing for more…

Diana Brennan: Diana wasn't as sentimental about love as her younger sister. So there didn't seem to be any harm in her tying the knot with the brooding single dad she had once loved from afar…

Isabelle Brennan: Though this society woman knew better than to take the name of a half-breed rancher, sassy Isabelle was ready to take on the challenge of being Kyle 'Running Horse' Brennan's wife to save her family ranch. And if her marriage is the match she hopes it will be, Isabelle will show generations of Brennan brides just what it takes to turn a marriage of convenience into a forever kind of love!

CHRISTINE RIMMER

A reader favourite whose books consistently appear on the *USA Today* best-seller lists, Christine Rimmer has written over thirty novels for Silhouette®. Her stories have been nominated for numerous awards, including the Romance Writers of America RITA Award and the *Romantic Times Magazine's* Series Storyteller of the Year Award.

JENNIFER GREENE

Jennifer Greene has been married to her hero for over twenty-five years, which is why she's such an exuberant believer in love stories. Known for her warm characters and real-life humour, Jennifer has won numerous honours, ranging from RWA's Hall of Fame Award to *Romantic Times Magazine's* Lifetime and Career Achievement Awards. She loves children, dogs, cats, antiques and, of course, books.

CHERYL ST JOHN

Cheryl's first historical book was nominated for the Romance Writers of America's prestigious RITA Award. Cheryl is a married mother of four and a grandmother several times over. You can write to her, sending a self-addressed envelope, to: PO Box 12142, Florence Station, Omaha, NE 68112-0142, USA.

MONTANA WEDDINGS

Christine Rimmer
Jennifer Greene
Cheryl St John

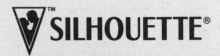

™ SILHOUETTE®

*All the characters in this book have no existence outside the imagination
of the author, and have no relation whatsoever to anyone bearing the
same name or names. They are not even distantly inspired by any
individual known or unknown to the author, and all the incidents are
pure invention.*

*First published in Great Britain 2001.
Silhouette Books, Eton House, 18-24 Paradise Road,
Richmond, Surrey TW9 1SR*

MONTANA WEDDINGS © Harlequin Books S.A. 2001

The publisher acknowledges the copyright holders of the
individual works as follows:

SUZANNA © Harlequin Books S.A. 2000
DIANA © Harlequin Books S.A. 2000
ISABELLE © Harlequin Books S.A. 2000

*Special thanks and acknowledgement are given to Christine Rimmer,
Jennifer Greene and Cheryl St John for their contribution to
Montana Weddings. This book was originally published as
Montana Mavericks: Big Sky Brides*

ISBN 0 373 04724 X

107-0901

*Printed and bound in Spain
by Litografia Rosés S.A., Barcelona*

CONTENTS

Dear Reader,

Looks like there are going to be more weddings under the Big Sky as Silhouette® brings you MONTANA WEDDINGS, an anthology with three brand-new stories by reader favourites Christine Rimmer, Jennifer Greene and Cheryl St John, and featuring an exciting new family. The Brennans are ranchers who go way back. In fact, this anthology brings you the contemporary marriage-of-convenience stories of Suzanna and Diana Brennan, as well as a historical romantic tale featuring their great-great-grandmother Isabelle Brennan.

MONTANA WEDDINGS is just one of the brand-new MONTANA BRIDES stories we have in store for you in the coming months. In August 2001, Silhouette Special Edition® presented a sexy new story by Jackie Merritt, which introduced the other half of the exciting Kincaid clan. Then, starting this month, the lives and loves of the Kincaid heirs will be told over twelve books, when the newest continuity series, MONTANA BRIDES, begins in earnest!

We at Silhouette hope you enjoy this anthology, as well as the rest of the forthcoming MONTANA BRIDES, where more of your favourite authors will take you back to the town where passions run deep...and love lasts forever!

Happy reading!

The Editors

SUZANNA

Christine Rimmer

For Tom and Ed

Prologue

Trailing satin ribbons, Sierra Conroy McLaine's wedding bouquet of white Derringer roses sailed through air. All the single girls reached up eager hands.

"It's mine!"

"I've got it!"

The bouquet found its highest point. Excited, happy cries followed it down.

"Oh, look! Here it comes...."

Suzanna Brennan closed her eyes. She didn't need to look. She *knew*.

And she was right. The roses dropped right into her outstretched arms.

"Suzanna!" one of the girls cried. "Suzanna's got it!"

There was more laughter—and a few rueful sighs.

Suzanna opened her eyes and looked down at her prize. So beautiful, those velvety, snowy-white blooms. And it was so *right* that she should be the one to catch it. After all, according to local superstition, any girl who caught a bridal bouquet of roses from the Derringer garden would marry soon and happily.

Her engagement diamond sparkling on her hand, Suzanna brought the flowers close for an intoxicating whiff. A little hint of heaven, the smell of those roses.

Lucky me, she thought. Lucky me, I've got it all. In five months, on March twenty-fourth, *I'll* be the one tossing the bouquet....

Chapter 1

"Those eggs are not going to eat themselves."

Suzanna stopped pushing the food around on her plate and looked across the breakfast table into blue eyes much like her own. Say it, she silently commanded herself. Just open your mouth and tell him. You swore that you would. This very morning, you swore it.

And yesterday morning.

And the morning before that.

It had gotten to be a habit, for the past month or so. Every morning Suzanna got up and threw up—and then promised her own grim image in the bathroom mirror that this was the day she would tell her father about the baby.

So far, every day, she had broken that promise. And today was turning out the same as all the other ones. She just couldn't make herself do it.

"I guess I'm not too hungry," she muttered, as she silently called herself a yellow-bellied coward.

"A body needs fuel," Frank Brennan coaxed.

So Suzanna made herself spear up a bite of the eggs. She stuck it into her mouth and chewed, fighting an unnerving feeling of queasiness. Over the past few weeks, she had discovered that she didn't much care for eggs anymore. She didn't much care for food, period, of late. Pregnancy and guilt had conspired to ruin her appetite.

To her surprise, the eggs went down all right.

Her father was still watching her. She could see in those eyes that he was worried about her. Wondering what was wrong with her. And waiting for her to tell him. But she just couldn't. Not today.

Tomorrow. Yes. Tomorrow, she would do it. Tomorrow...

Doggedly, Suzanna ate more eggs, washing them down with milk. Concentrating on her breakfast had a definite advantage—it gave her an excuse to stop looking into her father's eyes.

"The new man's due today," he said.

She looked up again, frowning, her mind still stuck on that important promise she never managed to keep.

"Nash Morgan," her father reminded her. "The new horse trainer." A teasing light pushed the worry from his eyes a little. "I think I mentioned him once or twice."

They shared a smile. "Yes," Suzanna said. "I believe you did." Sometimes it seemed that Nash Morgan was all her father talked about since he'd met the man and hired him a few weeks back at the Yellowstone Quarter Horse Show.

On the Big Sky, the ranch that had been in Suzanna's family for several generations now, they raised horses, quarter horses known for their stamina, good looks, steady dispositions and plain cow sense. The Big Sky had a well-deserved reputation for producing fine, well-trained stock. And Frank Brennan was always on the lookout for a certain kind of trainer, for a man who had "the touch," as he called it, a man who knew how to "think like a horse." Such men were rarities, Suzanna's father always said. And Frank Brennan believed that Nash Morgan was just such a man.

Suzanna's father had had to do some fancy talking and pay a very high salary to get this paragon to come and work for him. Nash Morgan, apparently, was in the market for his own horse ranch now. But Frank had a plan. If the man worked out the way Frank thought he would, he hoped to talk the trainer into investing his talents, his capital—and his future—in the Big Sky.

"If he gets here before lunch, you can show him around," her father suggested. "See he gets settled in, tell him where to park his rig—and put him in the cabin.'' Her father referred to the separate cottage several hundred feet behind the main house, where business guests always stayed. ''I don't want him in the bunkhouse with the rest of the men. I want him to feel comfortable and I want him to—''

''Dad, the cabin's all ready for him. I promise, I'll make him feel welcome.'' That, at least, was a vow she knew she could keep.

Her father left to join the other men at the corrals a few minutes later. Suzanna cleaned up the kitchen and got the stew meat simmering for lunch. Then she went to the office off the living room and worked for a couple of hours, paying bills and checking on feed orders.

Suzanna had a business degree, and she'd been putting it to use, handling all the bookkeeping for the Big Sky, since her final return home from college out in Sacramento last January. She'd met Bryan Cummings there, in Sacramento. But Bryan was long gone now. He'd joined the Peace Corps three months ago, back in March—on the day they were supposed to have been married, as a matter of fact.

So much for the luck of the Derringer roses.

At least she had her education, she kept telling herself. She wouldn't have to worry about that *and* about trying to raise a baby on her own.

As a rule, taking care of the books always soothed her. Suzanna enjoyed the orderliness of numbers, the way there was always a right answer and all a person had to do was find it. But today, the columns of figures on her computer screen couldn't hold her attention. She kept making errors, entering data incorrectly, punching up the wrong commands, blinking back to the present to find herself staring into the enormous stone fireplace opposite the old mahogany desk where she sat. No fire burned there now.

She looked toward the window. A mild, clear June day. Outside, beyond the shadows of the wraparound porch, the endless Montana sky was blue as her father's loving eyes.

Maybe she should get out and ride. She could choose one of the two-year-olds just graduating from the round pen, where every Big Sky colt's real training began. She could give the animal a little break from his lessons—and get her mind off that promise she was going to have to keep one of these days very soon.

With a sigh, Suzanna shut down her computer and left the office. She wandered up the stairs to the second floor. And then, instead of going into her room to trade her sneakers for some heavy socks and the old beat-up boots she used for riding, she found herself standing on the landing at the top of the stairs, looking at the pull-down ladder that led to the attic.

The heavy satin rope that would bring the ladder down was anchored along the wall. Suzanna unhooked the rope and gave a tug, caught the center joint and swung the bottom section of rungs to the floor. Then she started climbing.

Suzanna loved the attic. On a mild day like today, it was toasty warm and smelled rather pleasantly of wood and dust. It was also full of several genera- tions' worth of treasures, things that the Brennans didn't really need anymore yet somehow couldn't bear to throw away. The two small windows at ei- ther end let in enough light to see by, but Suzanna pulled the chain on the bare bulb overhead anyway.

Dust motes danced in the air around her as she surveyed the rows of boxes stacked along the eaves, boxes full of Christmas decorations and old clothes, of dishes and linens and toys and board games. In addition to all the boxes, there were floor lamps with their shades missing and chairs with wobbly legs. The two-story dollhouse, which had first belonged to her big sister, Diana, and eventually to Suzanna herself, stood in a corner beside a sagging, faded easy chair.

And to the right of the dollhouse, beneath the east window, sat her great-great-grandmother Isabelle's cedar hope chest. The old boards creaked beneath her sneakers as Suzanna approached the chest. When she reached it, she knelt and took the key from where it hung on a nail beside the window.

"This is too self-indulgent," she whispered aloud to the silent stacks of boxes and the broken-down furniture. "I shouldn't...."

But she did. She stuck the key in the tarnished brass lock, gave it a turn and lifted the lid.

A wistful smile curved Suzanna's lips at the mingled scents that wafted up to her, lemon and lavender, oranges and cloves. Over the years, the women of her family had taken care of the trunk and its contents. The satins and laces had been lovingly cleaned and mended whenever necessary. And a variety of sachets kept everything smelling sweet.

Right there on top was the dress, Great-Great-Grandmother Isabelle's wedding gown of silk and Irish lace. Like the trunk's lining, the gown had mellowed to ivory over the years.

"Almost..." Suzanna whispered.

Almost, she had worn this dress. Almost, she had lived the dream she'd cherished since she'd been a little girl playing with the dollhouse inherited from her sister—to walk down the aisle in the wedding gown her great-great-grandmother had worn on the day she'd married Kyle Running Horse Brennan, over a century ago.

Now, *that* had been a scandal: the pretty, Eastern-educated Cooper girl's marriage to the handsome but penniless half-breed who worked as foreman on her father's ranch. But Isabelle had bravely defied the disapproval of her neighbors. She had married for love and never regretted it.

There had been a string of happy Brennan marriages down the years since then. Suzanna had thought hers would be the next one. She'd had a dream of a Brennan-style wedding, of a Brennan-style lifetime of love.

And when that dream had slipped away from her, she had gone just a little…well, there was only one word for it.

Crazy.

Yes. She'd gone a little crazy, thinking that even the Derringer roses hadn't been powerful enough to make her wish come true. Thinking of how she'd *saved* herself for her wedding night with Bryan. And now the wedding night was here, and Bryan wasn't.

Crazy. That was how she'd felt. Crazy enough to go and have herself a wedding night anyway.

With some footloose cowboy.

Some cowboy whose real name she didn't even know.

She'd been twenty-two on the day Bryan left her at the altar. She was *still* twenty-two, but she felt a lot older now. Years older. And sadder. And wiser. And *guiltier*…

"Fool," she whispered to the ivory lace. "Silly, dreamy-eyed, *reckless* fool…" She let out a small moan of self-disgust.

And downstairs, the doorbell rang.

Suzanna glanced over her shoulder toward the ladder to the second floor.

It must be her father's new horse trainer.

She lowered the lid of the chest and was about to turn the key when she spotted the tiny bit of lace sticking out. She raised the lid again and swiftly folded the lace out of the way.

That was when she noticed that a section of the trunk's lining, right near the lock, had come loose from the wood. She'd have to come up later and figure out the best way to repair the damage. She slipped her finger into the gap between satin and wood—and felt something wedged between the lining and the wall of the trunk.

Suzanna leaned closer to peer into the narrow space. Envelopes. They were yellowed with age like the trunk lining, like her great-great-grandmother's wedding dress.

She had to pull loose more of the lining to get them all out. There were six of them, each one addressed to Mr. Kyle Running Horse Brennan in a flowing, rounded, very feminine hand.

Apparently, she hadn't matured as much in the past few months as she'd thought. That dreamy-eyed fool must still live inside her. Because her heart pounded hard in pure elation.

From Isabelle. The letters were from Isabelle. Suzanna would have known it even if the return address hadn't told her so.

Could it really be possible? Might she actually be holding Isabelle's love letters to Kyle in her hands— love letters hidden away for over a hundred years now?

Downstairs, the doorbell rang again.

Suzanna ordered her heart to a more dignified

rhythm. The love letters would have to wait—if they really *were* love letters. By now, Mr. Nash Morgan must doubt that anybody was home. In a minute, he'd wander off toward the corrals in search of the welcome she wasn't providing. And her father would wonder why she hadn't had the courtesy to answer the door.

Suzanna shut and locked the trunk. She hooked the key on its nail. Then she flew to the light, pulled the string and rushed down the ladder, levering it up so quickly that it clapped hard against the frame.

She didn't even bother with hooking the rope back into its place on the wall. She just left it dangling and raced to her room where she yanked open the bottom drawer of her bureau and tucked the envelopes beneath a stack of heavy winter sweaters.

The doorbell rang for the third time as she pounded down the stairs. "I'm coming, I'm coming," she muttered under her breath. She could see the tall form of a man through the etched and frosted oval of glass in the center of the front door.

"I'm coming!" She called out that time, so he would know she was on her way.

She paused at the bottom of the stairs to smooth her hair and tuck her shirt more neatly into her Wranglers, running her hand nervously over her stomach, thinking that nothing showed yet, thank goodness. Finally, she put on a smile and pulled open the door.

"I'm so sorry, I was—" The words turned to dust in her throat.

And her heart froze in her chest, just stopped dead—and then began beating triple time.

Oh, sweet Lord. It was *him*. The man she'd met on what should have been her wedding night. The man she'd known only as Slim.

It couldn't be....

But it was.

The father of her unborn child was standing right before her on her own front porch.

Chapter 2

Like someone blinded by a hard burst of piercing light, Suzanna blinked. Maybe she was just imagining—but no. When she dared to look again, he was still there. Still Slim. She would have known those leaf-green eyes anywhere. For an awful moment, she was certain that she would throw up on his worn rawhide boots.

Suzanna swallowed hard, pushing down the urge to be sick, using every ounce of grim determination she possessed. It worked, to a degree. She still felt dangerously unsettled, but the immediate danger of losing her breakfast had passed.

Slim took off his hat. "Nash Morgan, ma'am." His voice was low and soft, with a sort of a purr in it, just the way she remembered. He smiled, a true cowboy's smile, friendly but not forward. A pleased-to-meet-you sort of smile.

He didn't know her! Dear Lord, he'd forgotten.

But that couldn't be, could it? He had, after all, spent a whole night with her. The lights might have been low—in that roadhouse and then later, in that room at the motel. But they hadn't been *that* low. He'd gotten a good look at her. At *all* of her.

And besides, she'd seen that flash of recognition in his eyes when she first opened the door—hadn't she?

He held out his hand. She took it automatically, felt the heat of it, the strength in it, the roughness of calluses along the palms and finger joints. A blush tried to creep up her neck as she recalled the way those hands had felt gliding along her naked skin. She ordered that blush down.

"Mr. Morgan." She smiled at him, a big, fake smile that she prayed he wouldn't recognize as such. "Our new horse trainer."

"That's right."

"Welcome to the Big Sky." Her hand still lay enclosed in his. She pulled it free.

"Frank's daughter, right?"

"Yes. That's right. Suzanna." She was positive now. He didn't remember. She'd been just another warm and willing woman to him. How many must there have been for her to have vanished from his mind after only three short months?

Suzanna decided it would be safer not to ask herself such a dangerous question right now.

Beyond his shoulder, down the stone walk and past the white picket fence that defined the yard, a dark green pickup and a gooseneck trailer waited in the bright late-morning sun.

She gestured toward the vehicle. ''There's room in the wagon shed for your rig.'' She tipped her head toward the structure in question, several hundred feet to her right, near the well and the slowly turning windmill that loomed above it.

He was staring at her so strangely. Did she look as stunned and sick at heart as she felt? She babbled more suggestions. ''There's a tack room in the closed-off end. You're welcome to store whatever riding gear you've brought in there. You have horses in that trailer?''

He shrugged. ''It's empty.''

''Oh. Well. All right, then just put it with the pickup.''

''I'll do that.'' He started to turn away.

''Oh. And…'' He stopped. Looked at her again, waiting. She gulped. ''When you're done, come on back and I'll take you to your quarters, see that you get settled in.''

''Good enough.''

She watched him stride down the steps and along the walk, admiring in spite of herself the proud breadth of his shoulders and the way that the sun picked up auburn lights in his thick dark hair.

It didn't take him long to come striding back.

This can't really be happening, Suzanna kept thinking, as she went through the motions of making him welcome.

She led him to the cabin. He looked around and shook his head. "This is real nice. But I'd prefer to stay with the other men."

"But my father thought you'd be more comfortable if you had your own—"

"As long as I'm here, those men will be training your horses by my methods. I want to get to know them. You learn a lot more about a man who bunks next to you."

So she took him to the bunkhouse, gave him a bed and showed him where he could stash his personal belongings. The whole time, images of their night together kept trying to sneak into her mind, stealing her breath and threatening to make her voice crack.

Clear as his tanned face before her now, she could see him—first at that roadhouse outside of Billings where they'd met, bending across the felt-topped pool table to sink a shot, glancing up to give her a teasing smile. And then later, his face above her, those eyes that didn't know her now burning, green fire, into hers in the motel-room bed.

Finally, she led him to the corrals and left him with her father and the other men. She thought as she went to the house that she had never in her life been so glad to walk away from someone.

Her father appeared at twelve-thirty. "So Nash refused to take the cabin." Frank chuckled. "Got himself a narrow cot when he could have had a nice big comfortable bed. Now, there is a man dedicated to his work."

Suzanna chuckled, too, and hoped it sounded more sincere than it felt.

Then her father told her he wanted to invite the men in to share the stew at one. Normally, the men took their meals in the bunkhouse. But this was a special occasion, since it was Nash's first day.

What could she say? Suzanna served up the stew and tried to act as if nothing was bothering her as the men talked horses and wolfed down the food.

She did her best not to look Nash Morgan's way too much. But memories kept grabbing at her.

Memories of the way it had been that night. The way *she* had been, just plain crazy in her mind and heart, after Bryan didn't show up for the wedding.

Diana, who'd taken time off work and come all the way from Chicago to be her maid of honor, had stayed by her side that whole afternoon. Finally, when dark came, Suzanna had told her big sister that she couldn't bear being cooped up in the house a single moment longer. She had to get out and drive. And she needed to be alone for a while.

At first, Diana had tried to dissuade her. But Suzanna wouldn't listen.

Finally, her sister gave in. "Be careful," Diana warned, shaking her head, sounding like the mother she had been to Suzanna after their real mother had died so young. "Don't do anything crazy...."

"I won't," Suzanna promised. "I just have to get out."

She'd climbed into the Bronco her father had bought her when she went away to Cal State and she'd hit the road, driving reckless and fast in a hopeless attempt to outrun her humiliation, her anger, the hot pressure of the tears she was not going to let fall.

She considered driving north, toward Whitehorn, the town where she'd gone to school and where many of her friends lived. But she wasn't in the mood to see friends that night, to have them look at her with pity in their eyes. Most of them had been there, for the wedding that didn't happen. And news traveled fast in Whitehorn. Anyone who'd missed the actual event would know the whole story by now.

So she went east on the interstate, exiting the main highway about twenty miles outside of Billings. She drove two-lane blacktop for a while, going nowhere in particular. And then the roadhouse, Fanny Annie's, had loomed up on her right. She'd swung across the centerline, kicking up a high cloud of dust when she pulled into the dirt parking lot.

She knew at a glance that Fanny Annie's was one of those places a woman probably shouldn't enter alone. But she went in anyway. Just strolled through the doors and started drinking long necks and playing eight ball—with Nash Morgan, though she hadn't known his name at the time.

The truth was, she'd never asked for his name. And he'd never asked for hers. He'd called her Deadeye as a joke, because every time she took a shot, those balls never went where she meant for them to go. And she had called him Slim. She'd thought that the name fit him.

Raised on the Big Sky, where the cowboys came and went, Suzanna had known a number of Slims in her life. They had hips that matched their names and they wore faded denim and you could see the shape of lean, hard-worked muscle beneath their worn Western shirts. They had good hearts and a tender way with women and horses. And they never stayed around that long.

She hadn't started out to end up in bed with him. It had just moved on to that, somehow. What with the craziness in her heart and too many long necks and…something about him that felt so consoling. He was a stranger, and a stranger was just what she needed that night, someone who didn't know of her shame and embarrassment. A teasing, handsome stranger—one who somehow reminded her of coming home.

"Suzanna." Her father's voice snapped her back to the here and now. "Pass those biscuits down here. Nash needs more."

Nash laughed. "I wouldn't say I need 'em, but they sure are good."

Suzanna pasted on her most gracious smile and passed the biscuits down the table.

"My baby girl's got a light hand with biscuits and a good head for figures, too," Frank announced proudly. "She's gone and dragged the Big Sky right into the twenty-first century since she came back from college. Got this whole operation on that computer of hers. Anything you need to know about what's on hand or what's on order, you just ask her. Has it all at her fingertips, and that's a fact."

Nash made an admiring, agreeable noise.

"And you better be nice to her," Frank warned. "She's the one who'll be cutting your checks."

"I'll remember that." Nash looked right at her, causing her queasy stomach to lurch and her heart to start banging against her rib cage.

Suzanna kept on smiling, letting everyone know that she was just dandy, just a happy little biscuit maker with good computer skills. By the time the men finally returned to their work at a little after two, her face felt stiff and the muscles around her mouth ached from all that grinning.

She put a casserole together to heat up later, though her head was pounding and her heart felt like a big ball of lead inside her chest. She cleaned up the kitchen. Then, finally, she went upstairs to lie down with a cool, damp rag over her eyes.

Later, over dinner, her father asked her right out if something was bothering her. It was a perfect opportunity to tell him the truth.

She didn't. She said she had a headache. Then she listened, smiling that smile that made her face ache, as her father went on about what a find Nash Morgan was, how he'd had Darcy's Laddy, a spirited three-year-old who'd been giving them trouble, eating out of his hand in the space of an hour.

For the next few days, Suzanna hid out in the house. Immobilized, that was how she felt. Stuck in a low, dark place, with only her own indecision and self-loathing to keep her company. She felt sick to her stomach—and not just because of her pregnancy. The sickness came from dread at the prospect of running into her baby's father again. Being cooped up in the house drove her right up the wainscoted walls, but still, she couldn't bring herself to go out, not until she was ready to face Slim—er, Nash.

And she did know that she would have to face him, to tell him about the baby, even though it appeared that he had forgotten her by the morning after he bedded her. No matter if it turned out, as it most likely would, that he didn't want a thing to do with her or his child. Whatever he ended up thinking or saying when he learned the truth, he *was* the father and he did have a right to know.

So now there were two men who deserved to be informed of the mess she'd gotten herself into. One had raised her and loved her all her life. One had spent a single night in her arms.

But Suzanna said nothing. She was stuck—stuck in that low place where her stomach churned and her head pounded and she couldn't seem to make herself do what had to be done.

More than once, her father tried to get her to tell him what was eating at her. Each time, she brushed off his concern. She was just tired. She had another headache. There was nothing really wrong....

By Thursday morning, Frank Brennan had heard enough lame excuses. And he told his daughter so.

"By God, girl. Something is wrong with you, and I will know what."

"There's nothing."

"Don't lie to me."

"I'm..." *Pregnant,* she thought, pregnant by Nash Morgan, that top-notch horse trainer you hired and won't stop talking about. "Fine. Honestly. It's just a little twenty-four-hour bug, that's all." Ha, she thought. A twenty-four-hour bug? Talk about an understatement. This was a bug she'd carry for six more months. And when she got over it, she'd have herself a child to raise.

"Fine?" Her father, always soft-spoken, raised his voice. "*Fine?* You think I don't have eyes in my head? You've been draggin' around this place for weeks now. And the past few days, it's gotten nothin' but worse. You haven't left the damn house since Monday. I want you to tell me now. What is going on with you?"

"Dad, I—"

"Are you still mooning over that idiot social activist from California who left you flat on your wedding day?" Her father glared down the table at her. "You'd better not be, that's all I've got to say. You're lucky to be shut of that fool, and it's time you got smart and realized as much."

"No, I'm not mooning over Bryan, Dad." That, at least, was the truth. But what she said next was not. "Nothing's the matter. I'm fine."

"Fine," her father repeated again in pure disgust. "You think saying that word is gonna make it true? Something's wrong with you, and if you won't tell me what, I'll take you into Whitehorn today. We'll pay a visit to Doc Winters. Maybe he can figure out what's ailing you."

"I am not sick, Dad. I don't need a doctor."

They stared at each other, a battle of wills.

Frank was the one to lower his gaze first—but he hadn't surrendered the field, only changed tactics. "All right then. If you're not sick, I want to see you out and about. You can take a colt or two out for a nice, quiet ride—and get a little fresh air for yourself at the same time. Nash is completely in charge of the training schedule now. You talk to him this morning. He'll tell you which horses he wants you to ride."

Dear Lord. Nash. He wanted her to talk to Nash. "But, Dad, I—"

"You get out and ride, Suzanna. Or we are payin' a visit to the doc."

* * *

She found Nash at the round pen, where he'd just finished putting Bucky Boy, a fine sorrel two-year-old out of their treasured King broodmare, Chocolate Jessie, through his paces.

When he saw her, he dismounted, then he spent a few seconds talking softly to the animal. Bucky Boy stood very still, as if he really were listening, then he turned his head and seemed to be whispering in Nash's ear. Nash laughed and rubbed the horse's forehead affectionately. Then he led Bucky Boy out of the pen and turned him over to one of the other wranglers.

Finally he came toward her, those long, strong legs of his eating up the ground between them. He touched his hat brim in a sort of salute to her.

"Miss Brennan." He said *miss* the cowboy way, so it sounded like there were z's instead of s's at the end of it, a little like Ms., but softer, longer, more drawn out. "Frank said you'd be riding today."

Suzanna nodded, feeling awful, so awkward and formal, hurt slicing through her all of a sudden that he didn't remember, that they really were strangers in spite of the fact that she'd once lain naked in his arms, even though she carried his baby beneath her heart.

She coughed to clear the sudden obstruction from her throat. "Yes. He said I should check with you before choosing a horse."

He led her to the tack room, where the big training schedule was mounted on one wall, a line for each colt and filly, the days marked off in squares. Her father had always kept that chart, but often the wranglers got lazy about filling in the blanks. Since Nash had come, though, each blank space was crammed with notes and instructions for what the trainers should concentrate on in the next session.

"I like to have a plan," Nash said. He was standing behind her as she looked at the chart. His nearness sang along her nerves. She breathed deeply and told herself to relax.

He went on. "Every horse is different, and this way we don't just pick up on the weak points and drill them to death." He chuckled. The rough, warm sound sent a naughty thrill coursing up her spine. "A colt is a lot like a schoolkid, if you think about it. A colt needs a good teacher. And a good teacher always works from a lesson plan."

Suzanna made a noise of agreement, which was all she could manage right at that moment. She could see him out of the corner of her eye. And she could smell him. He smelled the same as she remembered, an earthy, warm, healthy sort of scent— a scent she realized she would have recognized anywhere. A scent that hollowed out her midsection and made her want to lean back against him.

She stiffened and turned. "I…it looks real good."

A half smile lifted the left side of his mouth, the mouth that had kissed her, deep and wet and long.

The mouth that had roamed her whole body so that she had moaned and writhed beneath him, begging him not to stop, crying out for more.

She shifted her glance. ''Well. If you'll just tell me which of your students could use a little field trip today, I'll get out of your way.''

His eyes caught hers again—and wouldn't let go. ''Did I say I wanted you out of my way?''

''Well, no. No, of course you didn't. But you know what I mean.''

He shrugged and turned to the wall hung with bits and bridles. ''Get your gear and we'll get going.''

She didn't move. ''Uh. *We?*''

He chose two snaffle bits and a pair of cinch straps, each with a flat-sided ring. ''I'll ride out with you to see how you do.''

''But—''

He turned, snared her with that green glance once more. ''But what?''

''It's not necessary. Not necessary at all. I've been riding Big Sky colts since I was knee high to a gnat, for heaven's sake. You just tell me what you want me to watch for on any colt you give me and I'll—''

''You got some major objection to riding with me?'' All of a sudden, his eyes were flat as paving stones, all the gleam gone out of them—and they still wouldn't let go of hers.

''No. No, of course I don't mind riding with you.''

"Then grab a saddle." He pointed to the row of lighter-weight cutting-horse saddles, not far from the wall of bits and bridles. Then he asked with a definite note of challenge in his voice, "You need someone to haul your saddle for you?"

"I do not."

"All right, then. Let's go."

It was a perfect morning for an easy, quiet ride, warm but not hot yet, with a nice breeze blowing off the white-crested Crazy Mountains to the northwest. The grasses moved, rippling soft and silvery in the path of the wind. Black-eyed Susans and purple-headed bull thistles turned their faces to the yellow ball of the sun.

They rode for an hour, hardly speaking, roughly following the winding path of Bear Tooth Creek, the ranch's major water source. Suzanna kept thinking of what she had to tell the stranger on the horse beside her. She also wondered sourly if he approved of the way she handled her mount. But then he must, mustn't he? Or he'd be giving her instructions in that low, rough-velvet voice of his.

"There's a nice shady spot up ahead," Nash said eventually. He pointed at a cluster of cottonwoods along a wide place on the creek. "We'll stop there." He clucked to his horse and took the lead. Her stomach suddenly churning with foreboding, Suzanna followed.

In the shade of the trees by the sloping bank of

the creek, Nash dismounted and hobbled his horse. Suzanna did the same. Their horses drank from the creek and then nipped at the low grass along the bank. Suzanna watched them, though they weren't doing anything she hadn't seen a thousand times in her life. But watching them meant she didn't have to look at Nash.

He made small talk. In that soft, gentle voice of his, he remarked on how much he liked her father, how the Big Sky was a fine operation and the other handlers were good men. He talked about the colt and the filly grazing idly along the bank. About how Dingo was still slow to pick up a lead and Baby June tended to laze along rather than walk out as she should.

Somehow, Suzanna managed to make intelligent noises in response. But her mind was a whirlwind.

There *was* something in the way he kept looking at her, something in the knowing curve of that mouth, which had once kissed her with such wild passion. His glances and his half smiles were clues, it seemed to her.

Clues that communicated without his saying as much that he *did* remember, after all. That the way he'd seemed not to know her had been only an act. That she really had seen recognition in his eyes in that first moment on the porch Monday morning.

All of a sudden, he asked, ''What's on your mind right now?''

She'd been staring at the horses again. But his

question had her whipping her head around, made
the skin down her arms and at the backs of her knees
go hot and prickly with something that felt very
much like fear. "I...what?"

"What are you thinking?"

"Well, nothing," she baldly lied. "Just...I was
just listening to what you were saying, that's all."

His expression said he didn't buy that for a minute. "You want to know what *I'm* thinking?"

No! her cowardly heart cried. *I don't. I do not
want to know....*

But he told her anyway. "I'm thinking that you're
a much better rider than you are a pool player, Deadeye."

Chapter 3

Deadeye.

Oh, God. He *did* remember.

Suzanna's stomach lurched dangerously. Sweet Lord, she was not going to be able to stop it this time. She was going to be sick....

She sucked in a breath, closed her eyes and bent over, getting ready.

Nash touched her shoulder. "Suzanna..."

She put up a hand, waving him away. Her stomach lurched again—and settled, at least somewhat.

She opened her eyes. She could see Nash's boots planted firmly not two feet to her left.

With a sigh, she let herself sink to a sitting position on the bank.

After a moment, Nash dropped down beside her. She shot him a furtive glance, then quickly looked away.

He asked, "You all right?"

She didn't answer. There was no need. He could see that she was very far from all right.

"Look," he said. "As far as I'm concerned, what happened was between us. If you're worried that I'm a man who likes to talk about things that are nobody else's business—"

"I...no. No, it isn't that."

"Then what?"

It was the moment, the moment to tell him. She looked at him hopelessly. "I..." The words just would not come.

She hung her head.

And he put his arm around her. Strangely enough, it felt utterly natural for him to do that. And so comforting. She let out a hard sigh and buried her face against his shoulder. He pulled her closer, stroked her hair.

A long time passed. Nash held her, and she huddled against him, breathing the wonderful scent of him, glad for his strong arms around her at the same time as she found it impossible to raise her eyes and look at him.

"Come on," he said at last, putting a finger under her chin, making her raise her eyes to meet his. "Come on, it can't be *that* bad...."

She hitched in a tight breath. "But it is. It really is. You don't understand...."

"Then maybe you'd better tell me."

"I..."

"Come on. Tell me."

Something in his eyes undid her. She blurted out the truth. "I'm pregnant."

Lord, it sounded awful, just to say it like that. She shied away from him a little, and he dropped his arm from its comforting position across her shoulder. For a time, they sat very still, not touching, staring toward the mountains, neither knowing what to say next.

Finally, Nash picked up a pebble and tossed it overhand into the water. Suzanna watched the ripples move out when it dropped through the glassy surface.

She wondered if he was thinking the same thing she was thinking, that it was a pretty bum deal for her to go and get herself pregnant when he'd only made one little slipup the whole night they'd spent together.

He *had* used protection. But there had been that one time, near dawn, when some last, frantic eagerness had taken them both. He had reached for her and she had pressed herself against him—and the necessary precautions had been the furthest thing from their minds.

He asked carefully, "Was there...anyone else besides me?"

She shook her head fiercely.

"Then it's mine."

She nodded, biting her lip to hold back the hopeless little moan that was trying to squeeze itself out of her throat.

"We'll get married," he said.

She looked right at him then. "I don't even *know* you."

"It doesn't matter. It's the right thing to do."

"No," she said firmly, then decided that maybe that sounded a bit harsh. She tried to soften it a little. "I mean, no, thanks. It's...very nice of you to offer, but...I just couldn't marry someone I didn't love."

He gave her a long look, one that made her extremely uncomfortable. Then he said flatly, "Think about it."

She turned her gaze toward the mountains again, to get away from those eyes of his. "No, really. I don't have to think about it. I don't love you and I—"

He stopped her in midsentence, skipping right on to the next order of business. "Frank doesn't know yet, does he?"

"Uh. No. I...I've been meaning to tell him."

"But you haven't."

"Not yet."

"Well, I think we'd better do it tonight, then."

We. He intended to be there with her. To face her father with her. Gratitude washed through her in a warm wave.

She made herself turn to him. His eyes were waiting. "I... You don't have to do that."

He looked at her steadily. "Yeah. Yeah, I do." He touched her shoulder, and she knew that *he* knew exactly how she felt. He understood the dread inside her at the prospect of telling Frank Brennan what they'd done. "You're three months gone," he said. "It can't wait any longer."

"I know." She sighed the words.

"We'd better get it over with then. Tonight, like I said."

What else could she answer? "All right."

"I'll come to the house."

"Okay. Um, come at six, for dinner. We'll tell him after. It will be better that way, not quite so abrupt." It wouldn't be better. Nothing could make such a thing better. But still, if the poor man insisted on standing by her when she broke the news, he ought at least to have a nice dinner first.

Her father came in at five-thirty. Nash had already told him he'd be dropping by for supper.

Frank seemed to think that was a dandy idea. "I'm glad you asked him." Her father winked at her. "And he does like your biscuits."

Suzanna drew a fortifying breath. "Well. I made plenty."

The meal went smoothly enough. Her father and Nash seemed to have a lot to say to each other. They talked business. Frank brought up the two-week trip he'd be taking near the end of the month, first to the annual Wyoming quarter horse show in Gillette, and then on to visit a friend in Colorado.

"I'm real glad you'll be here, Nash," Frank said. "Between you and Suzanna, I'll be leavin' the Big Sky in capable hands."

Suzanna kept her eyes on her plate and wondered if Nash would be around by then. Would her father have so much faith in his new trainer after he heard what they had to say to him? And would Nash want to stay? She did admire him for sticking by her tonight—but she couldn't expect him to want to hang around watching her stomach get bigger and bigger with the baby they'd made. He'd made his obligatory offer of marriage, and she had turned him down. Really, it might be better for everyone if he decided to move on down the road.

But then again, the more contact she had with him, the more he seemed like a man who wouldn't walk away from his own child. So maybe they'd have to work something out, arrange things so he could see the baby now and then.

Oh, who could say? The truth was, she didn't know what Nash Morgan would do.

The dinner was over too soon for Suzanna. She cleared the plates and served peach cobbler and made herself eat it as she'd eaten her pot roast and vegetables, forcing the food down to keep her father from looking at her with a worried frown between his brows.

Finally the time came. She sent a swift, questioning glance at Nash. He nodded—and all she wanted to do was leap from the table, grab the empty dessert plates and flee to the kitchen.

She made herself stay put.

And Nash said, "Frank, there is something you need to be told."

Her father pushed his plate away and looked from Nash to his daughter. "Sounds like something serious."

"It is." Nash waited. Suzanna understood that he was giving her a chance to say the words.

"What?" Frank demanded. "You two are makin' me nervous."

Nash cleared his throat.

And somehow Suzanna found her voice. "I'm going to have a baby, Dad."

The silence that followed was downright deafening. Her father's face went dead white, then flushed with hot color. He turned a brutal glare on Suzanna, a look that made her long to slide off her chair and scurry under the table like a naughty child, to curl herself up in a ball under there—and never, ever come out.

And then Frank Brennan swore, a single, very ugly word. "That weaselly little rat bastard," he muttered. "I should have known."

Suzanna gulped in a breath, then found herself echoing in a numb voice, "Weaselly?"

"I didn't trust him. Never. Not for a minute, from

the first day you brought him here. All that talk of
the homeless and hungry. All those big-shot ideas
about changing the world. Charity begins at home,
that's what the Good Book says. And a man who
gets a girl in trouble and then runs off to join the
damn Peace Corps is no man at all in *my* book.''

"Bryan?" Suzanna heard herself murmur dazedly.
"You mean Bryan?"

"Who the hell else would I mean?" asked her
father in utter disgust. Another crude epithet followed. He glowered. "You been in touch with
him?"

"I…no. I don't have any idea *how* to get in touch
with him. And anyway, Dad, it wasn't—"

"Well, okay. Okay, fine. I wouldn't want that
damn fool for a son-in-law anyway, and that is a
plain fact. If he ever sets foot on the Big Sky again,
I'll skin him for the polecat he is and stretch his
sorry pelt on the tack room wall."

"Dad—"

Nash cut her off. "Just a minute," he said quietly.
"Who's Bryan?"

Frank snorted. "Who's Bryan? I'll tell you who
Bryan is. Bryan's her fiancé—her *ex*-fiancé. Left her
flat, the weasel. Three months ago, on their wedding
day, last March the twenty-fourth. Joined the damn
Peace Corps, wouldn't you know?"

Nash cast her a glance. Suzanna read its meaning.
She'd never said a word about Bryan to him—not
during that night three months ago, and not today,

either, when she'd had a clear opportunity to say anything that needed saying.

"March twenty-fourth," Nash said, his soft voice even softer than usual. Too soft, actually. Accusingly soft. "That was supposed to be your *wedding* day?"

Lord. How could she have thought he'd forgotten? It was painfully clear that he remembered everything—including the calendar date of the night he'd spent with her.

She swallowed. "I...I suppose I should have explained."

"Yeah," he said. "I suppose you should. But then, I guess there were a lot of things you didn't explain."

That got her dander up. "Just you wait a half a minute, here, mister. You didn't do a lot of explaining, either, if memory serves. You didn't even—"

"Stop." Frank fisted his hand and hit the edge of the table with it. Plates and flatware jumped and clattered. "Don't you two go getting into it. There is no sense at all in us turnin' on each other—which reminds me." He swung his gaze on his daughter and asked in a tone midway between curiosity and fury, "Suzanna, why the hell did you have to go dragging Nash into this mess?"

Suzanna had that urge again—to crawl under the table and hide. She slid a glance at Nash. Those green eyes were on her, waiting for her to tell her father the truth.

And she knew she must do exactly that.

But how? Where were the right words to say? How could she explain to the conservative man who'd raised her that she'd gone out on what should have been her wedding night and had sex with a stranger?

"I…"

"Speak up, girl. Answer me, now."

"Well, because I…"

"Yeah?"

"Because he, um, well…"

Nash must have grown tired of waiting for her to get the words out. He said wearily, "Because the ex-fiancé is *not* the man at fault. *I* am."

Frank Brennan looked as if he just might keel over from the shock of that news. "You, Nash? You?"

"Yeah, Frank. Me."

"But you don't even *know* each other. You just met this past Monday."

"We met before. The night she was supposed to have married that other guy. At a place called Fanny Annie's, a few miles outside of Billings."

Her father stared from Nash to Suzanna and back again. His face showed disbelief and disappointment and a host of other emotions too painful to contemplate.

"Oh, Dad," Suzanna cried. "Dad, I'm so sorry, I—"

Frank waved a hand at her, as if he couldn't bear

the sound of her voice, of her excuses. Then he sank down in his chair. Slowly, he lifted both big, blunt-fingered hands. He raked them through his thick graying hair. "Oh, Suzanna. This is not like you, to pick up a stranger, in some roadside bar."

"It was…a really bad time for me, Dad. I was feeling so crazy, just out of my mind and I—"

"Never mind." Frank shook his head and let out a deep sigh. "So. What are you gonna do now?"

And Nash said very calmly, "Now, she's going to marry me."

Chapter 4

A slow smile spread across Frank Brennan's tanned, lined face—a relieved, indulgent kind of smile. He sat up straighter in his chair. "Well," he said. "I gotta admit, I feel a lot better hearin' you say that, son. But I guess I should have known. You're not a man to run from his responsibilities."

Frank turned his smile, only slightly dimmed, on Suzanna. "So, I guess everything will work out all right, after all. The fact is, you and Nash will make a great team. I have to admit, the thought that you two might get together has already crossed my mind a time or two. And now, well, things could be a damn sight worse, couldn't they? You'll get married and I can rest easy—and not only because my little girl's baby will have a father, but also because I can be certain the Big Sky will end up in capable hands when it's time for me to pass on the reins.''

Nash said, ''Frank. We're not talking about your ranch, here. We're talking marriage. Period.''

''I know, I know. You're right. I understand. You two will get married. We can worry about the rest as time goes by.''

Suzanna realized she'd better speak up before the two of them planned out her whole life for her. ''Wait just a minute here.''

Both men turned to her. ''What?'' they said at the same time.

She looked from one strong-jawed, masculine face to the other. The men muttered, ''What?'' again, simultaneously as before.

Suzanna's father was frowning at her. She dared to turn to Nash, to look him square in the eye. He stared right back, calm as you please. She demanded, ''How could you do this?''

Nash shrugged. ''Do what?''

''I told you I can't marry you. I told you this afternoon.''

''You *what?*'' Frank bellowed.

Suzanna answered her father, but she kept looking right at Nash. ''I told him I couldn't marry him.''

Her father loosed another expletive. ''Now, why would you go and say a crazy thing like that?''

Suzanna ignored him. ''Look,'' she told Nash.

"We don't love each other. We don't even *know* each other."

"It's a good match," her father said stubbornly. "And you need a husband right now. Love will come later."

She whirled on him. "How can you say that? I'm a Brennan, Dad. And Brennans always marry for love."

Frank grunted. "This is no time for silly sentimentality."

"Sentimentality?" Suzanna echoed the words in outrage. "That's what you call it now? You're the one who told me all the old stories. I learned them sitting on your knee. How Great-Great-Grandmother Isabelle married Kyle Brennan because she loved him with all of her heart, even though—"

"Suzanna, I know the old stories."

"Then how can you suggest that I marry a man I don't love?"

"Because he's the father of your baby. Because he's a damn fine man. Because it's the best thing and it's the *right* thing."

"It is not. It's the *convenient* thing."

"Whatever," her father said gruffly. "It's the best solution to a bad situation."

"No, it is not. It's wrong, that's what it is. And I can understand that you don't think much of my judgment right now. I have made a pretty bad mess of things. But I am still a Brennan, born and raised. And I will marry for love, or I won't marry at all."

Her father's face had flushed deep red again. "You will do as I tell you—in this, at least."

Suzanna held her ground. "I will not."

"You are in trouble, girl. You are having a child. Your baby's father is willing to marry you. Don't be a damn fool about this, on top of everything else."

She squared her shoulders and stuck out her chin. "I am sorry you think I'm a fool, Dad. But I don't love Nash, and I'm not going to marry him. It's not right."

"It *is* right."

"I won't do it. I can raise my baby on my own just fine. If Nash wants to help, well, we can talk about that. But not about marriage."

Frank shoved his chair back and loomed above her. "I have had enough of this moony-eyed foolishness!" He was shouting. "You will marry Nash...or else!"

"No, I won't. I won't, I tell you."

"Wait a minute, here." It was Nash's voice, quiet and low, utterly calm.

Both Suzanna and Frank shut their mouths and turned to him.

He rose to his feet and said to Suzanna, "Thank you for a fine dinner. I'm headed back to the bunkhouse now. You think about my offer and let me know what you decide."

Then he stepped away from his chair, pushed it gently under the table and went out the back way.

Once the door shut behind him, Frank glowered at Suzanna. "You'd *better* do some thinking, girl. Some hard thinking. And when you're through thinking, you'd better come to a reasonable decision."

Suzanna glowered right back at him and didn't say a word.

A stare-down ensued.

In the end, her father tossed his napkin on the table, growled good-night and retired to his room.

Suzanna cleaned up the dishes.

Then, desperately needing emotional support, she picked up the phone on the kitchen wall to call her sister in Chicago.

But she hung up without dialing. Diana, who was five years Suzanna's senior, truly had been like a mother to her through her growing-up years. Diana had bandaged her hurts, nursed her when she got the chicken pox and shared all her secrets.

But it wouldn't be fair to draw her into the middle of this situation. Since Suzanna and her father were totally at odds, confiding in Diana would be tantamount to asking her sister to take sides. And even if Diana held to the middle ground, she would be bound to worry. If she got too concerned, she might just decide she had to drop everything and pay a visit home.

No, bothering Diana with this wouldn't be right.

The time had come for Suzanna to handle her difficulties on her own.

She trudged up the stairs, her feet as heavy as her heart. In her room, she dropped to the edge of the bed and kicked off her shoes.

If only there was someone she could talk to about this. Someone to reassure her, to tell her she was right not to want to marry a stranger, even if that stranger did happen to be the father of her child.

She hung her head and stared at her socks. If only she could...travel across time. Take a little trip to the past. Have a nice, long talk with her great-great-grandmother Isabelle about love and marriage and—

The letters.

Suzanna's head came up. She stared at the bow-fronted bureau across the room, where she'd put the letters on Monday when Nash Morgan had come knocking on the door. She'd yet to read them, had more or less forgotten them in the misery and upheaval of the past few days.

Suzanna rose from the bed and padded across the hooked rug to the bureau. She knelt and pulled open the bottom drawer. With hands that shook just a little, she withdrew the six envelopes.

Then she went to her desk at the window that looked out on the front yard. She switched on the lamp and sat down to read.

An hour later, Suzanna carefully refolded the last yellowed sheet and put it in the envelope from which she'd removed it. She neatly stacked the envelopes in a corner of her desk. Then she put her head on her arms and cried.

She had hoped they would be love letters. And they were. Love letters written a year after Isabelle and Kyle's marriage, while Kyle was away on a trail drive and Isabelle looked after the Big Sky. Isabelle's passion, tenderness and commitment shone forth in every line. She had loved her husband deeply.

Suzanna switched off the lamp and sat back in her chair. She stared blindly out the window, where twilight had brought the bats and swallows out to dip and sail through the darkening sky.

"For love," she whispered to the night as the last lonely tear tracked its way down her cheek. "To marry for love. Is that so much to ask?"

The night gave no answer. After a while, moving very slowly, feeling weary right down into the center of herself, Suzanna rose and got ready for bed. She settled beneath the comforter with a heavy sigh and waited for sleep to steal all her cares.

But in spite of her weariness, sleep wouldn't come.

The next day at breakfast, Suzanna's father hardly spoke to her. He ate his meal in silence, then without a word took his plate to the sink, rinsed it and stuck it in the dishwasher rack.

He headed for the back door, but then couldn't

resist turning and demanding, "You made a decision yet?"

She looked at him pleadingly. She really did hate to have this hostility between them. "Dad, I—"

He grunted. "Never mind. I can see you haven't." He left her there.

She lasted through that whole day and another never-ending, mostly sleepless night. Her father barely spoke to her during the day. And later, as she lay in bed, she thought about Nash, wondered what he was thinking out there in his narrow bunkhouse cot. Did he already regret speaking up and offering marriage? Or did he remain steadfastly determined to do the right thing?

Saturday morning, as she was zipping up her jeans, she finally admitted to herself that they were getting tighter. Soon she'd have to buy herself some pregnant-lady clothes.

It was another pretty morning, clear and cool with the promise of a hot afternoon to come. Suzanna decided she'd drive into Whitehorn later, since the pantry needed filling. But first, before it got too hot, she would go riding. She'd have to face Nash to do it, in order not to disrupt his precious training schedule, but she could manage that. She could manage that just fine.

She put on her boots and grabbed her hat and went out to the corrals, but Nash wasn't there. One of the handlers told her that Nash and her father

were in the near pasture, putting a first lead on one
of the foals.

It wasn't that far to walk. Five minutes later, she
found them. They had a set of pipe panels surrounding the mare and the sweet little chestnut foal.
They'd used the mare, who was accustomed to such
goings-on, to maneuver the frightened foal into a
corner. Then her father, halter in hand, slid between
the foal and the back panel, blocking escape on that
side. Nash stepped up and wrapped one arm under
the foal's neck and the opposite hand firmly around
the base of his tail. Frank slipped on the halter.

Watching them, Suzanna thought that they
worked together as if they'd been doing it all of their
lives. Her father was holding the lead rope, stroking
the little fella about the face and neck. Nash was
making soothing sounds, talking softly, saying re-
assuring things. The foal tried to toss his head and
cried out for his mama.

The mare gave a low, rough snort, a questioning
sound.

Nash said gently, "It's all right, girl. We won't
hurt your baby."

The mare snorted again and shook herself. Turning her back on the proceedings, she moved a few
steps away.

Really, Nash Morgan was a wonder with a horse.

And Suzanna had to admit that he'd been pretty
terrific with her, as well. So tender and passionate
on their one night together, he'd made her first time

a beautiful thing. There was also the way he had held her so kindly, day before yesterday, down by the creek, when she'd almost lost her breakfast right in front of him. And he hadn't made a single mean wisecrack when she told him the baby was his.

And then he had faced her father with her. A lot of men wouldn't have been willing to do that. He'd stepped right up to accept complete responsibility. He'd offered to marry her—well, *insisted* on marrying her, really.

He *was* a good man.

It occured to Suzanna right then that maybe she needed more than some jeans with elastic in the waist. Maybe she needed to face the fact that love wasn't everything. Once, she'd thought she'd loved Bryan Cummings—and look where that had gotten her.

She wasn't her great-great-grandmother. She was only herself, Suzanna, who had made a few mistakes and now ought to be finding the best way to set things right.

Nash Morgan was a good man. She could do a lot worse than to become his wife.

Chapter 5

Her father looked up and saw her. Nash cast a quick glance her way, all he could manage with the foal in his arms. Frank said something to Nash, and Nash slowly backed away from the nervous foal, leaving Frank holding him by the lead. Right away, the foal whinnied and tried to back up.

Nash said, "You okay?"

"Go on." Frank spared him a wave. "The day I can't handle a haltered foal is the day I need to find myself another line of work." The foal yanked on the lead. "Easy, boy," said Frank. "Take it easy, now…"

Nash moved the panel aside and stepped through the gap. He skimmed off his hat. "Something I can do for you, Suzanna?"

She made herself smile. Her mouth kind of quivered at the edges, but it was the best she could do. "Well, I was wondering if maybe you'd go for a ride with me."

They just naturally seemed to head for that same spot along the creek. And when they dismounted, Suzanna felt almost as nerved up as she had the other day.

But somehow she did it. She told him, "I have considered your offer, and I've decided that I will marry you." Her stomach seemed to drop toward her boots as it occurred to her that he very well might have changed his mind. "Er...that is, if the offer's still open."

"It is."

A slightly frantic laugh escaped her. "Whew. That's good. I mean, okay. I mean..."

The tangle of words died in her throat as he grasped her arm and pulled her toward him.

She landed against his chest with a soft little, "Oh!"

He looked at her, roving her face with that green glance of his. "You want me to let go?"

She felt terribly flustered. "I...no. I don't. Really, it's just..."

"What?"

"I...I'm nervous, I guess." She added silently, *And you feel so warm and big and good. So exactly as I remember you feeling...*

"A man usually kisses a woman, doesn't he? When she says she'll marry him?"

"Well, yes. I mean, that's how I understood it. I mean—"

She wasn't really sure what she meant. But it didn't matter, because he lowered his mouth and started nuzzling hers and she didn't have to say anything more anyway.

She didn't *want* to say anything more. He truly was a wonderful kisser. He kissed the same way he talked to a horse. With complete concentration. And also with respect. He knew never to force the issue. He just made the whole experience so lovely, a woman would have to be a total fool to say no.

He nipped her lower lip, then scraped it softly between his teeth. She sighed, her mouth opened a little and the tip of his tongue went roaming there, at the entrance, teasing her with the idea that he just might come all the way inside.

And then he did come inside. He swept the tender wet surfaces beyond her lips with a tongue that knew exactly what to do when it was inside a woman's mouth.

She sighed some more, pressed herself closer to him, there beneath the cottonwood tree. She felt the ridge of his arousal against her belly and she melted down there, her body knowing what was needed of it, going open and ready. His hands roamed her back as the kiss grew ever deeper.

Oh, yes. She wanted him. As she had wanted him

that very first night when he'd come up to her at the long bar in Fanny Annie's and asked if she was open to a little company.

She'd turned to him and looked in his eyes, and suddenly all her misery and humiliation seemed to have happened to some other woman. Suddenly, she felt good about herself. Good about being there in the smoky, loud bar. Good about everything.

A little wild, maybe. A little too ready to risk what she shouldn't.

But good. Very good.

She slid her tongue around his, moaning at the contact, at the wetness and the heat.

Too soon, he pulled back. "Just a kiss," he said, as if reminding them both that they weren't going any further.

She dragged in a big breath and let it out slowly. "Yes. Just a kiss…"

He had her by the shoulders, his strong fingers digging in a little. "This Bryan guy. He still special to you?"

"No." It was easy to say. After all, it was the truth. "I…I realize now it wasn't love with him. It was just…"

"What?"

"…a dream I had. Love and marriage. Walking down the aisle in my great-great-grandmother's wedding gown."

"You hate him now, for walking out on you?"

"No. I just…don't have that much feeling at all

for him. A little sadness and a whole lot of embarrassment that I made such a bad choice in a man."

He looked...what? Satisfied, maybe. "Good." He was still holding her shoulders.

"What?" she asked, all at once feeling nervous again.

"There were a lot of things you didn't tell me that night. Like your name."

"You didn't tell me yours, either."

"Okay, so we're even on that score. But what about it being your first time? That was a real shocker."

"Well, it didn't seem to stop you."

He had the grace to look abashed. "You didn't tell me to stop. And I didn't want to stop, so..."

"Nash. It's okay. All I'm saying is, you didn't volunteer much information yourself that night. It wasn't a night for talking. We had a lot of fun. And we ended up doing a few things we shouldn't have. And the vital information just never got exchanged."

He smiled a little ruefully, then grew serious again. "You left in the morning, when I was still sleeping."

"It seemed...the best way."

"I wondered if I'd dreamed you or something."

She understood that. Sometimes she'd wondered herself if that night had really happened. At least, at first. But then, when she'd realized she was pregnant, she'd been forced to admit that it had been very, very real.

She glanced at their two sets of boots, so close together, pointing toward each other on the mossy bank. Then she lifted her face to him once more. "You didn't dream me, Nash."

He looked at her for a very long time. Then he shook his head slowly. "No. I reckon I did not."

Her father was waiting when they got back to the home place.

"Well?" he demanded when they rode up.

In a formal tone that plucked at Suzanna's heart-strings, Nash said, "Your daughter has decided that she will be my wife."

That night after dinner, the three of them firmed up the details.

Frank was in an expansive mood. "You'll have that big wedding you always dreamed of after all, Suzanna. Diana will come home and—"

"No, Dad." She cut in before he could get rolling.

Her father drew back in surprise. "Why not? I thought a big wedding was what you always wanted."

"Maybe it was. Once. But I'm through with that kind of foolishness now. And I don't want to drag Diana back here all over again just to see me get married. I think we'd better make it simple. And soon."

Frank looked at Nash, who said nothing for a moment, then shrugged. "I guess Suzanna knows what she wants."

Frank spoke. "A nice honeymoon, then. On me. How's that? Two weeks, wherever you two want to go."

Suzanna and Nash both vetoed that one.

Nash said, "Listen, Frank. Thanks a lot, but I'll pay for my own honeymoon."

And Suzanna added, "I really don't want to make a big deal of this, Dad." She glanced questioningly at her husband-to-be. "Just a few days away, that's what I was thinking."

"Whatever you want."

"Someplace nearby would be nice," Suzanna said. "Since it will only be a short stay."

Nash shrugged again. "I've got a friend who owns a bed-and-breakfast in Buffalo, Wyoming."

Suzanna had been to Buffalo and remembered it as a lovely little town. "Wyoming sounds fine."

"All right, then. Wyoming," Nash said flatly. "We can get the blood tests this week, then get married at the county courthouse next Friday. We'll stay in Buffalo till Tuesday. That'll get us back before Frank leaves for the horse show in Gillette."

"Take your time," her father said. "I can skip the horse show this year."

"There's no need for that," Nash said. "We'll be back on Tuesday." He was still looking at Suzanna. It wasn't a cold look—but it wasn't warm, either.

"All right?" He seemed so distant all of a sudden, not at all like the tender lover who had kissed her at the creek that very afternoon. She wondered if something was bothering him and decided that she'd ask him later.

She said brightly, "Yes. That's fine."

Next, her father announced that he intended to give Nash a share in the Big Sky. The year before, when Suzanna had turned twenty-one, Frank Brennan had seen his lawyer in town. He'd had it fixed so the Big Sky belonged half to him and the other half equally to his two daughters. Now that Nash would join the family, Frank had decided to split his own half with his new son-in-law.

"We'll see the lawyer this week," Frank declared expansively. "We can do it when you two go in for those blood tests and—"

Nash said no before Frank could finish. "I won't lay claim to another man's land—even if I am marryin' his daughter."

"But, son. You'll be part of the family now and—"

"Forget it, Frank. I earn what I own, or I pay for it. If I decide I want a piece of your ranch, then I'll buy in. I won't have you handing it to me as a wedding present."

Her father tried to make him see reason, but Nash wouldn't budge. Suzanna couldn't decide whether to be thrilled at the high level of Nash's integrity— or to start getting worried. She did believe that Nash was an honest man. And an honest man might hesitate to take a chunk of his father-in-law's land if he had doubts about how long his marriage would last.

Frank left them alone a little while later.

They walked out to the front porch together. Suzanna sat on the swing suspended from the porch eaves. Nash hitched a leg up on the railing a few feet away.

Suzanna toed the porch boards, making the swing creak a little on its heavy chain. Far away, a coyote howled at the new moon, which seemed to hang from a star in the indigo sky. In the near pasture, one of the mares let out a high, nervous whinny in response to the sound.

"How old are you, Nash?" she asked.

"Thirty-one. You?"

"Twenty-two." The swing creaked some more. "Strange, isn't it? We're getting married in less than a week, and I just learned how old you are."

He took off his hat and dropped it to the porch boards. "Not so strange, really. Not given the circumstances."

She swallowed. "Yeah. I guess you're right about that. You...ever had the urge to settle down before?"

He didn't answer right away. Her stomach tightened, and she found herself expecting him to say something like, *No, and to tell you the truth, I don't really want to settle down now.*

But he didn't. He replied simply, "I've never been married. Never even been close to it before."

Her lips felt dry. She pressed them together and ran her tongue along the inner seam. "Why not?"

In the light of the porch lamp, his eyes were dark as the bottom of a well. "What are you after here, Suzanna?"

She felt her face pinkening, felt like a person prying into someone else's private business. But he was to be her husband, wasn't he? And didn't that make his private business *her* business, too? "I just...I want to know about you, that's all."

"You want my life story, is that it?" His tone was gentle, as always, but she thought she detected a thread of sarcasm in it.

She answered frankly. "Yes, I want to know everything about you that you're willing to tell me."

Another nerve-racking silence, then he said, "All right."

He began rattling off facts. "I was born in Laramie. My father died when I was seven. I was ten when my mother remarried. My stepfather didn't like me much. He had a mean streak and a big leather belt and he exercised both on me regularly. I never graduated from high school, ran off when I was seventeen, at the beginning of my senior year. That was when my mother died. I didn't see much sense in sticking around there after that.

"I've been on my own since then, working as a ranch hand and then finding I had a certain way with horses. I've called myself a horse trainer for the past eight years and now I'm to the point where I can ask a premium wage for my services. I've got a pickup, two good saddles, an empty gooseneck trailer. And fifty thousand dollars in a bank in Billings against the day that I can buy my own spread.'' He chuckled, a mirthless sound. "My big dream is to get my own place, which I'm always telling myself I'll do real soon. Fifty thousand doesn't go that far, though. Not in the ranching business. Sometimes, I gotta admit, my big dream seems about as likely to happen as…meeting a pretty virgin college girl in a roadhouse and spending the night with her.''

If Suzanna's cheeks had felt pink before, now they felt bright red. Nash was watching her, his eyes intent.

He asked, ''Why'd you choose me that night, Suzanna?''

She felt embarrassed to tell him—but it was only fair to reveal a few of her own secrets after the things he had just said to her. ''I…looked at you and forgot how unhappy I was. That night, I forgot everything but what it felt like being with you. And, well…''

''Well, what?''

''You made me think of home.''

His eyes were velvet-soft and so was his voice when he said, ''That's not such a bad start, I guess.''

She made a noise of agreement low in her throat,

then dared to ask, "If you want your own place, why didn't you take what my dad offered you?"

His broad shoulders tensed, and the softness left his expression. "I think I made that pretty clear."

Yes, she thought, *you certainly did.* "Because you want to earn what you own. But was that the only reason?"

"It's reason enough."

"It just seemed like something was bothering you when we were talking about the wedding and the honeymoon and...everything."

She waited. He only looked at her, his eyes well-deep once more. She wondered at the way she felt with him. There was a low, constant hum inside her, a waiting, eager kind of feeling, something she'd never experienced with any other man. Arousal would probably be the word for it. Yes. She felt aroused. And utterly at home—yet curiously on edge at the same time. As if she knew him to his soul. As if she didn't know him at all.

It was terribly confusing.

She murmured, "If I said something that offended you while we were talking about the wedding—"

He stood and came toward her. "You said what you wanted, right? What you were willing to do. A plain ceremony, nothing fancy. And a little trip to Wyoming afterward."

She stilled the swing and stared at him. The whole night seemed to hang suspended, between her eyes and his. "I...yes. Nothing fancy. And a trip to Wyoming is great."

"So that's what you'll have." He held out his hand.

She put hers in it and he pulled her up, into his arms.

He kissed her, pressing her against him, so that she forgot everything but the way his body felt along hers. When he let her go, she wanted only to grab him close again.

He stepped back, bent and scooped up his hat. "Good night, Suzanna." He went down the steps and across the lawn, vanishing into the shadows around the side of the house.

She stood there, watching, until he was gone. Then she dropped to the swing again and leaned back in its swaying embrace.

Later, she went into the house and called Diana. She told her big sister the truth. That she'd gotten pregnant the night of the day that Bryan Cummings had left her at the altar. She was marrying the father of her baby—who, as it turned out, was also the new horse trainer their father was so impressed with.

Diana immediately offered to come home. But Suzanna said no. Diana tried to argue. Suzanna remained firm. It was only a simple legal ceremony, after all. Nothing to make a big fuss over. And she and Nash were going away for a few days right after.

"You know I'll come if you need me," Diana said.

And Suzanna answered that yes, of course, she did know. And she was fine. There was no cause for worry.

Suzanna hung up the phone and felt sad. It really would be nice to have Diana there, when she and Nash said their vows. She reached for the phone again.

But she put it back in its cradle before she hit the redial button. After all, Diana had her own life. And Suzanna was a grown-up now. She needed to get beyond silly sentimentality. She'd dragged her sister all the way home to play maid of honor one time already this year. It was enough. This time, the ceremony would be very short. A couple of "I do's," a kiss, and maybe a simple gold band. Not a big deal.

No maid of honor required.

Chapter 6

They were married as they'd agreed, the following Friday morning in a plain civil ceremony. Her father and one of the other horse trainers stood as witnesses. They had lunch afterward at Whitehorn's newest and nicest restaurant, the State Street Grill. Then Suzanna and her husband climbed into his pickup and headed for Wyoming.

Buffalo, Wyoming, was a charming little town. It reminded Suzanna of Whitehorn, with lots of picturesque brick buildings on its wide main street and proud, craggy mountains not far away. Cottonwood fluff blew in the air, just like at home, and the prairie rolled off forever into the distance, the grasses still early-summer green.

Suzanna loved the Clear Creek Inn on sight. It was as old as the house she'd grown up in, with similar dark woodwork, high ceilings and generous-size rooms. Their hostess, Nash's friend, greeted them in the front parlor on their arrival. An attractive red-haired woman who appeared to be in her mid-forties, Emma Marie Lawrence instructed Suzanna to call her Marie and smiled affectionately at Nash—maybe a little too affectionately.

"You two come on now," Marie said. "I'll show you to the room I've saved especially for your honeymoon."

All too aware of the big four-poster lace-canopied bed just a few feet away, Suzanna hovered near the door after Marie left them alone.

"Marie seems...real friendly," she said. Nash set down their suitcases near the mahogany armoire on the far wall and then turned to look at her. She coughed. "So. How do you two know each other?"

He chuckled. "Suzanna. You been listenin' to too many Garth Brooks songs."

She made a face at him. "What is that supposed to mean?"

He'd worn new jeans to marry her in, olive green in color, neatly creased and stacked just right over his tooled dress boots. He hooked his thumb in his watch pocket and slung out a hip, pure cowboy—and purely insolent, she thought.

"Marie's a friend," he said. "And that's all. I worked for her and her husband before he died.

They owned a ranch, ran cattle, about twenty miles out of town.''

Suzanna twisted her wedding band on her finger. It felt so new on her hand—new, but not really strange. She could get used to it very easily.

It struck her again how little she really knew of the man she'd just married. He'd had a hard life—she understood that from what he'd told her the other night. And yet there was that softness about him sometimes, that natural gentleness.

''You...really do like women, don't you?'' The question escaped before she realized it wasn't exactly what she meant. She hastened to amend. ''I mean, you're good with them...er, *to* them, I mean....''

He chuckled again. ''I think that's a compliment you're stumbling all over.''

''Yes, it is,'' she said, relieved he hadn't taken it wrong.

He suggested gently, ''Could it be that you're also asking how many there have been?''

She looked at the pretty Oriental-style rug between them. ''Well, yes. I suppose that I am.''

''More than one.'' He didn't chuckle that time, but she could hear laughter in his voice. ''And less than a hundred. How's that?''

Her head came up. She could feel the color in her cheeks. ''It's not very specific, if you want the truth.''

Now he looked rather solemn. ''I'll tell you this.

I take my promises seriously. Today, I promised to be true to you. And I will.'' He looked at her sideways then. ''You gonna be true to me?''

Though she knew it was a tad unreasonable, she felt vaguely put out with him for even having to ask. ''Of course I will.''

''You sure? After all, I was your first and only…so far. Maybe you'll end up regretting that you didn't try out a few more before ending up with me.''

''Well, I will not. Not the way *you* mean, anyway.''

''And what way do I mean?''

He honestly was beginning to irritate her. ''That's not fair.''

''You started it. And why wouldn't you wonder about other men? You said yourself that you're not in love with me.''

She glanced away from the strange light in his eyes, then made herself face him. ''Why would I want some other man touching me, with the way it was that night between us?''

His smile was slow, the sweetest thing she'd ever seen. ''You liked how it was that night, between us?''

Her belly was hollowing out, and that lovely, shimmery feeling had started moving all through her. ''Yes. I liked it. I liked it very much.''

He cast a glance toward the four-poster. ''That's a nice, big bed.''

She had to cough again. "Yes. I noticed that."

"Got something in your throat?" He started toward her. "Let me have a look."

Opposing urges struck simultaneously—to run forward into his arms or to back up against the door. She gave in to neither and held her ground. "There is nothing in my throat."

"Well, good." He reached her. "And as long as I'm here, I might as well kiss you." He put his finger under her chin and tipped her face up. "Would a kiss be agreeable to you?"

That wasn't hard to answer. "Uh, yes. A kiss would be very nice."

He obliged, settling his mouth so tenderly over hers. She felt his smile against her lips, and she sighed.

He kissed her for a very long time. It felt just wonderful. And it seemed perfectly natural that he would begin undressing her as he kissed her.

Slowly, he undid the front buttons on her dress. Then he peeled the dress open and slid it over her shoulders. It dropped to the floor.

She stepped to the side, free of the dress, and he went with her, his lips still playing over hers, taking her slip straps in those gentle fingers of his and guiding them over her arms. She held her mouth to his eagerly, kissing him back as she shimmied the slip down and over her hips.

Next, she kicked off her shoes, her heart pounding

deep and hard, all of her warm and quivery and hungry for the pleasure she knew he could bring to her.

Being married to someone who knew how to kiss definitely had advantages, she decided, as he took away her bra and then pushed at her panty hose. She had to break the kiss to wiggle out of them.

When she tossed the wad of nylon aside, he was looking at her. She felt just fine, having him look. He had looked at her on *that* night, and it hadn't bothered her at all then, either. Of course, then the room had been swathed in shadow. Now, the sun shone golden and bright beyond the lace-curtained double-hung windows.

But even with the light so bright and unforgiving, she didn't mind. It seemed a natural thing, to be naked with him.

He brushed the back of his index finger over her breast, which she knew was fuller than it had been the last time. The nipple was pebbled up, hard and pouting with her excitement.

He touched her belly. "I can see the roundness now."

She looked at his hand, then laid her own over it, thinking of the baby, so tiny inside her, the hands of both father and mother pressed so close right then. Could he—or she—feel that? Was it possible the baby knew?

She looked at Nash again.

He said, "Your eyes are shining."

"It just hit me. There really is a baby inside me.

And everybody who should know about it does know about it. I don't have to be so…miserable anymore. I don't have to be so worried. I can just…''

He hooked his free hand around her neck, under the waves of her hair. ''You can just what?''

''Well, I can get on with living, I guess.''

His hand was warm and rough on her neck, massaging, making her sigh a little. ''And that's good?''

''Yes. That's wonderful.''

He caressed her cheek, ran the side of his finger over her lips. She opened her mouth a little and touched that finger with her tongue. And then, with a low sound, he hauled her close again. He kissed her deeply, then lifted her high and carried her to the bed.

He laid her down carefully, as if she were the most fragile of women. And then he stood back to remove his clothes.

Once he was naked, too, she held up her arms to him. He came down to her, laid his hard, lean-muscled body against hers. He kissed her breasts and her belly, where their baby lay sleeping. And then his mouth went lower. He parted the tender folds and kissed her in her most private place, slow and gentle, then deeper, until she clutched his head and moaned and writhed on the white sheets.

It wasn't long before she hit the peak. Pleasure pulsed and cascaded through her, clear and pure as water from some deep mountain spring. He held her hips in his rough hands and continued his endless, intimate kiss until the waves of pleasure faded to a soft, lovely glow.

Then he slid up her body and he filled her.

He rode her slow and sweet at first, putting his big hands on either side of her head, tangling his fingers in her hair. He looked at her as he moved within her, his eyes moss-green, full of color and light.

Again, her climax rolled through her, starting slowly this time and increasing in intensity. Her body bowed toward him. He rode her harder. She wrapped her legs around his lean hips and clutched him to her heart, hitting the peak a second time as she felt his completion taking him. They cried out together as fulfillment sang through both of them at once.

I love you. I love you, Nash. The words came into her mind and echoed there, insistent, unwilling to fade.

But of course, she didn't say them. She was not the foolish, romantic child she had once been. She desired him. She loved making love with him. They were going to have a baby. And he had married her to do the right thing.

Love was something else again. Love took time to build. After what had happened with Bryan, she'd learned her lesson. A woman could fool herself too easily when it came to loving a man.

A while later, they bathed and got dressed and took a long walk along Clear Creek Trail, which wound its way through the heart of the town. Box elders and willows shaded their progress, and they picked out patches of wild roses, yellow monkey flowers and the little five-petaled faces of blue flax along the way.

Blackbirds and magpies chattering at them as they went, Nash talked of the future. He told her that he and her father were making plans to improve on the already solid reputation of the Big Sky. They were going to make some changes to the breeding program, become even more selective as to which mares they used for breeding stock. And they planned to buy a few more top-quality stallions. With Nash around to supervise the training, Frank hoped to enter more of their horses in quarter horse shows and rodeo competitions.

''We want to build ourselves a reputation for raising more than just solid working horses,'' Nash said. ''We want to be known as the best quarter horse outfit around.''

Suzanna listened and encouraged him and thought that maybe all her fears had been groundless, after all. Until now, he might have been the kind of man who'd spent most of his life moving from one ranch job to the next. But right then, he sounded like a man who liked where he was and had no intention of leaving. Her heart felt lighter the longer he talked.

They ate at a nice place on Main Street, and they talked money. How much it would cost to buy those stallions they needed. How much they had—and how much they'd need to borrow. Since she handled the books, Suzanna had a pretty good idea of what it was going to require.

Her heart soared when he teased that he knew where they could get fifty thousand easy. It wasn't near enough, he said, but it would help, wouldn't it?

"It certainly would," she agreed with alacrity, thinking that his willingness to invest his life savings was just more proof that he truly did intend to settle down for good—on the Big Sky, with her and their child.

They lingered over dessert. He talked of some of the outfits he'd worked for over the years and asked her how she'd liked college out in California.

"I'll tell you this," she replied. "I always knew I'd come home."

He looked at her quizzically.

She leaned toward him across the table. "What does that look mean?"

He shrugged. "We're having such a good time. I don't want to ruin it by asking the wrong thing."

"Go on, say it," she told him. "I can take it, whatever it is."

He looked doubtful, but he did confess. "I was just wondering what that fiancé of yours knew about horse ranching."

"You were, huh?" She wrinkled her nose at him.

"Yeah. I was."

"Well, then, I'll tell you. Bryan Cummings didn't

know a thing about horse ranching—and he didn't *want* to know a thing about it, either.''

''Then why did *you* want to marry him?''

She fiddled with her teaspoon, stirring the tea the waitress had brought her, though by that time it was too cold to drink. ''To be embarrassingly honest, I hadn't thought a lot further than the wedding and the honeymoon. Bryan had a job lined up in San Francisco, working for an organization called the People's Antipoverty Brigade. I was going to move there with him. But in my heart, I knew that somehow, eventually, I would convince him to give all that up and move to Montana with me.'' She tapped the teaspoon on the side of the cup and set it carefully in her saucer. ''Pretty foolish, wasn't I?''

Nash said nothing, only watched her with a bemused expression on his rugged face.

She added, ''The fact is, the best thing Bryan Cummings ever did for me was to run off and join the Peace Corps on our wedding day.''

A smile was flirting with the corners of Nash's mouth. ''But you didn't think so at the time.''

She lifted her chin. ''No, I did not. At the time, I went a little wild.''

''I guess you did.'' He reached across the table and took her hand. ''Wild enough to pick up some no-account cowboy and spend the night with him.''

''I beg your pardon.'' She captured his thumb inside her fingers and gave it a squeeze. ''That cowboy was not a no-account. That cowboy was my future husband.''

They laughed together, and Suzanna knew with absolute certainty that everything was going to work out just fine. She was happy at that moment, holding Nash's hand across the table, happy in a way she hadn't been in a long, long time.

Maybe, she thought, she'd never been quite this happy. Never known this lovely, *fulfilled* kind of feeling, with her baby lying peacefully under her heart and her husband's hand surrounding hers and their shared laughter in her ears.

They returned to the Clear Creek Inn at a little after ten. Suzanna had barely shut the door behind them when Nash reached for her and started kissing her and taking off her clothes.

She kissed him back and unbuttoned his shirt for him, laughing a little at her eagerness to do again what they'd already done just a few hours ago.

He barely got his jeans and boots off before he was lifting her, guiding her legs around him and sliding inside her. Her body gave him not the slightest resistance. She was wet, primed for him.

She held his broad shoulders and let her head fall back, moaning. He put his mouth at her neck, licking and sucking, walking backward until he got to the bed.

Once there, he sat down, with her in his lap, her legs wrapped tight around his hips. It felt so wonderful, she couldn't help but cry out. Maybe she cried a little too loud, because he put his hand over her mouth as those waves of fulfillment cascaded through her again.

Then he finished, too, and she returned the favor, kissing him to keep him from shouting the house down. Finally, they collapsed across the bed, snickering together like a pair of very naughty kids.

They fell asleep sometime after midnight, dropping off with their arms and legs twined together, so that Suzanna's last thought before sleep claimed her was that it was hard to tell where she ended and he began.

It seemed to Suzanna that the three days that followed were a little bit of heaven on earth. They explored the wilderness area outside town together, visited the huge, spring-fed tree-shaded public pool—the largest in Wyoming, everyone said. They studied the contents of the glass display cases in the Jim Gatchell Museum, then walked the narrow halls of the historic Occidental Hotel, where the Virginian finally got his man.

They talked and they laughed. They made love at every opportunity. And they slept close together.

Oh, how Suzanna loved that, dropping off with Nash all wrapped around her—and then maybe coming half-awake a little before dawn, with his arm across her waist, his broad chest warm and solid at her back. She felt so *close* to him then. As if they'd been sleeping that way for years and years. Just an old married couple, close and safe and intimate in the big canopy bed. She would drift back to sleep with a smile curving her lips.

Monday night, the last night of their brief honeymoon, they stayed awake very late, making love and then whispering together about nothing in particular, then making love again. When they finally fell asleep, it was after two.

Suzanna woke sometime later to a feeling of...absence.

Nash had left their bed.

She opened her eyes and dragged herself up against the headboard.

He was standing at the lace-curtained window, looking out at the night.

"Nash? What's wrong?"

He dropped the edge of the lace panel and turned to her, the muscles of his powerful shoulders gleaming silver, limned in starlight.

"Nothing." His voice was flat, lacking emotion, the way it had been that night they planned their marriage, when she had sensed that something was bothering him, though he'd later told her it wasn't so. She peered at him through the darkness, seeking...what?

She couldn't say exactly. And she couldn't see his eyes. The only light came from outside, behind him. He seemed a stranger all over again at that moment, a stranger in her bedroom in the dark. She could have switched on the lamp, but something held her back from that, some feeling that he wanted the darkness and too much light would only make him turn away from her.

She waited, longing for him to come to her. When he just stood there, she couldn't bear it and held out her hand.

He did come then, the shape of him so perfect and male and beautiful to her, lean and economical, all hardness and ready power. He took her hand and sat on the bed beside her, leaning his body across hers, bracing his other hand on the mattress near her hip.

At last, she could see his eyes. He looked at her probingly. "It's good," he said. "This thing between us."

Much better than good, she thought. But all she said, very softly, was, "Yes."

"You really think it's going to last?" He tried to sound offhand, yet there was such intensity in his eyes.

She took time before she answered. It seemed very important that she give him a thoughtful reply, not just toss something off.

He spoke again before she could come up with the words she sought. "In my experience, nothing lasts all that long. Look at us, that first night. It was good then, wasn't it?"

She nodded.

He finished. "And then, in the morning, you were gone."

She licked her lips, swallowed. "Nash. I thought you understood how confused I was that night."

"I do understand. I'm not blaming you. I'm just saying that you did leave."

"I'm not going anywhere now. We're married now."

He looked so sad. "A marriage is a promise. And sometimes, even when people have the best intentions in the world, promises get broken. When my real father died, I remember my mother trying to get me not to worry. She promised she'd take care of me. And I believed her. I knew she loved me a lot and she'd never have done anything to hurt me. But in the end, she married my stepfather, and she didn't take such good care of me, after all. She broke her promise, even though she never meant to. He was so damn mean. She never could stand against him, even for my sake."

"Oh, Nash. I'm so sorry." She put her hand on his shoulder, a touch meant to soothe. He still bore very faint, pale welts there, fine lines of scar tissue, where the cruel belt had struck. She could feel them, just barely, beneath the pads of her fingers.

Carefully, he shrugged out from under her touch, a gentle but firm rejection of her sympathy. She let go of his shoulder—but not of his hand. That she held tighter than before.

She told him steadily, "I won't break my promise

to you, Nash. And I know we can make it last. If we stick together, if we work hard to stay open to each other, to build a good, honest life.''

He looked at their twined hands. ''A good, honest life.'' He glanced up. ''Sounds real solid.''

''I think it could be. I think we could make it that way.''

''You think what we have is solid?''

''I said, I think it could be solid.''

''You're only twenty-two. You've got a college education and you come from a good family. If I hadn't slipped up and forgotten to wear a condom that one time, you would never have—''

''Nash.'' She reached out, brushed his dark hair off his forehead.

''What?''

I love you. There were those words again.

But wouldn't that be too easy, just to say those three words?

She needed time to make sure the words were true. To *earn* the right to say them to him, the same way Nash wanted to earn what he owned.

''We're married,'' she said, instead of *I love you.* ''And I want to make it work. I honestly do.''

He squeezed her hand, and his eyes seemed to lighten a little. ''All right.'' He looked at her for a long moment, then he leaned forward and kissed her, a kiss that started out sweet and quickly turned hungry.

Soon, neither of them felt much like talking anymore. He slid under the covers with her and he loved her again.

And later, when she wondered what had gone wrong, she couldn't help thinking that whatever it was, it had started right then, when she'd awakened to find him at the window and hadn't known what to say to ease the doubts in his mind.

Chapter 7

They drove home after lunch the next day. Nash was quiet during the drive, but then Suzanna didn't feel much like talking herself. They'd been up so late the night before. She was tired—and a little sad, as well. Their honeymoon had been lovely. Too bad it had to be over so soon. She wouldn't have minded a little more time just for the two of them, time to get past the doubts that had troubled him last night.

At home, the ranch would make its demands on them. They'd have their nights together. But long, leisurely hours in each other's company would be harder to come by. She was jealous of that, she realized with some surprise. Jealous of the hours they couldn't be together.

Which was silly and childish and extremely self-indulgent. They had a horse ranch to run, for heaven's sake. Life was not a honeymoon—darn it, anyway.

She must have sighed or done something to betray her melancholy mood, because Nash turned to her with a worried frown. "You all right?"

She sent him a wan smile. "Fine. A little tired, I guess."

His frown deepened. "Maybe you'd better call Doc Winters when we get to the ranch."

Now she was frowning, too. "What for? You know I saw him just last week. He said everything was fine." Nash had gone with her for her first pre-natal visit, on the day they got their blood tests.

"But if you're feeling sick—"

"Nash, I'm not sick. I've been feeling just fine for days, as a matter of fact." And she had. The morning sickness that had dogged her for over a month had faded the past week or so. "I'm just a little tired." *And our honeymoon is over and I wish that it wasn't.* "I need a nap, not a visit to the doctor."

"I still think you should—"

"I said I am fine." She hadn't meant to snap at him. It just came out that way, impatient and angry-sounding.

He turned back to the road.

"I'm sorry," she said softly.

"For what?"

"Sounding so mean."

He shrugged and said it was okay, but he didn't say another word the rest of the way.

When they got home, he insisted that she go upstairs and take the nap she needed.

She didn't argue with him. She thought a nap was an excellent idea. An idea that would be even more excellent if her husband agreed to take a nap, too.

She gave him a look from under her lashes. "I will, if you'll come with me."

He shook his head. "I'd probably better go on out and find Frank. I'll let him know we're home, see what needs doing around here and get after it."

She knew he was right, of course. Besides the breeding and training of horses, there were always fences that needed mending and ditches that required burning. Not to mention hay fields to tend and cattle to look after. The herd they kept was small but necessary. You couldn't train a good cow horse without cattle for the animal to practice on.

Suzanna made a sour face. "Oh, all right. Go on and get back to work." She thought of their room at the Clear Creek Inn and had to suppress more sighing as she wished they were still there.

Nash went upstairs with her briefly, to their new room, the one in the southwest corner that had once been Diana's. It was a little larger than Suzanna's old room, and it had its own bathroom, too. Last week, before the wedding, Nash and Frank had moved Suzanna's queen-size bed in there, along with her bow-fronted bureau and an extra dresser for Nash.

Suzanna kicked off her shoes, stretched out on the bed and watched her husband change into work clothes. He came close and bent down to kiss her on the forehead before he left.

"You could at least give me a real kiss, since you insist on leaving me here alone," she muttered grumpily.

He chuckled. Was that the first time she'd seen him smile all day? "A real kiss, huh?"

"Uh-huh. On the lips. Like you mean it."

He did just that. Then he stood tall above her. "Rest now," he commanded.

"Oh, all right." She sat up, punched at her pillow, then flopped down again.

"Don't worry about dinner," he said before he went out. "Frank and I can rustle up something."

"No way will I be on my back at dinnertime. I'll cook. And you'll eat it."

He really was grinning now. "Yes, ma'am." And then he left.

Suzanna closed her eyes.

When she opened them again, it was after five and she felt rejuvenated. She got up and went downstairs and pulled some cube steaks from the freezer.

Nash and her father came in at a little after six, both covered in mud acquired while hauling a stubborn bull out of the pond in the south pasture. Suzanna sent them upstairs to get cleaned up and had the dinner on the table when they came down.

Frank asked how his daughter and his son-in-law had enjoyed their stay in Buffalo. Suzanna told him all about the beauty of the northeastern Wyoming countryside, about how homey and comfortable they'd found the Clear Creek Inn.

Her father's smile was knowing. "Sounds like you two had yourselves a real good time."

Suzanna felt the warmth in her cheeks. Why, she was blushing like some silly fool. She shot a glance at Nash, who said calmly, "Yes. A real good time."

"Well, I'm glad to hear it," her father replied, his tone grave, his eyes gleaming.

Suzanna picked up her fork and paid attention to her cube steak. Soon enough, as always, the talk turned to horses.

After they'd eaten, Nash and Frank went out to look over the training schedule together. Nash needed filling in on how the colts had performed in his absence.

Suzanna didn't know what time her father came in, but Nash didn't appear till after eleven.

Suzanna was already in bed. She sat up and turned on the lamp when she heard the bedroom door creak slowly open. Her husband stood in the doorway, his boots in his hand, squinting against the sudden burst of light.

"Er, sorry. Thought you'd be asleep...."

She knew immediately what he'd been up to. "Having a few belts with the boys, huh?"

He shoved the door shut and set his boots down. "They had to have a li'l toast, to the new bridegroom."

She shook her head. "Looks to me like it turned out to be more than one toast."

His mouth flattened out. "You mad?"

She smiled. "No." And she wasn't. She'd been irritated earlier, when he hadn't come in by eight or by nine. But then she'd given herself a stern talking-to. They weren't at the Clear Creek Inn anymore. He had his work to do, and he had a right to a little free time of his own, as well.

Besides, she'd reasoned, harping at him wasn't going to help lure him to her side. She had better ways to do that. Like wearing her prettiest little shorty nightgown, the pink one with the matching pink lace panties, which Nash had told her made a man think only of getting to what was underneath.

She lifted the covers and held them open for him. "Come on to bed."

Something happened in his face. Something almost too painful to witness. She dropped the covers and leaned toward him. "Nash. What's wrong?"

He cut his eyes away. "Nothing. I think I'll brush my teeth first."

"Are you sure you're—?"

He didn't even let her finish her sentence. "I said

there's nothing.'' His voice was rock-hard. ''Turn off the light. I'll be there in a minute.''

She obeyed him, rather numbly, wondering what she had done to make him look at her that way, as if she'd cut him to the quick somehow. She'd only smiled at him, held open the covers, sweetly suggested that he come on to bed.

She heard his feet whispering across the floor. The bathroom door opened and then clicked shut. There were the sounds of water running, of the toilet flushing.

Finally, the door opened again. A wedge of light fell briefly across the bed, then winked out. He came to stand over her in the dark. She heard the rustle of his clothing as he undressed.

Then he slid in next to her.

They lay there in silence.

Strangers, she thought. Strangers all over again…

Right then, their honeymoon closeness seemed like no more than a dream. A wishful fantasy of her yearning heart. The same as their first night had sometimes seemed to her, far away, unreal, something magical and wild that had happened to someone else.

''Nash,'' she whispered into the darkness. ''Something *is* wrong. Just tell me. Just—''

He lifted up and canted over her so suddenly that she gasped. ''I told you. Nothing.'' She smelled whiskey and toothpaste and that arousing scent that was only him. The three-quarter moon shone in the front window, its silvery light catching in his eyes. Feral and dark, those eyes. The eyes of a stranger.

But then he breathed her name. "Suzanna." He looked at her mouth.

A small, lost cry escaped her.

He took that cry, lowering his lips to hers and drinking the sound as if it were liquid, her need, her confusion, her desire to share again what they had so briefly known.

Together.

His rough-tender hand found her thigh and trailed under the short hem of her gown. He traced the elastic of her lace panties with a finger, then hooked that finger under them. She lifted herself, her mouth still locked with his, so that he could pull them down.

Then he raked the gown upward, the lace abrading her skin in the most erotic way. He found her breast, his hand closing over that fullness with heat and undeniable possession. She surged toward his touch—and he let go, only to take that burning touch lower. He found the female heart of her, found it ready, open, weeping for him.

He swallowed another of her lost, hungry cries as he slid on top of her, positioned himself and, with a quick pulse of his hips, came into her.

She cried again, the sound muffled, as her other cries had been, by his consuming kiss. He pushed into her, pulled back—and waited. She whimpered. Still, he held himself just slightly away.

She could not bear that, the feel of him inside,

but not fully. Hers but not completely. And he went on kissing her, driving her wild with his lips and his tongue, while down there he kept himself just a little away.

With a low sound of pure need, she shoved her hands under his arms, swiftly, forcefully, so that he had no time to stop her. She grasped his hard hips and pulled him sharply in to fill her again.

He moaned into her mouth then. She surged up, tighter, closer still.

And at last, he gave in to her. He moved with her, rocking into her, rocking back, rolling to the side, so that she was on top, then rolling again, to end up above her.

She rolled with him, clutching him close, wild and needful, alive to each separate, delicious thrust. She kissed him as he kissed her, in a never-ending, liquid pulse of purest sensation. The sensation spread out, a ripple in a pond of light, traveling wider and wider in a bright, burning circle, until it encompassed the room, the night, the moon and all the stars in the dark Montana sky.

Finally, he pushed in so deep, deeper than any of the thrusts that had gone before. She held him, felt his satisfaction taking him in a long, hard shudder. She shuddered in kind.

He said her name again on a low, endless groan.

And then it was over, leaving her limp, her body fulfilled, her mind and heart sad and just a little bit empty.

"Nash?"

He slid to the side and gathered her close, the way he'd done each of the four wonderful nights in Wyoming, so that her back was against his chest, his legs cradling hers.

"Sh. Go to sleep now." He brushed her hair aside, kissed her nape.

"But, Nash—"

"Go to sleep, Suzanna."

Almost, she tried again. Almost, she softly pleaded, *Please. Talk to me....*

But no.

Not tonight. She'd tried over and over again already tonight, and each time he'd rebuffed her. He'd made it so painfully clear that he wasn't in a talking mood.

Let it go for tonight, she thought. There will be time. Soon, very soon, I'll get him to talk to me, to tell me what's wrong.

Suzanna closed her eyes. She concentrated on relaxing, on how good and right it felt to have her husband's arms around her. Eventually, she managed to drop off to sleep.

Chapter 8

Frank left for Gillette on Thursday. From the horse show there, he'd go on to visit an old school friend in Colorado. He'd decided to stay in Colorado a bit longer than he'd originally planned. For three weeks, Nash and Suzanna would have the house to themselves.

Surely, Suzanna told herself, the privacy would be good for them. The intimacy they'd known at the Clear Creek Inn would be theirs again.

She tried, in the mornings before Nash left the house and in the evenings when they sat alone at the table, to reach out to him. At first, by asking what was bothering him.

When she saw that her questions only made him

close up tighter against her, she tried to talk of safer things. Of his plans for the breeding program, of which shows he wanted to see their horses enter in the months to come.

He would answer her questions, but he never really volunteered anything. More and more she felt that their conversations were like strained interviews. She asked, he answered—and then there was silence unless she asked something more.

For a few too-brief and shining days, she had thought she was coming to know him. Now she wondered if what they'd shared in Buffalo was all she would ever really have of him. A memory of closeness slipping further and further off into the past.

In the first few days after Frank left, when her work in the office was done and the house in order, she would get out Isabelle's letters and read them again and again. She was seeking some clue, some sign from her ancestor, something that would tell her what she needed to do to make her husband open his mind and heart to her again.

Isabelle wrote of an amulet given to her on her wedding day by Kyle's Cheyenne aunt, Mae, an amulet that Mae had promised would secure Kyle's love for all time.

Was that what Suzanna needed? An amulet to charm him? Unfortunately, no distant Cheyenne relative had appeared to provide one.

Suzanna racked her brain for new ways to reach

him. She went to the corrals every day, ready to ride any horse he would put her on, being helpful and hoping that he might ride with her.

He always had some reason he couldn't accompany her right then. He would tell her which colt to choose and what to watch for in the animal's behavior, and then he would leave her to ride out alone.

She tried enlisting his aid in fixing up her old room for the baby. On the last Thursday in June, when her father had been gone exactly a week, she drove all the way to Billings to get wallpaper books and fabric samples to share with Nash. He barely glanced at them.

"Whatever you want to do," he said, "that's fine with me."

Every night he went out after dinner and didn't come in until very late. She would lie in their bed alone and listen for the sound of his pickup leaving.

But he never went anywhere—except out to the bunkhouse with the other men. Suzanna knew what went on out there, and it was nothing to worry about, really. They played cards, watched TV, drank a few beers.

She kept telling herself that as long as he only went to the bunkhouse, it didn't really mean anything. He'd spent half the nights of his life in a bunkhouse, after all. He was used to hanging out with the boys. He felt at home there.

Now that was depressing. Her husband felt more

at home in the bunkhouse than with her. And depressing wasn't the only word for it.

It was scary, too. It made her fear that her original doubts about him ever truly settling down had been valid. That the real Nash Morgan was the cowboy she'd called Slim, good to horses and to women but not someone likely to stick around for too long.

Some night, and some night soon, he wouldn't just visit the bunkhouse. He'd get in his pickup and he'd head for a place like the one where she'd met him. He'd stay out all night and he'd come home smelling of whiskey and some other woman's perfume.

Maybe she'd forgive him. The first time.

But eventually, she'd run out of forgiveness.

And he would run out of patience with staying in one place.

He would leave her, with his name and his baby to remember him by.

Lord, it made her sad to think that.

Or at least, it made her sad at first.

But soon enough, as the days went by, she stopped being quite so sad.

She started to get mad.

She stopped trying to reach out to him, to get him to talk to her, to coax him to show an interest in the baby's room or to share with her his plans and dreams. She fed him his meals and she spoke to him only when necessary, and at night, when he came in late, she turned on her side away from him and pretended to be asleep.

On the first Thursday in July, when Frank had been gone for two weeks, Suzanna woke to the awareness that she did not intend to keep on like this.

She rolled over, toward the still form of her husband. He slept on his side, with his back to her. They both slept like that now, hugging their separate sides of the big bed, like strangers on a large, soft raft, floating in a vast sea of words not spoken.

Strangers.

Yes. Strangers so careful of intruding on each other's space.

It had to stop. She didn't care anymore if it drove him away for good. She was going to confront him. And, one way or another, she would make him listen to what she had to say—whatever it *was* that she had to say. She wasn't really sure yet what that should be. But she would find the words somehow.

As she glared at his back, he stirred.

Without turning her way, he pushed aside the covers and left the bed.

"Nash?"

For a determined woman with real anger in her heart, her voice sure did come out soft—barely a whisper, really.

Either he didn't hear it or he didn't want to hear it. He went into the bathroom and closed the door.

He got away from her at breakfast, too, slipping out while her back was turned as she went to clear the table. And then he didn't show up for lunch.

But he did come in at dinner. He went upstairs to clean up. She waited until he'd had time to get into the shower before she followed him.

When he emerged from the bathroom, he found her sitting on the bed. He gave her a quick glance, then ignored her as he swiftly dressed in clean clothes.

He'd sat in the corner chair to pull his boots on when she said in a clear, concise tone, "Nash, I don't know what I have done to make you turn away from me, but I want you to give me a chance to understand. I want you to tell me what it is that's been eating at you for the past two weeks." She stopped, breathed, swallowed and added, "Please."

He pulled on his right boot and then the left. Then he planted both boots firmly on the floor and looked at her.

He looked for a long time, his gaze running over her face. She had no clue what he might be thinking. Was he studying her to gauge how much she could take? Or *memorizing* her? That was what it felt like. As if he were storing her face in his memory.

But why would he need to do that? Unless…

No, she would not think that. She wouldn't. He was not planning to leave her. He couldn't be….

At last, he stood and told her gently, "Suzanna.

You haven't done anything. There's nothing wrong."

She gaped at him. And then she couldn't help it. She let a growling sound rise up from her throat and she said, "You are a liar, Nash Morgan. A damn liar, and you know it."

He sighed. He had the nerve to stand there in front of her and to *sigh*. "Suzanna…"

She fisted her hands, though what she really wanted to do was grab something and throw it at him. "You have been strange since the last night we were in Buffalo. I don't like it. I want it to stop. I want you to tell me—"

He raised a hand. "I'm going out."

She jumped to her feet. "No. No, you are not going out. You are going to stay here and—"

But he was already at the door to the hall. "Don't wait up."

"Nash!"

He didn't stop. He just kept on going, into the hall and down the stairs. She heard the front door shut.

She rushed to the window and watched him walk out the front gate. He left her line of vision as he headed in the direction of the wagon shed.

She knew what was coming.

And she was right.

Moments later, she heard the roar of an engine. His pickup appeared, swinging into the drive. He sped off, leaving a high trail of dust in his wake.

Chapter 9

Suzanna's righteous anger failed her as she watched Nash race away from her. She stood at the window for a long time, until all the dust of his leaving had settled. Until the shadows began to lengthen and the bats came out.

Then, at last, she went downstairs, cleared the clean dishes off the table and put the untouched dinner away in the refrigerator. That accomplished, she climbed the stairs, took off her clothes and soaked in the bathtub for an hour and a half.

Then she put on another shorty nightgown—the blue one this time—and she got into bed.

The hours crawled past. She did try to sleep, but sleep wouldn't come and relieve her of her misery.

So she just lay there, staring at the ceiling, rolling over, hitting her pillow to try to fluff it up a little, lying down, staring at the wall.

It was after two when she heard his pickup again. She threw back the covers and raced to the window. He stopped in the turnaround outside the picket fence. She watched him emerge from the driver's side, slam the door and approach the gate. He strode up the walk and then disappeared beneath the overhang of the front porch.

She was standing by the window, in the dark, when he came in the room. He paused in the doorway.

"Mind if I turn on the light?"

"Go ahead."

She blinked at the brightness when he flicked the switch. When she opened her eyes again, he was striding to the closet.

He got out his big, battered canvas duffel, carried it to a chair by his dresser and started pulling his clothes from the drawers.

Apparently, he was leaving her.

Her worst fear coming true.

She asked softly, "Have you been with some other woman tonight?"

He froze, turned to her. His eyes looked dead. "No."

She believed him. But it didn't make her feel any better.

"Where are you going?"

"Into town, for the night at least."

"And then?"

He paused in the act of pulling open a drawer. "Suzanna. Face it. It's time I moved on."

"Moved on?" She echoed his words as if their meaning eluded her. Then she cast about frantically for all the reasons he couldn't leave. "But…what about the Big Sky? What about all your plans? What about my dad? My dad *depends* on you."

He started piling socks and underwear into the duffel. "The Big Sky and your dad were getting along just fine before I showed up."

"But he—we…we *need* you."

"No, you don't. You needed my name. So our baby wouldn't be a bastard. And you've got it. For as long as you want it."

"No. No, that's not so. It's not just your *marrying* me. It isn't. I need *you,* Nash. I need you as my husband. Our baby needs you."

He shook his head. He didn't even glance at her. He only went on loading up that duffel bag.

Her legs didn't feel all that steady. She made them carry her to the end of the bed and then let herself sink down onto it.

He left the duffel. She watched him stride across the hooked rug and disappear into the bathroom. She stared at the open bathroom door, wishing, *yearning,* for the right words to come to her, the words that would make him change his mind and stay.

A few minutes later, he returned with his shaving gear. He put it in the bag with everything else.

She sucked in a tight breath and made herself speak with excruciating civility. "Would you mind, now that you're going, just telling me why?"

He froze—and he turned and looked at her. "Why?" he said. She wasn't certain what he meant. Maybe, *Why do you want to know?* Or just, *Why?* all by itself, just repeating her own question back at her.

She licked her dry lips and smoothed the lace of her skimpy nightie over her thighs. Her throat felt as if someone was squeezing it. She had to work to suck in a deep breath, but she managed it. Then she attempted to explain herself.

"It seemed, at first, that we were doing so well. I just don't understand, that's all. Where did it go wrong?"

"It doesn't matter." His voice held no inflection. But there was something in his eyes, something that told her it mattered very much.

"I think it does." She got the words out in a whisper. "I think it does matter, and for some reason, it's…terribly hard for you to say it. Harder than just picking up and leaving me."

He seemed to have forgotten the duffel and all the clothes he'd stuffed into it. He stood there, arms limp at his sides, staring at her.

She pulled in more air through her constricted throat and suggested quite reasonably, "After all, you've had a lot of practice at leaving. But telling your wife what she's done to...hurt you. Well, I'm pretty sure you have never tried that before.''

''It's not your fault.'' His voice was harsh—yet somehow tender at the same time.

''But there is something?''

A muscle worked in his jaw. ''Nothing you can do anything about.''

''Well. That may be so. But if you told me, it would...help me.'' She felt a smile quiver across her mouth as she added, ''Men keep leaving me, have you noticed? And it would be nice if someone would tell me why.''

''Suzanna...'' He took a step toward her, then seemed to catch himself and stayed where he was. ''I haven't got a clue why that fool you were going to marry before joined the Peace Corps.''

''Well, okay. But you. Why are *you* leaving?''

His mouth worked. She really thought he was going to tell her the truth. Then he loosed a crude oath and muttered, ''Just...leave a man a little pride, won't you?''

''What? I don't—''

''Just let it be!'' He shouted the words.

She ordered strength into her legs and made herself stand. ''No, Nash. I can't. I really can't do that. I want you to tell me. I *need* you to tell me. Why are you leaving me? What have I done?''

He swore again, and his expression was thunderous. "All right. All right, since you just have to know." She waited, not even realizing she was holding her breath until he said, "I love you. All right? Damn it, I love you."

Chapter 10

Suzanna let the air out of her lungs in a rush and sank to the edge of the bed. "You...I...what?"

"I love you." He said it again, like he was rubbing it in. "I love you, and damn it, I *hate* loving you. It's nothing but a stone heartache for me."

All she could do was sputter. "B-but, if you love me, then why—"

He sliced the air with a hand. "You want to hear it? You want to hear *all* of it? Is that what you want?"

"I...yes. I do. I really do."

"You want to hear how, after that first night, I couldn't forget you? How all I did was think about you, think about the way you were that night...so sweet and so wild?"

"The way I was that first night? Since that first night, you—"

"—couldn't forget. That's right. Like some messed-up, lovesick kid, I couldn't forget. I told myself for weeks that it was only the whole idea that I was the first one for you. That I was just getting old enough that I needed someone to yearn for, needed the one that got away to dream about while I lived my life in other men's bunkhouses and wondered if I'd ever really get my own place."

"You…thought about me? All the time?"

His mouth curled into something she could only have called a snarl. "Yeah. I thought about you. I was pining for you." He gestured widely, a move that seemed to take in the room and the big, generations-old house, the acres and acres that made up the Big Sky. "And this job I took here? You want to know the real reason I took it?"

"Yes. I do. I—"

"I took it because good old Frank pulled a picture out of his wallet, a picture of his younger daughter on Chocolate Jessie, that King broodmare of yours." Nash let out a pained laugh. "Poor Frank. He thought I was impressed by the look of that horse. Well, it wasn't the damn mare that made me sit up and take notice. I came to the Big Sky with my stupid heart in my throat, just for a chance to see Deadeye again."

He shook his head as if he couldn't believe the extent of his own foolishness. Then he started across the room in the direction of the closet, muttering over his shoulder as he went. "And you...you denied me right from the start. You pretended not to know me that first day."

She couldn't let that pass. "But, Nash, you acted like you didn't recognize me, either."

He stopped in the middle of the room and turned to her. "What the hell was I supposed to do? You looked sick to your stomach at the sight of me."

"Well, Nash. I'm pregnant. I *did* feel kind of sick."

He swore some more. "Come on. You didn't *want* me to know you. So I let you off the hook— for a while, anyway. Then you wouldn't even admit to your father that the baby was mine."

"I was trying to admit it. I was doing my best to tell him and I—"

"You would have hemmed and hawed until hell froze over. I had to tell Frank. And then you went on and on about how you wouldn't marry me, wouldn't get yourself hooked up with a stranger, a man you didn't love. And when you finally did agree to be my wife, you refused a *real* wedding with me. For me, you wouldn't wear your grandmother's dress, you wouldn't call your big sister to come stand up beside you. You were eager enough for a big wedding with that college boy who walked out on you. But a big wedding just to marry me? Hell, no."

She said, rather cautiously, "I thought you said you didn't *blame* me."

"I don't. I'm just telling you, telling you how it was."

"But I was trying to be more *mature* this time. I was trying to—"

"Whatever." His broad shoulders rose and fell in a shrug that dismissed her arguments before she could even phrase them. "I realized it that last night in Buffalo. It came crystal clear to me then that every day we were together, I only loved you more. And you…you don't love me. You like what I can do to you in bed. And you want to do the right thing, because of the baby, to be a good wife to me."

"Is that…so awful?"

"Hell, no. It's not awful. It's just…not enough. It's not love. You don't have the same feeling for me that I do for you. You never would have married me if it hadn't been for the baby. But I jumped at the chance to make you my wife."

She tried to speak. But he spoke first. "I jumped too damn fast, I realize that now. All my grown life, I've had sense enough to keep my heart to myself. And I know why. Because it hurts. It hurts like hell. To love someone who doesn't love me back, that's just no good for me. It steals my peace of mind. It leaves me thinkin' all the time that you've got five extra years of education on me. Leaves me thinkin' that we live in your father's house and I work your father's horses, that I haven't given you much of anything but a plain gold wedding band and a baby to tie you down."

That made her mad. "What are you talking

about? I *want* our baby." She held up her left hand and shook it at him fiercely. "And I am proud to wear this ring."

He wouldn't believe her. "This was all a giant-size mistake, trying to make a marriage work between us. You can do better than a man like me, and we both know it. And the best thing I can do for both of us is to head on down the trail." He turned and strode the rest of the way to the closet. She watched him in misery, wanting to shout at his back that she loved him, too—but certain in her heart that he would never believe her.

She should have told him, that last night in Buffalo, that night when he'd tried to reveal all this to her, that night when she'd been so careful, so *reasonable,* so *mature.*

From the closet, he collected his dress boots and his winter jacket and his few good Western shirts. Then he shut the closet door and started across the room.

"Nash," she began, and then said no more.

He wasn't listening. He hooked his shirts and jacket on the back of the chair as he tucked the boots into the duffel. Then he zipped it up and grabbed the handle, scooped up the shirts and jacket and slung them over his shoulder. "I'll drop by tomorrow to pick up my saddles and my trailer. And after that, I'll keep you posted as to my whereabouts. You'll get regular checks from me. Put them in a college fund for the kid or something. And once the baby's born, you can send me the divorce papers. I'll sign them and ship them right on back.''

Oh, Lord. He was leaving her. Really leaving her. ''Nash. Please…''

But he turned his back on her. He strode away from her and disappeared through the door.

Suzanna sat on the bed and listened to his boots echoing down the hall. It was the sound of him leaving her—this time for good.

She felt poleaxed. Hit square between the eyes with a big, heavy club.

Nash *loved* her? He loved her and that was why he'd kept himself from getting close to her?

The more she considered that thought, the more dazed she felt. So she went on sitting there, on the end of their bed, turning her thin gold wedding band around and around on her finger, utterly confused by the emotions churning inside her.

Shock. And worry. And anger. Why didn't he tell her all this before?

And…joy. Yes. Joy.

Because…well, because, after all, she did love him, too.

Down in front, she heard his pickup start up.

That crazy fool. What did he think driving off would prove? Nothing. Absolutely nothing. He had another think coming if he thought he could get away from her!

She jumped to her feet and sprinted across the floor, flying down the hall, taking the stairs two at a time. He was turning the pickup around when she flung back the front door and raced down the porch steps, the lacy hem of her little blue nightie floating high on her thighs.

"Nash! Nash, come back here!"

He swung the truck around, started heading away from her.

She ran faster, her hair flying out behind her, bare feet slapping the paving stones, down the front walk, through the white gate.

"Nash! Nash, you get back here!" Her feet pounded the dirt drive. And she was breathing kind of hard. She had no air left to waste on shouting. She ran for all she was worth, her heart seeming to pound his name through her blood.

Nash. Nash. Nash. Nash…

Thirty yards down the drive, he must have glanced in his rearview mirror and seen her.

The pickup slowed to a stop. She ran faster, right up to his open side window.

He leaned out at her, scowling. "What the hell has gotten into you, woman?" he growled.

So she told him. "*You,* Nash Morgan. You've gotten into me good. I love you, and if you leave me now, I will hunt you down in every roadside bar from here to New York City."

He blinked. "You're crazy."

And she nodded, gasping for breath, clutching the ledge of the window, thinking she'd hold him there with her bare hands if he dared to try driving off again.

"I am," she said, panting. "Crazy in love with

you. I'm gone. There's no hope for me. And I'm calling my dad, Nash. Calling him in Colorado. I'm going to do it right now, at two-thirty in the morning, as soon as you come inside with me. I'm telling my dad that he was right, that you were just the man for me. That I love you. That I went crazy on what was supposed to be my wedding day—and while I was being crazy, I found you.''

She paused, gulped in air, pressed one hand against her racing heart. ''And I'm also telling him that I want that big wedding, after all. That I'm marrying you all over again. A real, honest-to-goodness wedding this time. I'll be carryin' Derringer roses....''

She stopped, panted some more, frowned at him. ''You know about Derringer roses? White roses from the garden of the Derringer ranch?''

''Damn it, Suzanna, you're out here half-naked.''

She shrugged. ''It's important. Those roses. They bring good luck.''

''Suzanna—''

''And I'll wear my great-great-grandmother's wedding dress. Somehow. If I can just fit into it, with my stomach the way it's getting. And...'' All of a sudden, tears were filling her eyes. She dashed them away. ''Please. Oh, please, Nash. Believe me. You really are the best thing that ever happened to me, and I don't want to lose you. I *need* you. Our baby needs you. And the Big Sky needs you, too.''

He said, ''Move back, Suzanna.''

Her heart stopped. "Why? No. I won't. I won't let you go!"

He smiled. He actually smiled. That tender smile of his. She understood now it was a smile of pure love. "Suzanna. I only want to get out of the truck."

She stared. "I...oh. Oh, all right." She let go of the door and stepped back.

He got out.

And then he took her in his arms and kissed her.

Far away somewhere, a coyote howled.

She whispered, "Marry me, Nash."

And he said, "I believe that I will."

A month later, on the first Saturday in August, Nash and Suzanna had their big wedding, right there in the house that had been in her family for so many years.

Suzanna wore Isabelle's dress—altered temporarily to accommodate her growing stomach with delicate lace panels Suzanna had found in the old trunk upstairs. She carried a bouquet of very special white roses. With a satisfied smile on his craggy face and a tear in his eye, her father gave her away.

Diana was there, too. She'd come home to be her baby sister's maid of honor for the second time.

Late in the day, after the cake had been served and an endless series of toasts raised to the new bride and groom, Suzanna and Nash climbed hand in hand to the top of the stairs. Below them, in the front hall, Diana had gathered all of the single girls and guys.

Nash leaned toward his bride and whispered in her ear. "Garter first, right?"

She turned her head just enough that their lips briefly met. "Right."

Everyone applauded as he knelt before her. Taking her time about it, looking into her husband's beautiful green eyes, Suzanna lifted the delicate lace. Nash's teasing hand glided up the inside of her thigh. She suppressed a sigh of pleasure as she felt him unhook the garter and slowly slide it down.

He stood. Below them, a sea of familiar faces gazed up expectantly. Nash tossed the garter over the banister.

The scrap of blue silk and white lace sailed out—and dropped into the plump, outstretched hand of a blue-eyed, dark-haired child.

"Molly," someone shouted. "Molly Derringer's caught it!"

Nash chuckled. "Blew that one."

But then the little girl turned to the tall man standing next to her. "Here, Daddy. You take this."

Trey Derringer, a handsome widower, held out his hand.

Everyone laughed and applauded and then started calling encouragements.

"The bouquet, Suzanna!"

"Throw it!"

"Throw it now!"

Suzanna, bemused, stared at her sister—who just happened to be looking at Molly Derringer's dad.

"Diana!" Suzanna shouted.

Her sister jerked her glance upward—just in time to see the bouquet coming at her. She caught it, but only to keep it from hitting her in the face.

"Cheater!" someone called out, but good-naturedly.

There was more laughter, more happy cheers.

Nash bent close again and murmured for her ears alone, "You did cheat. You didn't give any of those other girls a chance."

"No," she said proudly. "I certainly did not."

"It was a good shot," he allowed.

"Just call me Deadeye," she said, and lifted her mouth for his tender kiss.

* * * * *

DIANA

Jennifer Greene

Chapter 1

Diana Brennan pushed open the school door and stepped outside. For a second she closed her eyes and breathed in the crisp Montana morning.

It was hard to believe that just weeks ago she'd been a sane, practical, unshakably responsible kind of woman. She'd loved her third-grade teaching job in Chicago. She'd paid her bills, came early to work, ate healthy, was seeing a couple of decent guys.

Now *phfft*. Here she was, in Whitehorn, Montana, on September first, her whole sane life down the tubes. Did a rational woman quit a job she absolutely loved? No. Would an intelligent woman come home for a family wedding and abruptly shuck everything—her job, her income, her apartment, her

guys—just because she discovered she was homesick? Of course not.

It wasn't a pleasant thing, discovering at the
young age of twenty-seven that one was suffering
from lunacy. At fourteen, sure, she'd been a lovesick, mortifying, romantic dreamer—but what adolescent wasn't a lunatic? She'd grown up. Matured.
Competently and capably taken charge of her life.
Only, at the moment, she seemed to be standing on
the school steps, having applied for substitute teaching work that at best was going to cover her car
payments, sniffing the air as if she didn't have a care
in the world.

Worse yet, she felt like whistling.

Off to the west, the Crazy Mountains were bathed
in sunlight, the sky a spectacular ice blue, the air so
fresh it stung the lungs on an inhale. Her dad would
be working the horses by now. Hay would be cut
today, alfalfa harvested, every live body on the
ranch stretched to the work limit at this time of year,
and her dad did the training in the morning, the most
rambunctious horses first while he had the most patience. She couldn't smell the fresh-cut hay from
here, couldn't hear cows bawling just outside of
town, couldn't see or smell the long, rolling sweep
of meadow and western larch on the road to the
Brennans' Big Sky ranch…but it was all there in
her mind's eye.

She should never have come home for her sister
Suzanna's wedding. There'd been no threat of lu-

nacy before that. She hadn't been a harebrained romantic dreamer, not since her mom died years ago, and for ages she'd talked herself into believing that she loved the excitement of big-city life. Possibly there were a few teensy signs that she was fibbing to herself. She never tried applying her rent money toward a down payment on something she owned. The nice guys came and went; she shied from anything too settled with them, too. But as much as she loved her dad, there was just nothing she really wanted to do on the ranch. She *loved* teaching. She'd been so positive she was happy in Chicago.

Only every single day since Suzanna's wedding, she'd gotten up in the morning and inhaled that Montana air. All this time, she didn't know how fiercely she'd yearned for it, how addictive the smells and tastes and scents of home would be. Surely this problem of lunacy would pass soon. She just had to get her head together and decide what to do next. She'd get practical again. She'd get serious. But right now being home felt *right,* as if her heart recognized all along that it had unfinished business in Whitehorn before she could ever really try settling anywhere else.

Suddenly she heard a child's high-pitched shriek.

Something about the little girl's shrill soprano was familiar but that wasn't why Diana swiftly spun around, her eyes snapping open. She knew children. Which meant she knew children's shrieks. There was a mountain of difference between an earsplit-

ting, Mom-I'm-sick-of-shopping shriek and a cry of
pain or a whine of fear.

This was a shriek of outrage—but Diana also
heard an underlying real fear in the child's cry,
which was why she instinctively responded. Fast.
Her boots charged down the steps, aiming right toward the source of those shrieks, her blue-eyed gaze
darting around the playground.

The school was divided into two wings. The ad-
ministration wing where Diana had just applied for
substitute teaching work also held the preschoolers,
who were separated from the elementary-age kids
for the obvious reason. The urchins hurtling around
this section of fenced yard were all bitsy size, the
swings and slides smaller and safer for the squirt
set. She saw braids and freckles and runny noses
and apple cheeks and way-cool big jeans and flop-
ping shoelaces.

Her gaze swiveled past the swing sets, then back
again, honing swiftly on the mean-eyed boy in the
red plaid shirt. He was the problem. The little girl
with the head full of bouncy dark curls on the swing
set was his prey. Diana saw him yank on the girl's
hair. Yank hard. So hard that the little girl screamed
again and instinctively reached to try and free her
hair from the bully's clutches—but that unfortunately meant that she had to loosen her grip on the
swing handles.

Diana galloped faster. There was no hope of preventing the little girl from taking a backward tum-

ble. Thankfully the preschool swings were set low to the ground, so the child shouldn't be hurt too badly, but it was still going to be a good fall. The bully was already pumping in the other direction, but from the corner of her eye, Diana caught sight of a long denim skirt—the preschool teacher, who was finally catching on to the problem.

"I'll get her!" she called. When the teacher spun around, Diana motioned toward the bully to identify the culprit and direct the teacher's attention, so she could concentrate solely on the girl.

She reached her in seconds, but the little brunette moppet had already crashed in the dust by then. Diana saw big blue eyes drowning in a whole lake of tears, saw skirts splash up and show off frilly underpants. The head full of magnolia-brown ringlets was sprinkled with good old Montana dust, and the cherry-bud mouth let out a boisterous screech of pain worthy of an Academy Award for sound effects. Diana dove in fast. The swing was waving and weaving like a drunken sailor—ready to slap back and hit the little one again.

"There, there. You're going to be okay, Molly."

She used one hand to steady the swing and scooped the child into her lap with the other. The warm body promptly snuggled to Diana's—although she was still wailing as if a murderer were torturing her. Diana almost smiled. Some kids were born victims. Not this one. This child was never going to take even the slightest injustice without letting the whole world know she was ticked—and yes, Diana recognized her almost instantly. She was Molly.

Trey Derringer's daughter.

Diana had never met Molly before her sister's wedding, but all it took was one look for her to feel a kindred-spirit connection to the child. Remeeting Molly's dad, though, had been a lot more emotionally complicated. Trey was the mortifying crush she'd had when she was fourteen. He'd been her white knight, her Rambo, her dream boat, her prince, her leather-clad biker bad boy—and every other darn fool fantasy an idiotic adolescent girl could think up. That was back in the days when she'd been a full-time romantic lunatic.

Everyone had some embarrassing growing-up moments. Trey had just been her worst—yet a single glance had still brought all those stupid, lustful, yearning feelings back. Maybe there was something lethal in the fresh Montana air. She'd been sane in Chicago. She'd been doing fine all these years. Come home, and in a matter of hours her life had started turning into shambles—she was even drooling after an old crush again, for Pete's sake.

But at that instant, her only concern was Molly. "Remember me, Mol? I'm Diana Brennan. We met in the bathroom at the wedding for my sister, Suzanna, just a couple weeks ago? You had cake in your hair? And you were thinking about murdering the ring bearer who was teasing you. There, there, you're going to be fine, honest. Just let me see...."

But Molly was wrapped around Diana tighter than peanut butter clung to jelly, and she wasn't finished with the boisterous, heartrending sobs. "I hate all boys!"

"Believe me, I understand."

"I hated that Jimmy Rae who put cake in my hair. And I hate Walter Tucker even worse. All boys should drown in a bathtub with grape Kool-Aid and Vicks VapoRub thrown in. I hate you! You're so ugly! My daddy'll get you!" she shrieked to said hateful, ugly bully, after which she turned much more delicate tears on Diana. "You saw what he did? Pulled my hair and made me fall?"

"I sure did."

"Would you kill him for me?"

"Um, I'll make sure your teacher knows that he pulled your hair on purpose." The tears weren't flowing quite so exuberantly. Diana could feel the little one looking her over, remembering, measuring her. And she was still checking for damages and trying to do repairs. She brushed the grit from those piles of soft, springy curls. Tugged down the dress. Fell in love.

Oh, man, Molly was impossible *not* to fall in love with. All the other preschoolers wore jeans or play pants. Miss Priss was dressed like a duchess, with flounces underneath, flounces on top, pink rosebuds on her socks and pink bows in her hair. Her daddy wasn't going to have to worry about this one following any crowd. But she was so pure girl that

Diana would be checking out convents and chastity belts if she were her mom. Four years old, and the boys were already chasing her.

"I'm gonna get that Walter Tucker," she informed Diana with most unladylike zeal. "He's gonna be sorry he was ever born. He's gonna eat dirt. He's gonna... Hey, now I remember. You were talking to my daddy at the wedding, weren't you? You told him how Jimmy Rae put cake in my hair?"

"Yes." Diana hadn't found any injuries beyond a scuffed stocking, dirt and skinned pride, but she heard two more dramatic half-sobs. Molly seemed to be losing interest in the dramatic expression of pain, though, because she was suddenly studying her with shrewd old-woman eyes.

"Did you think my daddy was cute?"

"Um, yes." Diana sensed the trick question, but she still had to lie for the child's sake. No woman was going to label Trey Derringer *cute*. Trey was a panther, cut and dried, with hair black as jet, dark searing eyes and a long, sleek, athletic build. If life were fair, he'd have a pooch by now, but no. He'd looked sexy enough in a navy blue suit to make every woman at the wedding drool—except for the bride. Just then, though, Diana understood perfectly well that she was dealing with his daughter's biased opinion—and she'd have said anything to make the tyke stop crying, besides.

"Did you know that my mommy died?" Molly asked her.

"Yes, I heard." Suzanna had told her that Trey's wealthy young wife, Victoria, had died in a car crash two years ago. Undoubtedly that was why Diana had felt such an instant kinship for the child. "I'm sorry, honey."

"Why would you be sorry?"

Diana didn't miss a beat. She knew how blunt four year olds could be. "Because I lost my mom when I was a little girl, too. So I know how hard it is, sweetie."

"You don't have a mom, either?"

"Nope. I was fourteen when my mom died. And my sister, Suzanna, was around nine." Diana reached for the shoulder bag she'd dropped and started foraging for a brush and tissue. "Thankfully, just like you, though, we had a wonderful dad to help us through that rough time—"

"Yeah. My daddy's the best in the whole world. But I still need a mom, and I'm really tired of waiting. Are you married?"

"Um, no—"

"Are you 'gaged?"

"Engaged? No—"

"Well, do you like dolls? And telling stories?" The interrogation was curtailed for a few seconds. Molly first blew into the tissue Diana pressed to her nose, then lifted her face for some mopping up with a handkerchief.

"Sure."

"You're pretty." Molly announced this, then avidly scrutinized her head to toe, from her long denim dress and boots to her mink-brown short hair. "In fact, you're more than pretty. You're prac'lly gorgeous. You're not a digger, are you?"

The conversation had gone far enough, Diana mused wryly. Still she couldn't resist asking, "A digger?"

"Yeah. Like for money. Simpson keeps saying that women keep chasing my daddy because he has a bunch of money. We don't want diggers. We want someone who likes to sing songs and tell stories and wants to love us."

"Ah." Diana had no idea who Simpson was, but it was a pretty good guess that *digger* was a reference to gold digger. And she felt helplessly touched by the child's matter-of-fact seeking someone to love them. She stuffed the tissues in her shoulder bag and grabbed a brush. A little brushing and fussing and the little one looked almost back to normal—except for that rabid look in her huge, innocent blue eyes. Diana wondered if Trey realized his daughter was scouting women for him, and suspected yes. Molly wasn't a child to leave an adult doubting what her opinion was about anything. "Well, Mol, I'm a teacher—so naturally I like to sing songs and tell stories. Just like I'll bet your preschool teacher does, too. And right now, I think your recess is over and she's going to start missing you if you don't head inside."

"No, she won't. Ms. Hawthorne saw me with

you. And I'd rather talk to you, okay? Let's talk about sex.''

The little devil paused, obviously anticipating a shocked look from the nearest adult. When Diana failed to look embarrassed, Molly tried out a lofty look.

"It's okay. I know all about it. Everybody always starts whispering when that word comes up. Like they think I'm stupid and couldn't figure it out.'' Molly rolled her big blue eyes in clear disgust. ''It's something dads and moms like to do together. Everybody knows that. So. If you don't like to do it, say now, okay?''

"Well, you know, lovebug, we can talk about sex any old time…but right now, you really are going to be late unless you hightail it back to class. Come on, I'll take you in.''

Minutes later, Diana was winging toward home, having safely pawned off Molly into her teacher's care—but she was still chuckling at some of the child's precocious, manipulative antics. That one could keep two adults running without half trying, she mused. And she was so young to have lost her mother.

The dazzling noon sunlight almost blinded her as she turned onto Brennan land. The yearlings were kicking up their heels in the west pasture, a tractor leaving a wake of dust in the far east alfalfa field. All the sounds and smells were familiar from her childhood—and so were the memories of losing her

own mom. At fourteen, she had thought she'd die
from the grief.

She'd grown up that summer. She'd had to. Her
dad had been lost, and so had her younger sister.
She had no more time for a crush on Trey Derringer,
no time for romantic daydreams of any kind. Overnight she'd turned into a realist—which she needed
to do—but losing a mom was still the most heart-
tearing pain she'd ever experienced. Really, it was
impossible *not* to feel a special compatibility with
little Molly. Maybe she'd never gone mom hunting
quite like Mol—but she'd missed her mother so
fiercely and so long that she could still taste that old
pain.

She wondered if Trey realized how dedicated his
daughter was to the mom-hunting cause—and
thought, of course he must. And a shiver teased up
her spine at the thought of running into him again.
Best not. Making a fool of herself mooning after him
as a young teenager was understandable—the stuff
one could laugh at as a grown-up. But it wouldn't
be funny to make a fool of herself for the same man
a second time.

Not that she was even remotely afraid that could
happen.

"Diana! Telephone for you!"

"Thanks, Dad, I'll get it." She was hugging and
puffing, her arms precariously loaded with bedding
and pillows as she charged downstairs, but moving

would wait. All evening she'd been expecting a return call from some old Chicago teacher friends. Jogging swiftly, she dumped the armload on the cracked leather couch in her dad's library and then, breathless, grabbed the receiver on his desk. "Hello?"

"Diana…it's Trey Derringer. Did I catch you at a bad time?"

Well, shoot. Weakly Diana sank into the ancient desk chair, thinking that a sniper's bullet couldn't have caught her more unprepared. Trey didn't have to bother identifying himself any more than he'd needed to at her sister's wedding. She'd have known that lethally low, sexy baritone anywhere, any time. Unfortunately, even the sound of his voice was enough to make an adolescent girl's crush roll through her memory with the subtlety of a Mack truck. He could still do it to her. Invoke that feeling of lunacy.

Of course, she was mature enough to hide her feelings these days. Or die trying. "You didn't catch me at a bad time at all—actually, you saved me from a fate worse than death. I was moving."

"You're leaving Whitehorn again?"

"Oh, no, I'm staying home. At least for a while—I'm not sure about jobs right now. But I've been trying to move my things from the big house over to a cabin we have on the property. It's empty, no reason I can't use it, but the family's been giving me a hard time about it all day." She could hear her sister and new brother-in-law in the kitchen. "They all keep saying there's plenty of room here—which is true. But I don't want to be underfoot with Suzanna and Nash—"

"I wouldn't want to intrude on newlyweds, either."

"And it's different for Dad. He's off in his own wing. Also, when he and Nash start talking horse breeding... Well, let's just say they're both as happy as two pearls in the same clam. Anyway—I didn't mean to run on, but I can promise, you're not interrupting anything but a bunch of work I'm happy to take a break from. You had a reason for calling?"

"Yes. I just wondered if you realized that the two of us were wildly in love and engaged to be married."

She almost choked—but of course she realized this had to be some kind of joke and tried to keep her voice deadpan to play along. "Why, no, I had no idea. Thanks for letting me in on that news. Have we, um, set a date?"

"I don't know. I forgot to ask my daughter. Molly's the one who has all the details."

"Somehow I suspected that," Diana said with a chuckle. And then heard a sigh, heavy with relief and pure male.

"Thank God you're laughing. I should have remembered you had a great sense of humor. I almost didn't call," he admitted, "but I was afraid you'd hear all about our wedding plans and exotic love affair in town and wonder what on earth was going on. In fact, that's exactly how I heard. *Not* from my daughter. But when I got into town this morning, I started hearing details at the gas station, the school, the post office. And the Hip-Hop Café, naturally, was buzzing with anything resembling new town gossip.''

''Where else would news travel faster than the speed of light in Whitehorn? And yikes. It sounds like you've been taking quite a razzing.'' She propped her stockinged feet—with hole—on her dad's desk. Her gaze wandered around the library shelves, filled with books on horse breeding, vet medicine, ranch journals—but no fiction, and for sure no romance novels. The room smelled of pipe smoke and a soot-stained chimney and those old dusty books. The way a ranch library was supposed to smell. A little leathery, tough, hearty, no-nonsense sensible. The way she tried so hard to be.

''Well, I'm used to the problem. You're not. And I'm afraid you're going to hear about this love affair of ours sooner or later—''

''It's okay. I've met your daughter twice now, Trey. And I adored her both times.''

''Well, I do, too. But not when I'm inclined to kill her. When Molly lies…it's like she's in church. Everyone believes her. Those big blue eyes. The sincerity. Even as those whoppers are spilling out of her mouth. I don't understand where she got this inventing streak—''

"She's four, Trey. Nobody lies as well as a four year old. Even a con artist behind bars could take lessons. You didn't really think I'd take offense, did you? She's obviously auditioning women for a mom. I assume she's done it to you before."

"Actually, no. She hasn't." A sudden silence. "I just…thanks for being so understanding. And good luck with your move."

He'd obviously said all he wanted to and was about to end the call, which in principle Diana thought was a fantastic idea. Even the lighthearted conversation gave her heart a kick—as if they were friends, had a relationship, could easily talk together. Only her pulse was suddenly galloping like a runaway colt. She never had, never could think of Trey as a plain old pal. As quickly as she wanted to hang up, though, suddenly she hesitated. "Wait a minute—"

"You're busy, Diana. I don't want to interrupt—"

"But there's something else, isn't there?" She heard that something in his voice. "Something related to Molly that you didn't want to say? I'm touched that she likes me, Trey. Honestly, don't waste a second worrying that I would be offended or take news of our, um, wedding plans in the wrong way."

"I wasn't that worried. I remember you as a kid. You always did have the warmest heart in Montana."

Her heart started racing faster than a loony clock. For Pete's sake, he'd only offered her a small compliment. She decided it had to be best to take the practical bull by the horns. "You remember I had a crush on you, huh?" she asked dryly.

"I was honored."

"I'll bet. Every high school senior loves a fourteen year old following him around like a puppy dog, but it was partly your own fault. You were so kind. You never made me feel bad about it." She kept her voice light, and to her surprise, discovered her mood was becoming light, as well. It *was* a good idea to get this said. Partly so Trey knew she was mature enough to face an old embarrassment, and just maybe to convince herself of that, too. "I never had a chance to tell you. I'm sorry about your losing your wife, Trey."

"Thanks." Again, an odd silence, with the flavor of something troubling in his voice. "Actually, there is one other thing I'd like to bring up. I hate to ask you for a favor, but I would appreciate if you'd be…careful…about any comments you made about this imaginary engagement of ours."

"Well, sure. But I don't understand."

"It's just… Molly's my life, Diana. But since Victoria died, her parents have been trying to fight me for custody. That's no secret. If you're in Whitehorn long, you're bound to hear something about it."

Diana wasn't sure what to say. He was obviously

trying to be honest with her, but there was pain in his voice. Pain that was an unexpected intimacy to share with someone he barely knew—like her. And she suddenly didn't care about that old stupid crush. The sound of his pain touched her. "Are you afraid the Kingstons could win custody?"

"No, not really. No one could doubt that I can provide financially for Molly. And I'm her dad. There has to be a reason for the court to take a child away from a parent, and there is no reason. They've looked for all the obvious kinds of dirt—that I'd expose Molly to drinking or drugs or inappropriate behavior with a woman. But there's nothing like that and never will be."

She read between the lines. "But it could be troublesome, if Molly suddenly started telling stories of a woman in your life. Like me."

"There's no problem with an adult female being in my life, but there's a difference between that and Molly implying that she's been exposed to intimate behavior." He sighed, again clearly embarrassed. "I'm just asking that if someone teases you...if you'd be aware that anything you say could get back to the Kingstons. And could be taken in a very serious light."

"Good grief, Trey. That's terrible. Having to worry all the time what someone could say. Or that a friendship could be taken wrong."

"It's not your problem. And I sure didn't mean

to make it sound as if it were. I just had to ask you, to be careful—''

''I will be. Please don't worry.'' She hesitated, thinking that it was past time they both hung up. Neither could possibly have anything else to say. Yet somehow she just couldn't let the conversation go without opening her mouth one more time. ''Look. Is there any chance it would help if I talked to Molly?''

Chapter 2

Two nights later, Diana pulled into the Derringer driveway, feeling mad enough to kick herself. Where was her head when she agreed to do this? Inside a cuckoo clock?

She had no business offering to help Trey with his daughter. None. That whole telephone conversation had simply been flustering. She'd been startled to discover that she was the only woman Molly had glommed onto for a potential mom. Somehow that made her feel responsible. And she hadn't realized Trey's in-laws were fighting him for custody. And she naturally felt a kinship for a little girl who'd lost her mother, because she had, too. And somehow it just bubbled out. That offer to help.

Offering to help wasn't a bad thing. Volunteering

to spend more time around Trey was the bad thing. Did a dieter expose herself to crème brûlée? Did a drinker deliberately walk by bars? Did a broke woman go to a sale?

No, of course not. Anyone with a brain would avoid the dangerous substance. Yet here she was, gamboling like a carefree, nitwit yearling toward trouble.

And Diana's first glance at Trey's house only made her feel more morose. Reluctantly she turned the key in her dad's red pickup and stepped out. She'd dressed in a long khaki skirt with a vest and shirt, casual clothes that seemed appropriate for a dinner centered around a four-year-old child.

The casual clothes seemed all wrong. She kept forgetting that Trey had a ton of money now, because he'd grown up on the poor side of the Derringer family, and that's when she'd known him before. He'd worked every job on the ranch he could get as a kid—which had always been part of his allure for her. Growing up, she was always around horse ranches, which meant she was always catching sight of his bronzed, hot, sweaty muscles—mucking out stalls, working horses, pitching hay. It wasn't *just* his muscles that she'd drooled over, but his whole hunklike, heroic character. Not a spoiled bone in him. He'd made his own way, on his own brawn and brains, from the time he was a young squirt.

Only now he'd made it—made it so high that Diana felt even more awkward being around him. She hiked toward the front door, trying not to gawk at

the view, but the structure was less a house than a
Western palace. The place was built of stone, with
cool glass walls overlooking the mountains and a
balcony with a hot tub jutting out of the second
floor. Investments. She'd never been positive exactly
what that meant—but Trey made piles of money doing it, that's all everyone kept saying. Back when,
he'd aced a scholarship to some Ivy League
school—broke her heart when he left Whitehorn—
then landed some pricey-dicey job in an East Coast
investment firm, then presto, four years later, came
back home to start up his own. At thirty-two, he was
still practically a kid, for Pete's sake. And already
hauling in zillions.

Coming here was dumb. Dumb, dumb, dumb, her
agreeing to this dinner.

Yet the front door opened before she could back
out and skedaddle for the truck like the coward she
wanted to be. The unfamiliar man suddenly framed
in the doorway looked like the scary ogre in the
Beanstalk fairy tale. His height pushed past six and
a half feet, and he had to be carrying more than three
hundred pounds. His thinning long hair was shagged
back in a ponytail. He had a built-in inner tube
around his middle and tattoos running down his bare
arms. "Hey," he greeted her.

Hey? And this dude worked in a millionaire's
house? "Hi," she returned.

He offered her a beefy hand and a thousand-watt
grin at the same time. "I'm Simpson. Molly's
nanny, Trey's mechanic, the cook...hell, I don't

know what my formal job title is. I just live here. Come on in, we'll get you a drink— Oops, I guess that drink'll wait two seconds.''

Molly suddenly erupted from behind Simpson and catapulted toward her. ''Ms. *Brennan!* I'm *so* glad you're here! Simpson, isn't she beautiful just like I told you?''

''Yup, she is.''

Diana returned the exuberant grin, feeling like she was melting from the inside out. Okay. So this was dumb. But she was so crazy about Molly that there was absolutely nothing dumb or wrong about wanting to help the little one. And then Mol grabbed her hand and tugged. ''You just come on in and talk to my daddy. I'm gonna be so good and so quiet you won't believe it. And Simpson made us a *great* dinner, just for company—''

''I did,'' Simpson confirmed as he shut the front door. ''Meat loaf and mashed potatoes. And no, the peas won't be touching the meat loaf. Not on my dinner plates. Hot fudge sundaes for those who finish their suppers.'' His voice dropped two octaves. ''Just for the record, I had no vote in this particular menu—''

''But I did!'' Molly said happily. ''We had to have something specially good for you, Ms. Brennan!''

''And I'm so grateful. They sound like my most favorite foods of all times, munchkin.'' She could hardly take her eyes off the living room. She'd half expected a notably expensive feminine decor, because Victoria Kingston had been quite a socialite, yet it was obvious Trey had beat to his own masculine drummer. Everything was giant size. The fireplace was made of sandblasted granite with a spectacular bronze mantel. Huge couches and chairs were square in shape and terra-cotta in color, heaped with cushions big enough for Molly to curl up and nap on. The plank chestnut floor was softened with Turkish rugs. Red stone doorways and oak ceiling beams made the window view of the Crazy Mountains seem a natural part of the inside.

Trying to walk through the living room almost took a map. Diana couldn't help but be charmed. Not by the cool-guy decor, but by the nonstop messes. Some kind of marble board game was in midprogress, taking up the entire coffee table. A Barbie Vet Center blocked an aisle. A computer was blinking a game with basic-reader words on it. Spread liberally everywhere were coloring books and baby doll carriages, naked dolls and tea sets.

It was easy to see who ruled this place—and the only tyrant wielding any power around here was significantly shorter than four feet tall.

And then Trey suddenly stepped in from the terrace, his hand stretched out to greet her, striding through the debris as if he were an old pro at walking the gauntlet. Oh, dear. Oh, dear. Her brain picked up the chant and kept repeating the refrain. He was wearing jeans and a comfortable chamois shirt, his dark hair wind-brushed and his carved face ruddy from the brisk air. He was good-looking. That wasn't news. That wasn't the reason her pulse felt stunned. Truth to tell, she'd never cared that he was handsome in that dark panther kind of way. Good looks in themselves would never have made her blood pound.

But his smile did. Always had, and tarnation, maybe always would. And for some unknown reason, he smiled at her as if she mattered. As if he wanted to see her. As if he liked her looks, liked her program, was enjoying the visual stroll from her head to her toe and wanted her to know it. That slow, lazy crack of a smile was so darned intimate that Diana could almost believe he was attracted to her—but she'd have to be a total lunatic to believe that.

And she'd accepted having a problem with lunacy since she came home, but she refused to believe that she couldn't shake this idiocy with some guts and determination.

With his feet up and his stomach full, Trey took a sip of cappuccino, watching Diana with his daughter, trying to remember the last time he'd been this attracted to a woman.

Never, he decided. Which was a considerable period of time.

That Molly had chosen Diana for him especially struck his funny bone, because Mol had been a pistol and a half any time he'd had a woman over since her mother died—even if the sole reason for the visit was business. His family told him that the issue was jealousy. Molly'd had her daddy to herself all this time and she liked it that way. The surprise of Mol's taking to Diana so completely had naturally motivated him to take a look at her, too.

Truth to tell, he hadn't looked at a woman in an intimate way since Victoria died. But he was now.

A small fire lapped the logs in the stone hearth. This early in September, the evenings were usually still mild, yet this night there was a sting in the air, a hint of white on the mountaintops. Trey could already feel the chill of another lonely winter coming on, coming soon.

Backlit by the fire, Molly was scrunched on Diana's lap in one of the oversize chairs, a book of Shel Silverstein poems open between them, the two heads nestled together, both giggling. Trey had no prejudice about his daughter. With her shiny mahogany curls against that porcelain skin, she was the most beautiful child ever born—that was Trey's story and he was sticking to it. But for once, it was another female who'd snared his attention.

Diana's clothes were very nice—particularly if she were interviewing for a job as a nun. The khaki skirt concealed everything from waist to ankles. A loose, thick shirt revealed nothing of her upstairs figure, and the vest further hid the shape of her breasts, as well as advertised she was a homebody children lover. Everything she wore could have had a don't-touch-me-fella sign.

He got the message. But everything about her appearance—including her clothes—inspired him to know her better, and specifically to touch her. Preferably nonstop, and he hoped soon.

Her hair was a short, silky pelt brown. It framed her face, with a wave tucking under her chin. Her eyes were brown, too, only a deeper, richer, sultry brown, and that mouth of hers was just as sexy. She wore no gloss or lipstick. No makeup at all to call attention to herself. Yet her skin had a natural sun-kissed glow, a rise of color riding the delicate line of cheekbone, and when she smiled, the spirit and warmth in her eyes easily sent a man's heart slamming. Beneath all those figure-concealing clothes were long coltish legs, a long and low-waisted figure and a body that moved with her. There was no coyness to her walk, just grace. And so unlike Victoria, there was absolutely no look-at-me in Diana's appearance. Instead she radiated a natural feminine sensuality that tripped his nerves faster than a hair trigger.

He could have participated with the girls, but sitting back and watching the two of them was doing a good job of pulling at his heart. The amazing thing was that Trey hadn't been aware he had a heart to pull—except for his daughter. And after Di finished reading Molly the Silverstein poems, she gently, deliberately led Mol into a discussion. Belatedly he remembered that this discussion was the excuse he'd had for inviting her—which somehow he'd completely forgotten about.

"You know what telling the truth means, punkin wunkin?"

"Sure." Molly cuddled closer on Diana's lap.

"Okay. When you see a movie, and someone on the movie screen gets hurt, is that true? Is the actor really hurt?"

"No, that's pretend."

"You're so smart." Diana touched a fingertip to his daughter's precious nose. "And you're so right. That's pretend. Do you like the Cinderella story?"

"Oh, yeah."

"I do, too. But can you tell me if that story is real or pretend?"

"Pretend."

"Holy mackerel. You're right again. And when you told some people that your daddy was engaged to be married, was that true or pretend?"

Molly tried the big-innocent-eyes routine on Diana. God knows the kid knew it worked on him every time. "Listen," Molly said charmingly. "You could love my daddy so easy. He's wunnerful. I love him more than everything in the whole world. And then you could live here and read me stories every night, just like tonight. Wouldn't that be great?"

His daughter was talking about him as if he wasn't in the same room. Trey considered being embarrassed, but the thing was, Diana didn't seem to be. She just nodded.

"I hear you, punkin, but that didn't answer my question. When you told people your dad was engaged to be married, was that real or pretend?"

"It was pretend. I *know* I was making it up. But

it *could* be real. Is it the sex thing? You can do the sex thing, can't you?''

Trey's coffee mug dropped from his fingers to the carpet. Behind the chair, Diana made a hand gesture that Molly couldn't see, as if to privately communicate to him that everything was hunky-dory, stay cool.

''We're not talking about me, Mol. And we're not talking about sex right now, either. We're talking about you telling the truth, and first I want to be sure you know the difference.''

Molly hunched up her knees more seriously. ''Are you mad at me?''

''Nope. But there is a problem, Molly. The thing is, we're just getting to know each other. And I like you so much. But if I'm going to like you even more, it would help if I could trust you. And I can't trust you if you tell fibs.''

The princess tried arguing with her—Molly did have a teensy tendency to try arguing her way out of trouble—but Diana didn't let up, just kept gently teasing her into seeing what was right in terms a four year old could grasp. Trey marveled. Twenty minutes later, when Simpson poked his head in, naturally Molly didn't want to leave Diana's lap— much less go to bed. Eventually, though, she was conned. Simpson promising her a piggyback ride all the way upstairs was always an effective bribe. But the instant those two left the room, Diana leaped to her feet.

"Dinner was wonderful. I really enjoyed it, but now I should go," she said swiftly.

"No way," he said in his best slow, take-it-easy voice—but he was fascinated. As far as he could tell, Diana had nerves of steel. Hell, she could handle a four year old's questions about sex without even blinking, yet suddenly—now they were alone—nerves showed in her eyes and she was edgily bolting for the door. "You have to stay at least long enough for me to give you a brandy—or pay you in solid gold for a thank-you. I really appreciate how great you were with Mol."

The smile was a little flustered, but at least she stopped that mad flight for the nearest exit. "Not great. I'm just used to being around kids. You know I'm a teacher—"

"Uh-huh. But I'm her dad, and she can still run rings around me. In fact, I think I'm going to be an old man before she reaches her fifth birthday. I almost had a stroke when she suddenly brought sex into the conversation. How come you weren't mortified? I was." Simpson had brought in a tray of cognac and glasses earlier, but neither of them had touched any while Molly was around. Now, though, coaxing her to stay a few more minutes was simply a matter of pouring a few sips in a snifter—not so much it could possibly affect her driving later—and handing her the glass.

She didn't turn it down. She chuckled at his confession about being mortified, although she rolled her eyes as if she didn't believe him. "I think it's too late for me to be embarrassed by anything kids do. Besides, when little squirts use a word like sex, it's almost always because they figured out it has a shock effect for adults. It doesn't really mean anything more than that, Trey. Nothing to worry about.''

"I'm not worried. But I have to admit, my in-laws could well have a stroke if they heard Mol talking about sex or come out with any other suggestive words. I know they'd blame me."

He watched her hesitate. She obviously didn't want to pry, yet she didn't want to cut off the conversation about his daughter, either. Finally she said, "I never really knew your wife, Victoria, because you two were that far ahead of me in school. But I did kind of know the Kingstons, because they went to our church. They were never unkind, but they just seemed, um, stiff."

He set down his glass, but his gaze never left her face. "They are stiff. But that really isn't the reason that Molly's grandparents and I are at odds. And I hate making you uncomfortable by talking about this, Di, but I do feel it'd be easier in the long run if I just cleared the air and was frank with you. You'll hear it in town if I don't say it anyway. The Kingstons blame me for their daughter's death."

Her lips parted in surprise. "But how could they? I understand your wife died in a car accident. And she was the only one in the car, I was told."

He nodded. "Yes. She was alone in a car, coming home from a party. She'd been drinking. Skidded on an ice slick and crashed into a tree.'' He shook his head. ''The Kingstons blame me for Victoria being unhappy. They see it as my fault that she was drinking. My fault she went to that party alone. My fault she died.''

''I can understand their mourning their daughter. But not their blaming you,'' Diana said gently.

''Well, reality is that Victoria and I weren't happy, which her parents were well aware of. And when they started this custody fight, their primary argument was that I neglected my wife because I spent all my time making money, and I would neglect my daughter the same way. And they're right about their daughter. But not about mine.''

Diana opened her mouth as if to argue with him—the polite thing—yet instead she cocked her head and simply listened.

Trey never found it easy to talk about this. But there was no possibility of his developing any kind of trust relationship with Diana unless he were honest with her. ''I never meant to neglect Victoria in any way. But I grew up poor, where she grew up with wealth. I wanted money and everything money could buy, where she wanted to take things from her parents, have the two of us just live off them. I couldn't. It wasn't in me to live off someone else. But when I was working long hours, she went off with her own crowd, partying, drinking and so on— Diana, my daughter doesn't know any of this. Even if it would help me with this custody problem with her grandparents, I really don't want to down-talk

Victoria to Molly. Mol thinks that her mom was an angel. I want her to have that positive impression.''

"I understand."

"And so far, the Kingstons—Regina and Ralph—have worried the hell out of me, but there doesn't seem to be a real threat. The court's backed me. There never was a question about my financially supporting Molly. It was about whether I was too busy to provide attention and a loving home—the way two full-time grandparents claim they could. But Mol's my life, Diana. Yeah, I work, but—"

"Trey." Diana motioned to the mountains of toys and child entertainments strewn through the living room. "You don't have to tell me that you adore your daughter. And more to the point, I can see the way she is. Happy, secure, sure of herself."

"Spoiled rotten." He filled in another blank.

"Yeah, that, too." She grinned. "I imagine what you don't manage to give Molly, Simpson does."

Trey washed a hand over his face. "Yeah, well, Simpson's another one of the Kingstons' complaints. And I know how he looks with the tattoos, the long hair and all—hardly your typical nanny. I also realize that Mol needs a woman's influence, but it isn't that simple. Simpson is as crazy about Molly as she is about him. I can't see hiring a stranger just because of gender when he worships the ground she walks on."

"For heaven's sake, Trey. All anyone should have to do is look at Molly to be sure what you're doing for her is great, including Simpson. She's adorable. Full of herself, high on life and everything in it. What's to worry?'' Impulsively she reached over and touched his hand, the gesture clearly meant to express affection and sympathy, nothing more. But she seemed to notice her pale white hand against his sun-ruddy skin, and suddenly she was surging to her feet again. ''Good grief, it really is late now. I never meant to take up your whole evening, and I need to get home.''

Because he could see that she was serious about leaving this time, he walked her outside. The temperature had plummeted at sunset. The sky was a chilled-down navy blue, peppered with icy stars, and Diana had brought no jacket. She clutched her arms as she walked next to him to her father's red pickup with the Big Sky logo on the door.

''Diana, I want to apologize—''

''Apologize? For the wonderful dinner or the good company?'' she teased him. ''I fell in love with your daughter at my sister's wedding, if you didn't notice. She's a total darling.''

''Good. But I'm still apologizing for airing all our family linen. I never wanted to make you feel awkward…but I did want to be honest ahead of time. Because I'd like to ask you over again. To see you again. At least, if the total picture didn't scare you off.''

''You want to see me again?''

She dug in her shoulder bag for the truck keys, and when she found them and tilted her face toward his, her expression reflected both surprise and confusion.

She didn't get it, he mused. All evening he could feel the combustible chemistry between them, could see her eyes shying from his, then darting back, could see her cheeks flushing, had felt her pulse startle when his hand accidentally brushed hers. And yes, more than a dozen years ago, he remembered a coltish young girl who'd followed him around as faithfully as a puppy. She'd been so sweet, so painfully yearning. He wasn't a particularly sensitive teenager, but still he'd have shot himself before hurting her feelings, and hoped he never had. For sure he'd never let on that he was aware of her crush to avoid embarrassing her.

But that was then.

And this was now.

Her dark eyes looked like liquid chocolate in the moonlight, her smile alluring and luring both. Just looking at her, his gut tightened and his pulse started tripping like an ungainly teenager's. He couldn't help but be aware how different she was from Victoria.

He'd married once for practicality, because he thought it was time to be married, time to settle down. Truthfully, Victoria had picked him and done the chasing more than the other way around, but her country-club taste and blond perfection had been everything he had ever dreamed of. He expected to be a good husband. Expected to give one hundred percent. And he'd revered the ground she walked on in the beginning.

But it wasn't and never had been a marriage of love, and Trey would never make that mistake again. Both of them had been in hell before Victoria died. Neither, really, at fault. He'd never stopped trying, and if Victoria had, well, he'd blamed himself for that as long as he was going to. She'd wanted him, but she hadn't loved him, either. Ever. And he'd withered on the inside for a long time, feeling more and more alone, feeling wanted only for his money and what he could do, never for himself. Long before she'd died, he'd felt a chasm of silence from dying on the inside himself.

In the past couple years, he'd occasionally gone out, but not often. He carried a lot of problems that it wasn't fair to ask someone to share, he'd felt, but more than that, there hadn't been anyone he cared enough about to even try. Trey never wanted to make the same mistake. If he ever fell, he wanted nothing unless he could have it all. He wanted the flame, the magic, the power. He wanted a woman who made his knees shake with wanting. He wanted to feel crazy in love—and for her to feel the same— or he didn't want to waste time even stepping foot in the ballpark. And truth to tell, he never expected to find any such thing. He wasn't positive that kind of love existed—at least for him.

But damned if, for the first time in his life, he hadn't found a woman who finally did it. Made his knees shake. Her hair like a simple cap, skin so smooth she wore no makeup, no artifice to her, all bundled up in those figure-concealing clothes, making it so obvious that she hadn't come over for dinner with any intention of alluring him...yet she was alluring. That smile. Those eyes. The scent she wore, a tickle of flowers and a hint of a soft, summer wind and then something sexy right behind it, like a punch.

He could taste risk, just being in the same room with her. The kind of risk he'd never dared in his life before. The kind of risk he really hadn't known was out there.

Of course, he hadn't tested this amazingly fascinating problem with a kiss yet.

But that was next.

Chapter 3

"I just can't believe how chilly the night suddenly turned, and after such a warm day," Diana said with a nervous laugh. "I don't know if I mentioned that I drove up to the Laughing Horse Reservation this morning. My great-great-gramps, Kyle Brennan, was half Cheyenne...."

Diana wanted to give herself a morose kick in the keester. Why was she telling Trey all this? Why should he care? *Just shut up, Diana. Just get in the truck and say good-night and quit babbling like a nervous brook.*

But the problem was Trey, standing right in front of the driver's door. He'd always induced a white-hot sexual awareness in her, and this close was too close. Moonlight silhouetted his broad shoulders and rumpled dark hair and that slow, lazy smile of his. She could smell late-season roses and the ghost-clear night and her own nerves. Out spilled more babble.

"Anyway, I've been picking up some substitute teaching work, but not enough to make a living. And truthfully, what I'd really love to do is teach on the reservation, so I drove up there to see if there was any chance I could catch someone to talk one-on-one. In Chicago, I taught the high-risk kids. The little ones who were having trouble reading right from the start. And I doubt folks would normally think inner city and Native American country kids would have anything in common, but the problems that can make a child a high academic risk can be exactly the same. I had a great talk with the principal. She was on the same bandwagon with me right off. Unfortunately, there's just no funding for the kind of special-ed program I'd really love to put together."

She had to stop babbling long enough to take a breath. Her lungs hauled in a big chug of oxygen, but not enough to quell the light-headed, white-hot feeling.

The thing was, her specific problem had gotten worse. Trey was no longer just blocking the driver's door. He'd started moving. He lifted his arms as if he were reaching toward her. If Diana hadn't had a recent problem with lunacy, she'd have thought the man was going to kiss her...a thought that inspired her common sense to snap awake. For Pete's sake, catering to this lunacy thing had gone far enough. Old crushes didn't come back. Fantasy lovers didn't suddenly turn into the real thing. Sure, a woman could waste a few rag tail minutes daydreaming about Daniel Day-Lewis or Brad Pitt. What was the harm? You knew nothing was going to happen.

Only Trey suddenly bent down.

And he seemed to be studying her, staring at her face, looking at her in a strangely intimate way that made no sense at all.

And then his arms swept around her.

And the kiss that only a lunatic woman would believe could happen...was happening.

Holy hokum. Holy hooch. Her knees seemed to turn into dribbling noodles. Her toes and fingertips iced up. All the wonderful IQ points that had always handily glued her mind together suddenly flew out her ears into that big Montana sky.

His hands slid around her shoulders, scooped her back. His mouth tilted, then swooped. A butterfly kiss whispered down on her lips, soft, gentle, more a tease of sensation than the real thing...but that was followed by a hot stamp of a kiss that could melt a blizzard. No sound intruded on the still silence of the night, no cars, no birds, no humans. She heard nothing but the sound of his groan against her soft mouth, and her gulping in air. Or trying to.

Okay, okay, so she'd always been crazy about

him, but she'd only agreed to this dinner for Molly's
sake. She adored his daughter. There was no reason
to deny that. And after hearing about Molly's losing
her mom, Diana felt even more drawn to the urchin.
Mol had a fabulous dad. So had Diana. And Molly
was so wonderful, so fearless, so pure girl, the kind
of spoiled kid Diana had once been, too. Mol was
loved and lucky and blessed. Diana had that same
kind of background—yet all her life she'd ached for
her mom. A daughter who lost her mother too young
had a hollow spot that never went away. Diana knew
exactly how the little one felt.

And right now, she kept trying, fiercely, to think
about Molly.

Yet Trey suddenly lifted his head and smiled at
her in the darkness. Not a nice smile. Not a friendly
smile. More of a *Damn! I hoped you'd be this much
trouble* smile, and then he nuzzled down for another
kiss, spinning her around so he could lean against
the truck and splay his legs and pull her right into
the lariat of his arms.

Eek. A girl couldn't cook her goose on just a few
kisses, could she?

Nothing earth-shattering could happen as long as
they both stayed fully clothed out in the open, could
it?

Besides, a few kernels of rational common sense
finally seeped into her empty brain and started rattling. Obviously she could make herself behave any
minute. She always behaved. She was a teacher, for

heaven's sake. Respected. Respectable. A kid lover, a believer in families, a wanna-be mom.

The only reason she was having a teensy difficulty getting a grip was from the shock of Trey initiating a kiss, and not just any old peck of a kiss but this kind, the kind that started out sleepy and safe and somehow turned into drumrolls thundering inside her heart. He wanted her. Trey. Wanted. Her.

Really, it was way, way easier owning up to a problem with basic lunacy than admitting how much she was loving this embrace, loving him, loving this moment as if she'd been waiting for him her whole life.

Trey suddenly lifted his head, severing a kiss that had sampled her throat and earlobe and the side of her jaw before any kind of hesitation. His dark eyes were still kissing her, still savoring, but his expression had turned grave.

He didn't pull away. Instead, his arms tightened and he cuddled her in a hug for a moment longer. She could feel his arousal, feel the heat and electric tension pouring off his body, yet somehow that hug managed to communicate affection and comfort, as well. She had the sensation of a panther tired of dark, lonely nights and, instead of pouncing, trying to soothe the lamb in his clutches. A wildly crazy image, Diana realized. Trey wouldn't hurt her. She wasn't physically afraid of him in any way. Yet the instinct that he was dangerous for her was as real as the moonlight.

"You have to go," he murmured.

That should have been her line, her first words. She tried to pull back, and this time he let her. Yet his eyes still chased hers as if willing her to stay with him—when, of course, she couldn't. He said quietly, "It's been easier for me to stay uninvolved since my wife died. Particularly with in-laws watching every breath I take and hoping to find the grounds to judge me. But you know what, Diana?"

"What?"

"I think that you and I are going to get complicated real fast." A smile. A touch on her cheek. And then he watched her drive off.

Weeks later, Diana stood in her cabin window, towel drying her hair, mesmerized by the first snowfall. The snow fell like a hush in big, fat, crystal flakes, filling up the corrals, mounding on the fence posts, shining silver in the windowsills of her dad's house across the yard. Snow clouds hovered low in the witchy black sky. The first of October was early for a serious snow—even in Montana—but all she could think about was how much Molly was going to love waking up to this in the morning.

When a knuckle rapped on her door, she whirled in surprise. Her sister, Suzanna, poked her head inside. "Hey. You busy?"

"As if I were ever too busy for you. Come on in. How's my niece today?"

"Your nephew—" Suzanna pushed off her hat

and jacket, then patted her bulging tummy "—has been kicking me nonstop all day. I swear this boy already has attitude. But Dad and Nash are closed up in the den, talking horse breeding, the two of them happy as two peas in a pod, so I took off." She waddled toward the couch. "I've had a surprise I wanted to show you ever since you came home. Only first you insist on living in this pipsqueak-size cabin instead of in the big house with us, and then you're never here, besides!"

"You don't like the way I've fixed the place up?" From long habit, Diana studied her sister with the practiced skill of an honorary mother—but the glowing cheeks and deep contentment in Suzanna's eyes were ample testimony to how exuberantly happy her sis was. And happier yet when Diana produced a dish brimming with dark chocolate nougats—one of her sister's vices since the start of her pregnancy.

"Oh, God. Oh, God." Her sister spotted the nougats. And pounced. Unfortunately, though, even chocolate couldn't divert her train of thought right then. "You've fixed the place up wonderfully. But that has nothing to do with how little you're home—"

"Well, really, I'm lucky they're calling me so often for substitute teaching."

"I'm not talking about work hours, and you know it. You've been seeing Trey Derringer for weeks now. I want a full report. Skip the details and go right to the X-rated stuff. The more pregnant I get, the best I can do is hear about it vicariously.''

Diana's pulse suddenly climbed in her throat. Suzanna couldn't have any idea how fast and complicated her relationship with Trey had become— nor did she want to tell her. Suzanna was not only a new bride but expecting a baby in a matter of weeks. Diana had seen the two lovers together. No one could doubt they were happy, but something about the relationship had been stormy at the start— they hadn't opted for a big wedding at first, for one thing—yet Suze had been closemouthed about whatever the troubles had been. Diana didn't want to pry. And didn't need to, when she could see for herself that her sister was happy. But all the same, she'd never let her younger sister worry about her before and certainly wasn't about to start now. ''Well, I hate to disappoint you on the lascivious details, but really, I've just been spending time with Molly to help out. I admit I've fallen for his daughter big-time, but we've just been doing girl stuff—shopping and haircuts and that kind of thing—''

''Uh-huh. Sure. Like you expect me to believe a four year old put that new kick-ass swish in the way you walk or those stars in your eyes. Is Derringer serious? Because if he's playing with you, I'm gonna sic Nash on him with a bullwhip. I always did think he was a heap of man, but then there was so much talk. His wife was the fastest thing this town ever saw. And his in-laws are real public about their fighting for custody. And more to the point, you think I didn't know you had a thing for him when we were kids?''

"I sure did,'' Diana admitted smoothly. "In fact, when I'm around him now, I thank God I've grown up and don't believe in shining knights and wild romantic dreams anymore. You know you can count on me to be practical. Have you ever known me to do one irresponsible thing?'' If none of this were precisely true, Diana hoped it would be enough to reassure her sister. Just in case, though, she swiftly crossed the room and opened a drawer. She had another bag of nougats stashed for emergencies just like this. "Didn't you say you had some kind of surprise?''

"Yup. I found a treasure in an old trunk in the attic months ago. Letters. Love letters. From our great-great-grandmother Isabelle to Kyle. And I wanted to tell you right away, but you came home for the wedding first, and then Slim and I took off on the honeymoon, and, well, I just wanted to show these to you when the two of us had a little time alone.''

"You found love letters? Between our legendary Isabelle and Kyle? Sheesh, how'd you ever keep that secret this long? Let's see, let's see.'' Diana curled up on the couch, immediately becoming immersed in the fragile parchment letters as Suzanna divvied them out.

As young girls, both had always devoured the legend of their great-great-grandmother's love story. Their mom had first told it to Diana, and then Diana had told it to Suzanna a hundred times as a bedtime tale, how the young, gorgeous and pampered Isabelle had come west with her parents, then been stranded when she was nineteen because her mom and dad died. Still, she'd fallen in love with the dashing half-breed, Kyle Brennan. In those days, she'd risked her future and her reputation to marry a man of mixed race, and together they'd built up the Big Sky ranch.

Every time Diana had heard the story from her mother, she'd dreamed of that kind of a love—the kind of man you could trust beyond all rhyme or reason, the kind of love so strong that nothing else mattered. "Mom and Dad loved each other like that, you know," she told Suzanna, as they switched letters yet again. "I don't know how well you remember Mom—"

"Well, not as well as you. But you and Dad both helped keep her alive for me. And Dad still gets a softness in his eyes when he talks about her." Suzanna started carefully folding the finished love notes. "I didn't think love would ever happen like that. Not to me."

Diana's eyes shot up. "What do you mean? You married Nash—"

Her sister nodded, but her gaze was focused on the snowy landscape outside. "At the time I thought it was the right thing to do. For the baby.

For…everyone. And the first time I saw Nash with the horses… Well, I can't explain exactly. I felt I could trust Nash, and that mattered. I just never believed we'd always create sparks together. I remember saying my vows and wanting to cry. I felt like a fake. Not like a bride—at least not the bride our mom and grandmothers were. The thing was—''

When Suzanna hesitated, Diana coaxed her to finish. ''What?''

''Well, to be honest, I thought the romantic kind of love that our parents had—that I thought Isabelle and Kyle had way back—was old-fashioned. Corny. Wonderful to weave stories about, but nothing that happens for real today. People get divorced all the time. Nobody stays together. I just thought I should work on making a good relationship, but not count on ever feeling that corny type of being in love, you know?''

Diana felt her heart squeeze in a protective fist. ''Suzanna, the way you and Nash look at each other, I just assumed…I hoped—''

''Oh, yeah. I fell in love—hard. And so did he. Loving him is the best thing that ever happened to me…which is partly why I wanted to tell you all this. I'm worried about you, Di—''

''Me? There's no reason for you ever to worry about me!''

''Well, you take care of everyone else. But I never see anyone taking care of you. And I'm just saying, if this Trey's got your heart, go for it. I never expected to love anyone like I feel about Nash, not down deep at the soul level. And I just don't want you to settle for less. You deserve someone who'll love you for who you really are. Oh, God. Am I sounding corny?''

"Um..." Diana felt uncomfortable. Her sister was the baby in the family. It was always Diana who'd done the caretaking and mothering and lecturing. Suzanna had never done it to her. "You're being a sweetheart, sis. But I really don't want you worried about me—"

"Okay, okay. I'm not worried. Or I'll let you off the hook for now, because I still want to talk about the love letters. Come on, Diana, didn't you notice something was odd?"

"Um..." As fascinated as Diana had always been by the old family love story, she hadn't been paying that much attention. She was suddenly remembering Suzanna's wedding, and how her sister had hurled the wedding bouquet right at her chest. Whatever trouble Suzanna had found with Nash, the couple had obviously worked through it and found real love on the other side. Diana only wished she could believe the same thing could happen with her and Trey. She couldn't seem to stop worrying about her building worrisome feelings for him. But she forcibly returned her concentration to the family love letters. "To be honest, I didn't notice anything odd. The tone of the letters was wonderfully romantic and loving, just what we always thought. So what did you think was weird?''

"That there could even *be* any letters. Think about it. She's writing to him. To her lover. And judging from the number of letters, her Kyle was obviously gone for quite a while, right?''

"Yeah, so?''

"So when were they ever separated? All those years—you know the legend—once they met, they were never supposed to be separated. She was in a terrible mess when her parents died and she was left with a horse ranch that she didn't have a clue what to do with. So why would he have left her?''

"You're right,'' Diana mused. "That doesn't make sense.''

"I hate loose ends like that. And Isabelle's so much a part of our family. Every time we've ever talked about love and what family means, it goes back to her and Kyle.'' Suzanna stood, pressed her knuckles to the aching small of her back, then reached for her jacket and mittens. "I don't like their suddenly being a mystery in the family history when we were always so sure we knew the whole story.''

"Well, maybe my niece will unravel all the old genealogy when she comes of age.''

"Your nephew, you mean?''

Obviously they were done talking about serious subjects. Sister fashion, they fought over the gender of the baby, then whether Diana was going to walk

Suzanna home. Suzanna said she was pregnant, not ill, and it was dumb for Diana to get all cold when the big house was just across the yard, for Pete's sake. Diana listened to the rant—as she clutched her sister's arm protectively the whole walk. The night was dark and sleety, and her sister could too easily fall—which Nash obviously realized, too, because her new brother-in-law's tall, broad-shouldered figure emerged from the shadows before they were halfway across the yard. He'd come to make sure Suzanna made it safely inside.

"The two of you are a total pain!" Suzanna complained. "My God, I can't even walk a hundred yards without somebody babying me!"

Diana patted Nash's arm sympathetically. "I told you before—you should have married the nice sister instead of Ms. Crab here."

"Aw, she's not crabby. It's just that our daughter's been kicking her so many nights, she's getting short on sleep."

"Our *son.* I've told you guys a zillion times. I'm positive it's a boy."

"Excuse me, Diana," Nash murmured. And kissed his bride—which was the last anyone heard any further cranky complaints. Nash winked a goodnight at Diana.

Moments later, still chuckling at the newlyweds' antics, she let herself into the cabin. Abruptly her smile died. Normally the silence and privacy of the cabin were guaranteed to soothe her after a long day.

Heaven knew, she'd fought the family to stay alone here.

Her dad had built the cabin years ago because they had so many people coming and going during the breeding season. There were plenty of spare rooms in the big house, but that wasn't always comfortable for either the strangers or the family.

Her gaze skimmed the cabin as she locked up and started cleaning glasses and turning off lights. The place was set up like a studio apartment, with a corduroy couch and chair clustered in the small space in front of the fireplace. A bar served as dining table, desk and work space, and separated the living from the kitchen area. The kitchen had a hodgepodge of blue enamelware from the main house and cupboards always stocked with enough staples to put together a quick dinner or snack. Hiding behind an old-fashioned fabric screen was the bedroom area— a double bed, side table and storage trunk.

And that was it, Diana mused, but she'd done her best to make the place hers. She'd added the ivory down comforter and crocheted pillows, the nest of gardenia-scented candles, hung an Amish quilt and draped thick rugs to warm up the plank floors. But it was a frustrating lack of space for a woman used to her independence and autonomy all these years. And she felt like she was camping out, in between, not sure what rung on the life ladder she was climbing next.

Her sudden unsettled mood came from talking

with her sister, she knew. Maybe there was a sudden mystery about Isabelle, but Isabelle still had the courage to reach for love in spite of very difficult odds in her time. As had their grandmother and mom, and now, Diana suspected, her sister, too. The Brennan women had always found strength in themselves.

And growing up, Diana had understood where that strength had to come from. When her mom died, her dad had needed her to be strong. No one valued a weak woman. A woman stood up for what was right, took care of family, sacrificed for those she loved.

She didn't go mooning after wild hairs and moonbeams...the way she'd done years ago with Trey.

The way she seemed to still be doing with him now.

The telephone jangled just as she'd finished locking up and was pulling the sweatshirt over her head. She sank on the ivory comforter to grab the receiver on the far side of the bed.

"Am I calling too late?"

Oh, man. It was her own personal wild hair and moonbeam, and his question struck her as downright humorous. Was there ever an inconvenient time for chocolate? Winning the lottery? Being happy? Diana closed her eyes, knowing darn well she was thrilled to hear Trey's voice no matter what the personal risk to her heart. Just hearing his slow, magnetic baritone invoked memories of the first night when he'd kissed her and either warned her—or promised—that things could get complicated between them real fast. "No, Trey, the hour's fine. And how's our miniature femme fatale today?"

"Well, I guess she decided to tell the preschool teacher how to run the class. Specifically I think she had in mind revamping the disciplinary system on how little boys with cooties should be handled."

She started chuckling, and Trey recounted more of Molly's antics to make her laugh again. She always loved hearing about Mol, and she'd taken so strongly to Molly—and vice versa—that Trey's encouraging the three of them to spend more and more time together was no surprise. Except that the little one was invariably asleep by eight, and Trey had developed these sneaky, subtle tricks to make her stay just a little longer. Even after weeks, she felt startled when he initiated a kiss or embrace. And more confoundedly stunned at the power of the force field between them.

"You were going to drive up to the reservation today, weren't you?" he asked her.

"Yes." Diana snuggled into the comforter. "I guess that's pretty foolish when I know there's no funding for a full-time job. But the principal's been so enthusiastic about listening to the reading program I'd like to set up. And on days I'm not called to substitute teach, there's really no reason I can't go up there and tutor little ones every day if I wanted to."

"Except that no one wants to pay you." Trey had listened to her on this subject before.

She sighed. "Well, it's not like it's anyone's fault that there's no funding. And I love doing it. The money is a problem. If I'm going to stay in White-horn, I need to get serious about finding full-time work. I hate mooching off my dad—and I'm just too darn old to be dependent on family for a living."

"Something tells me your dad is perfectly happy you're there."

"Yeah, he is. And he keeps telling me to relax. Enjoy being home. Think through what I really want to do, and quit being in such a hurry." As she spoke, Diana realized this was exactly one of the things she'd never expected. That Trey would be so easy to talk to. Or that in such a short time, he'd know so much about her.

"You've suddenly gone quiet on me," Trey murmured. "You getting tired?"

"A little," she said, which was a total lie. The same confusion wrapped around her mind every time she talked to Trey. At first, she'd assumed he was being nice because Molly had taken such a liking to her. And after that, she'd assumed the lunacy that affected her in Whitehorn would simply go away if she gave it some time. Only time kept passing.

Enough time that right now, curled under the ivory comforter with the phone tucked to her ear, she could so easily imagine him. Curled under the blanket with her. Naked. In the dark. Kissing her like the other night. A good-night kiss that started in her car and somehow astoundingly ended up in the cold grass sparkling like diamonds in the moonlight, Trey's laughter sounding low and throaty, both of them breathing hard.

"Diana, will you be able to come over on Tuesday night? To help me with that costume thing for Molly's school play?"

There. Some sanity. She swallowed fast. Everything stayed wonderfully easy if they just kept talking about Molly. "No problem. I told you I'd be glad to."

"You're sure we're not imposing? I'm afraid Mol would ask for your full-time attention if we didn't put a lid on it. That doesn't mean I want you to feel obligated to say yes every time."

"Trey, I love spending time with her. Honestly. Unless you're worried that she's starting to get too attached to me—"

His voice caressed her ear like the stroke of velvet. "Oh, I think she is. And I know I am. Are you going to scare off if I finally come out and admit that the two of us are wooing you, Diana Brennan?"

Chapter 4

Trey didn't want to marry her. He wasn't wooing her. He couldn't be. It was just that problem with lunacy that had shown up since she'd been home— the one that cropped up every time she was around him. Like now.

Diana managed to look at the daughter rather than the dad, and reminded herself that Brennan women were strong. Strong, self-reliant and steady as rocks. And by God, she was going to shake this problem with lunacy or die trying.

"Do I look bea'ful?"

Diana rocked back on her heels and removed the pins from her mouth so she could answer. "More than beautiful. You look breathtaking, Mol. You're going to be the most beautiful pumpkin in the whole play—although I don't think we'd better let your daddy go shopping alone again.''

Said daddy glanced up from where he was hunkered by the fireplace, as if he sensed he was being insulted. ''Hey, I took Simpson,'' he said defensively.

''Yeah, and the two of you came home with how many yards of orange velvet? This is going to be the most expensive pumpkin that ever starred in a preschool play.''

Molly tugged at Diana's pale blue sweater. ''But I'm worth it, aren't I, Diana?'' she asked confidently.

''You're worth more than the sun and the moon,'' Diana agreed, with absolutely no hesitation. ''And okay. You're all done getting fitted. Would you like to practice your lines?''

''Yes! Yes! Daddy! Listen to me! And everybody has to be *quiet!*''

''I'm listening,'' Trey gravely assured her. ''Believe me, none of us would miss any of these rehearsals.''

And this, Diana mused, was exactly what she was here for. Molly. Maybe she'd been a romantic, ditsy dreamer as a kid, but when her mom died, she fiercely remembered how much her dad and sister had needed her. Really, it was the reason Molly seemed to need her now. Maybe the household was missing a mom, but Diana was the kind of person a child could depend on, which Molly seemed to sense. She'd always come through for people. It was who she was.

And Molly was loving every minute of the attention. The urchin twirled to the middle of the living room, where she paused dramatically. For this epic preschool play, Diana had padded pillows under the stitched orange velvet to make Molly's figure resemble a pumpkin. The orange tights matched perfectly. And once Molly lifted off the pumpkin-lid hat, dark curls tumbled wildly around her shoulders. ''Trick or treat!''

These three words, not surprisingly, were greeted with wild applause from her appreciative audience. Diana stood up, and between whistles, screamed, ''Encore, encore!'' Trey roared, ''Bravo!'' And Simpson put a beefy hand over his heart to express respect for Molly's acting ability and fervently hissed, ''What a star!''

Eventually Molly was conned into taking her costume off, after which a pre-bed tea party was served with real milk and virtual reality cookies on teensy doll-size dishes. When Trey finally stood up and gently insisted it was *really* time for bed this time, though, Molly threw herself in Diana's arms.

''Are you gonna come see me in the play?''

It was all too easy to snuggle the warm, wriggling body. Diana kissed the top of her head, conscious of her daddy standing barely a kiss away himself. ''If it's okay, I'd love to come to your play.''

"It's okay. I want you to. But you know what, Diana?"

"What?"

"I think you should be my mom, that's what. Then you could make me costumes every day. And we could play. And I could hide my peas in your napkin like we did at dinner."

Diana stroked the soft, dark curls. "You know what, Mol?"

"What?"

"I can be your friend. And help you with things like costumes. I don't need to be your mom to love you or be part of your life, did you know that?"

"Yeah. I guess. But I still think it'd be better if you were my mom."

"I'm honored that you think that, lovebug."

"All you have to do is marry my daddy, you know. It's easy. We get to get new dresses. Then we go to church and throw flowers. Then we go on a honeymoon. That's it. That's all you have to do—"

The rest of the instructions were muffled by a hand over her mouth, courtesy of her father, who carried the little one upside down to bed—which was the best way to keep her giggling. It took a few minutes before Trey returned, because he never rushed his good-nights with his daughter. But when he ambled in the living room, he threw himself on the couch next to Diana.

"She's a monster," he announced.

Diana chuckled. Simpson had typically disappeared a few minutes after Mol's bedtime, and the room felt entirely different with just the two of them. "Something tells me dads have used that particular descriptive term on their daughters before."

"I got a lecture on how to make you fall in love with me. Her best advice was chocolate ice cream." Trey swiped a hand over his face. "When I was four, I'm pretty sure the only thing on my mind was playing with trucks."

Again, she smiled, but her smile suddenly wavered. "Trey, do you think I'm spending too much time with her? I've been worried for the obvious reason. She really seems to be getting attached to me."

He stretched his arm on the back of the sofa, fingers dropping naturally on her shoulder. "Well, I'll tell you the truth. She's never done anything like this with any other woman. Which is partly why she's always startling me with the stuff that comes out of her mouth—I'm just not expecting it. And maybe I should be feeling more embarrassed, but I keep taking lessons from how you're handling this. She never seems to fluster you, Di."

"She doesn't. Not really." She felt his fingertips on her shoulder. Grazing. Skimming the curve of her neck. Exposing her collarbone to the charge of a couple dozen lightning bolts. "One of the things I love best about kids is their honesty. Obviously we have to teach them some tact and get them civilized

sooner or later…but that just comes with some
coaching en route.'' A fingertip strayed into her hair,
curled around his finger, made her feel shivery.
''And sometimes I think if you let them see you're
embarrassed, you're giving them the wrong message. That it's okay to be curious about certain
things but not others, and that their feelings are
wrong.''

''Well, I think you're incredible with her.'' His
dark eyes did the same thing. Grazing. Skimming.
Exposing her face—her mouth—to the charge of his
gaze.

''I think the credit goes to you, Dad, that she has
so much confidence and sense of self, especially for
a squirt that age.'' She leaned forward, thinking that
she'd dropped her shoes somewhere. She had to get
up, go home. One of these times, Trey was going to
discover she was having this problem with lunacy—
if he hadn't already. ''I don't get any credit for anything. I'm just around kids all the time. I'm used to
them. But back to my question. Do you think she's
getting too attached to me?''

Trey didn't protest when he saw her pushing her
toes into loafers. ''I don't know what 'too attached'
means. I think her relationship with you is fantastic
for her. She discovered that another adult woman
besides her mom can mean something special. How
could that possibly be bad?''

''But if I go away, Trey, she'd have to deal with
another loss.''

''Are you thinking about going away?''

It was a simple question. If he weren't so close, possibly she could have come up with a simple answer. She'd never realized how homesick she was in Chicago, how badly she wanted to be home…yet maybe going back to the big city was her best choice. In Chicago, everything was so much safer. Nothing there but crime and drive-by shootings and gangs to worry about. Here there were shifting timbers. All the petrifying alligators under the bed she'd feared as a child.

Here there was a strong, compelling man coming toward her, his dark eyes on her face, his mouth already open and tilted to take hers in. And then he did, with a kiss that took her breath. Somehow she never expected those kisses, never expected Trey to make any kind of pass. Even after all these weeks, she couldn't seem to believe he actually wanted her. And like before, by the time his lips connected with hers, it was too late.

Magic whispered in the air. The sough of his breath, the masculine scent of him, the feel of his hand cupping her head, angling her close to him…for her, everything about those moments was suspended in time. Outside, she heard the moan of a lonely wind. Inside, she heard only the soft hiss of fire and the potent shadows of firelight, illuminating his face, glowing on the lines of character and strength and power. It wasn't the boy she'd had a crush on—but the man who she'd fallen hopelessly, helplessly in love with.

His palm stroked her throat, down to the swell of her breast. Under her navy angora sweater, her heart started slamming, louder than a drum, louder than a wild wind and a blizzard gale both. Through her sweater, through her bra, she could feel her nipple tighten. Tauten. Ache. Her whole breast seemed to swell to the molding fit of his palm, and he made a sound, of desire, of need, and he suddenly pulled her closer, cradling her on his lap.

Her whole body was electrified. Blood pooled low, as if her womb were responding to an empty ache, a need to be filled. Whisper-soft kisses touched her cheek, caressed her nose, came back to settle long and compellingly on her mouth, taking in her tongue, taking in her last shreds of sanity at the same time.

Trey needed a mom for his Molly. She knew that. He appreciated that she was a good feminine influence for his daughter. She knew that, too. Possibly his in-laws would get off his back if he had a mother in house—or they'd give up fighting him for custody. Diana didn't believe for a second that Trey was being deliberately manipulative. A man couldn't kiss with that kind of tenderness, that kind of longing, if there wasn't feeling.

But she'd always understood what drew people to her. When her mom died, it had become so crystal clear how useless a romantic dreamer was. Her dad and sister had needed her to be rock steady, strong. That's what people always needed from other people. A doer, not a dreamer. Someone who was strong, not someone weak. Her identity, her whole self-worth, had long hinged on being the kind of person that others could rely on—the kind of person who never let a loved one.down. She *liked* the practical, responsible woman she'd turned into.

And she was scared of the blindly impulsive woman she seemed to become around Trey...but oh, this lunacy had a magical, exciting side, too. He'd kissed her before. She knew his taste, his scent, his textures. She knew his first kisses always seemed questing. Not tentative, but always asking. Did she want this? And only when he felt sure of an answer did he move into deeper, darker kisses, softer kisses, dangerous kisses. Kisses that dragged moans out of her and groans out of him. Hands were suddenly hustling to clutch, to claim. Skin temperatures soared fever high. Oxygen was sucked from the atmosphere. Annoyances—a couch arm, lamplight glaring, a distant telephone—struck her as infuriating and unreasoning frustrations.

She could feel how much he wanted her, feel how hard and pulsing he'd become as she twisted closer in his lap. Her fingers sieving through his hair only seemed to make his eyes darken with fire. The bones in his face seemed to tighten and tense, as if suffering pain...yet she caught smiles between his kisses, and a gurgle of low masculine laughter when her elbow accidentally poked him.

He liked this teasing. And so did she. She knew perfectly well that a grown man wasn't going to be happy volunteering for this kind of frustration forever, but she couldn't seem to think that far ahead. She only knew him when he was kissing her. And when she was with him, it felt like everything in the world could come right with desire this powerful, this fabulous, this silky pull from deep, deep inside her so huge that it obliterated any fears in her head.

"Trey? Diana? I wondered if you two might like a nightcap before— Oh. Hey, I'm sorry, excuse me."

Faster than a hair trigger, Diana's head jerked up at the sound of Simpson's voice. Yet, that swiftly, Simpson was already disappearing from the doorway and pulling the door closed behind him. And though her heart was suddenly hammering with the alarmed guilt of discovery, Trey was still only looking at her. Still only intent on her. He never even glanced up or seemed to notice that Simpson had been in the room.

"Diana," he started to say gently.

"I have to go. It's so late. I can't believe how late it is, I—"

As if she weren't making frantic movements to vault off his lap and stand up, he only looked more calm, more intent. "Why are you afraid of this?"

"Afraid? I'm not afraid."

His eyes searched hers. "I'm not playing around. Is that what you're worried about? That I'm not serious about you? But, Diana, being a single dad with a daughter as old as Molly, I couldn't sleep around even if I wanted to. And I don't have a great history behind me. I have no interest in a relationship with a woman unless I really believe we've got a shot at a real one."

A wave of protectiveness—all right, of love—swept through her. She reached over and kissed him. It was the first time she'd ever initiated physical contact between them, but she reassured herself that this wasn't a kiss of passion, but only one intended to communicate caring. "I know you're not playing, not in any manipulative or careless sense," she said softly. "And I care about you, too, Trey."

Enough to not want him—or Molly—hurt. At least by her. And if that meant keeping a physical distance between her and Trey, then Diana was determined. She simply had to try harder.

"Are we finally ready?" Trey called up the stairs. "Come on, punkin, shake a leg. We need to leave if we're going to get to the school on time."

"Well, I can't go, Daddy. My hair isn't right. The play'll just have to wait."

Trey stared at Simpson. Simpson stared back at him. "Um, can't you just brush it and come down, sweetie?"

"Daddy!"

Both men heard the tone of disgust. Simpson cleared his throat. "I think they come out of the womb this way. Don't argue with her. Go with it."

"Is there anything I could help with?" Trey called.

"No!"

Simpson motioned for him to sit on the third stair up, then plunked his three hundred pounds next to him. "Maybe it's the star temperament. Or stage fright. She couldn't be getting PMS before the age of five, could she?"

"I don't know. Diana would know. But then if Diana were here, we wouldn't be having the problem with hair to begin with."

Simpson smoothed his Mickey Mouse tie over the ample shelf of his stomach. The last time Trey had seen Simpson in a suit was for a funeral. Same suit. Same tie. "I could get us a bracer," Simpson suggested hopefully.

"Nah. The precedent is too scary. Think. If we need a drink before a nursery school play, how are we ever going to cope with the big stuff? Like high school graduation. And a wedding."

"Don't go there." Simpson shuddered. "One crisis at a time. At the moment, a nursery school play seems traumatic enough. Is Diana coming?"

"You already asked me that twice. And yes, she'll be there. But she wanted to drive separately because she was working until almost five on the reservation this afternoon. She was afraid we'd be late if we waited for her.''

"I think you should tell her what you did," Simpson said grumpily.

Trey sighed. They'd already argued about this several times. His friendship with R. L. Simpson went back to the days before Trey had money. Few outsiders understood how two totally unalike men could be close friends, but Simpson had been a wrangler on the Derringer ranch when Trey first knew him. An injury ended his cowboy days, but the injury hadn't stopped Simpson from befriending a green, hungry, dumb kid like himself back then. Maybe R.L. was tough around the edges and lacked formal education, but he'd stand in front of a semi to protect Mol—his loyalty was beyond absolute. Valuing his old friend, though, didn't mean Trey didn't occasionally find him a pain in the keester.

He tried explaining. Again. "If I tell Diana that I funded the program for the high-risk kids on the reservation, then she'll think I did it for her."

"Which you did."

"Yeah. But the point is that Diana's independent. And the reading program she put together for the high-risk Native American kids is really outstanding. She deserves credit. But she won't believe that if she thinks I pulled strings."

"You more than pulled strings. You paid for the whole damn thing."

Trey scowled at Simpson. "But that's the problem. She could feel beholden. Like she owes me. And that's the last thing I want Diana to feel for me.''

''Why? It was a great thing for you to do. Seems to me it shows that you care about her.''

''Simpson—we've had a four year old keep us waiting more than an hour to go to a nursery school play. You think either of us can claim to be an expert on the female mind?''

''Well…no.''

''I'm afraid of making a mistake with her. It matters too much. So just forget about it, okay? I do plan to tell Diana about it some day. Some day when she will understand in her own heart why I did it.''

The princess eventually came flouncing down the stairs. Both men were too smart to say anything about her hair and risk the four year old's wrath all over again, and they were late besides. Ten minutes later they barreled into the parking lot of the nursery school. Diana had parked her dad's red pickup and stepped out.

Just seeing her, his heart arrested and then pumped double time. The sky was all roiled up with snow clouds, heavy and dark in midafternoon, but even against that steel-gray background she looked gorgeous. She was wearing a red wool cape over a long swirling skirt and boots, her face flushed from hustling, her hair whipping in the wind as she charged toward them—swooping to kiss Molly first, then say, ''Hi there, sweetie,'' to Simpson, and when she got good and around to it, she smiled at him.

It was just a smile. And a stingy one. But it was still a personal smile—nothing like she was giving anyone else—and the flare of her color in her cheeks was clearly about awareness. Sexual awareness. The way her eyes met and ducked and then remet his echoed that vibrant, lusty sexual awareness…and so did that little swish in her behind when she took off with Molly, talking girl talk and rehearsal preparations and leaving the men in their wake.

"I'll help her get into the pumpkin costume, but you guys save me a seat, okay?" Diana called over her shoulder.

Anything she did was okay. Trey just kept thinking, *Oh, man, I don't want to make a mistake with her.* She didn't get it, he knew. She just couldn't seem to believe he was wooing her—much less that he loved her. Maybe she believed a single dad with a none-too-happy first marriage was a lousy risk. Maybe his money got in the way. He felt unsure exactly what made her so cautious…only that she lost that caution when he kissed her.

And so did he. His whole life he'd been lonely, and truth to tell that never seemed like all that big a problem—until he met Diana. Kissed Diana. Spent time with the first and only woman who'd ever spun his world the right way. Tonight, Trey mused. Tonight he was determined to escalate their relationship. To show her more of what he felt. To *risk* more of what he felt.

Something had to give. Trey felt like he was standing on a cliff edge, with a killer fall below and a perilous climb in the other direction. One way or another he had to move, because living in this limbo netherworld was untenable.

At the moment, though, the nursery school class was flooding on stage. Amazingly—for a play that only lasted ten minutes—there was standing-room only in the auditorium. One star actor tripped, fell to his knee and cried. One star actress socked the girl next to her. Costumes fell apart en route to center stage. Still, the audience stayed spellbound...except when individual actors spoke their lines, at which point certain biased folks in the audience leaped to their feet to scream and stomp and shriek approval.

"Do you believe how these grown adults are behaving for a little kids' play?" Trey whispered to Diana.

But when it was his daughter's turn to do her epic line...well, obviously Trey had to whistle and stomp and thunderously applaud louder than the other parents. They had nice kids, but he was clearly the only one with the real prodigy.

"Oh, my God," Diana said to Simpson. "He's pitiful. Even worse than the rest."

"Hey. Did you see her? Was she perfect? Was

she beautiful? Did she put the other kids to shame or what?''

He had a single red rose—thorns removed, of course—waiting for Molly when she came out, cheeks flushed like fever and her curls bouncing. ''Did you see me, Dad? Did you?''

''I did, and you were fabulous.''

''I get the rose? For real?''

''Yup, just for you.''

Simpson and Diana got to give her kisses, but Trey got to give her the piggyback ride to the car and then let her win the con job for ice cream even though it was before dinner. Most days he had panicked moments about what kind of parent he was, whether he was good enough, whether he had anything in him worth the precious charge of his incredible daughter. But some days, like this one, it was just so damn much fun to be her dad that the doubts all slipped under the cracks for a while.

Later, much later, after dinner and when Mol was finally put to bed, he climbed downstairs to find Diana pouring both of them short glasses of wine in the kitchen. ''I have to go home. Really full day tomorrow. But I figured you were exhausted, Dad.''

''Man, I am. This being in a play is hard work.''

She laughed. ''I don't know why you waste your time making money and doing all that silly investment stuff when it's perfectly obvious that you were born to be around kids.''

''Are you kidding? I couldn't survive a classroom

the way you do. Raising one is giving me gray hair…and she isn't even five yet. And we've been so busy, I never had a chance to ask you—how's it going with the new job?''

"Oh, Trey." Her face lit up like diamonds in the sun. "Those kids are so special, you can't imagine. They're just thriving. That's the whole point, you know? I don't believe there's any such thing as a child who can't read. Some just need an innovative and personal approach to get them moving. And the point is, if we don't catch those high-risk kids in the beginning, they start thinking of themselves like failures. Even by sixth grade, it can be too late. They already think of school and tests as their enemies by then…."

He'd heard her rant and rave at length on this subject before.

"So that's the whole thing. Never giving a child the chance to fail. Making sure they're successful from the start. Making sure they *can* read. And then inspiring them to want to get ahead. Kids *want* to learn. All kids. It's their nature. With a child like Molly, who's already so bright…"

He'd heard her rant and rave on that angle of the subject before, too.

"But I'm so worried that it won't be funded for another year. I'm trying to document everything, the progress of every single child who's participating, with as much detail as I can. You know. Really *prove* what a program like this is doing and is capable of doing—''

''I don't know, Di, somehow I just have a feeling that you won't have a problem with funding next year.''

''Well, you're more of an optimist than I am. I'm afraid to take any chances. I really am going to document every child's progress with absolute care, no mistakes, no leaving anything out. No fudging it, either. I think people have gotten suspicious about wasted money in educational programs because there's been cheating before. I want to show what these teaching methods can really do, especially for high-risk kids....''

He kissed her. Not because he wanted to shut her up. Not because he'd heard all this before—positively this was her favorite rant-and-rave subject—and he could finish some of her sentences by now. Truth to tell, she lit up so high when she was talking about teaching that he could have listened to her all night.

The kiss, though, it just wouldn't wait. He'd loved watching her with Molly. Loved watching her tease him for being hopelessly biased as a dad. Loved watching her shy, gentle ways of fitting in with his three-person family, never intruding, not even once, not ever, but just seeping into their lives the way a flower bud could bloom even through cracked soil sometimes.

She didn't seem to mind being jumped right in the middle of his kitchen.

Her lips softened under his. Then, slowly, her right hand lifted to his arm. Then, slowly, her left hand lifted to his shoulder. And this soft, slow, woman sound came from her throat. A sigh of need. Of willfulness and pleasure. Maybe nine o'clock in the middle of his kitchen, with ice cream bowls getting stickier on the counter by the minute, was a crazy time and place to kiss her, particularly when she was teaching tomorrow and obviously didn't need to be up late.

But she didn't kiss as if she were thinking about tomorrow's school day.

She didn't kiss like she noticed they were standing in the middle of a kitchen, either.

And Trey thought, *Now. It's now or never.*

Chapter 5

Could a heart actually shake?

His mouth. Oh, my, his mouth. Like silk-satin sex. Warm and wooing. Kisses that plugged straight into her emotions like a direct current to a lightning storm.

Diana didn't know how long she'd been telling herself lies. That she'd been spending all this time with the Derringers solely because she was crazy about Molly. That the kisses she'd shared with Trey before had been accidental, incidental. She'd have to be crazy to believe that a killer hunk of a multi-millionaire would seriously be attracted to your average plain old grade-school teacher.

She'd been trying so hard not to sucker into that kind of lunatic type thinking.

Only damn.

Hearts did shake. And she never wanted this lunacy to end. Possibly she was unsure what Trey felt,
but she was absolutely sure about what she did. All
her life, she'd dreamed of this. All her adult life,
she'd tried to talk herself out of believing in the fairy
tale, yet still she'd yearned for the kind of love that
would take her under, sweep her away, wasn't just
about sensible compatibility but about the one man
who made her feel different than every other man
ever had. Or could.

It was stupid, believing in anything so unrealistic.

She believed it all. Her hands climbed his arms,
wrapped around his neck, hung on. He picked her
up, still kissing her, blindly walked out of the
kitchen, still kissing her, began a precarious, perilous, stair-climbing journey upstairs, still kissing her.
The only thing she knew about his house's upstairs
was that Molly's bedroom was to the right.

He aimed in the opposite direction, down a pitch-
black hall. His shoulder banged against a wall. He
kept going, ducked inside a yawning black room
with big, burly shadows. Stopped. Used a boot to
close the door—not a slam, but none too quietly.
She whispered swiftly, "Molly—"

"—could sleep through an earthquake. Don't
worry. But if you plan on going home tonight, Diana, you'd better tell me in the next three seconds."

Within the next three seconds, she framed his face
in her hands and kissed him hot and fiercely.

Eventually shadows turned into discernible shapes. She could make out no colors in the room, nor did she need to. Silver shafts of moonlight slanted across a king-size bed. Her spine dropped onto something cool and feather bouncy. That quickly he followed her down, his weight and heat welcomed. Lips sucked at lips. Tongues twisted together. One openmouthed kiss hissed into another, moaned into another.

Clothes were peeled off. His boots first, then her long skirt. If there'd been time, she would have stopped to laugh, because he pulled one arm out of her sweater, then seemed to forget about it…and he got around to unbuttoning the skirt at her waist, skimming it down, but neglected to remember she was still wearing her boots. Both of them were more than half dressed when his hand dove inside silk, cupped her, teased her with a long, slow finger. And still his mouth kept coming with more kisses, each sweeter and more intoxicating than the last.

She ripped at his shirt, tore at his pants, yanked his tie off with strangling speed. That he'd dressed up for his daughter's nursery school play both charmed and frustrated her. There was so much more to take off, soft, ironed linen, trousers that landed with a woosh, too many buttons, too much material of all kinds. And when she finally managed to get him bare, he disappeared on her.

But not far, and not for long. First she sensed him at the side of the bed, hurling pillows, and then she heard his laughter wicked and low from the bed's foot as he yanked off her boots. After that he dove back in bed with her, hauling a comforter with him and draping it over their heads as if making a cocoon. He was already her cocoon. The darn man slept with his window open. The wind had started to howl, a typical Montana night wind talking all about the winter ahead, trying to bring that chill in.

But there was no chill. Not in Trey's bed.

So dark. All she knew were textures. The pleat of crisp hair on his chest. His stubbly cheeks, the muscles rippling under his shoulders, the tautness of his abdomen, and beyond those gruffly masculine textures was the sensual contrast of his mouth. His tongue was soft and warm. Evocative, tender, loving. This was so much more than sex. Maybe she was caught up in that want-to-believe world, but she tasted kisses of tenderness and sharing, kisses fierce with wanting and wooing both, kisses that yearned for far more than just physical release.

She told herself she'd die if he only wanted this one night, but the truth was, she didn't care. At that moment, being with him was everything. She'd loved him for so long. He was the prince in her every dream, the man she heard in every song of love. Tomorrow, she could go back to being sensible and responsible again.

Tonight, she wanted her man. She wanted to be the lover her great-great-grandmother had been—a woman who gave everything for love, who was strong and free enough to risk everything for the one man who mattered to her.

At some point, he clawed away from her and found protection, but that only took moments. Then he was back, feeding the rush and fire that both of them wanted. They'd been teasing for weeks and weeks now. Both of them had had enough. It was impossible to stop an arrow once the bow released it. It simply flew, straight and true. She flew, straight and true, toward the one man who'd started this aching, reckless, exhilarating longing for completion with him...only with him.

As he started a relentless rhythm, pleasure sheared through her, slicing past any fears she'd ever had. She'd never felt alive, not like this, not like with him. She called his name as if lost in a thick woods and desperate to be found...and then he found her, took her with him, out, up, higher than she could ever remember climbing, ever imagine feeling. When they both tipped off the sun, she felt the joyful emotion of belonging to him, with him, part of him. And then they both collapsed, still wrapped tight around each other.

Diana's eyes suddenly shot open as if she had been startled by the bang of a gun. But there was no bang, no noise at all in the quiet house—except for the deep, slow breathing of the man beside her. Trey's arm was tucked under her breast, effectively scooping her into the sheltering spoon of his body.

Warm, evocative memories flooded her mind of
their lovemaking, and a lump suddenly filled her
throat. Like a crazy woman, she suddenly wanted to
cavort on a rooftop singing love songs at the top of
her lungs. Instead—thankfully—she spotted the
clock on the bedside table.

The luminous dial claimed it was five o'clock.
Time for a woman to get sane. Fast. The last Diana
knew, it had been midnight. She'd intended to get
up and drive home just the minute she caught her
breath...only Trey hadn't seemed inclined to let her
catch her breath at midnight—or any other time.

Quickly, silent as a cat, she inched away from that
warm, evocative male body and stood up. Swiftly
she gathered her clothes—everything but her underpants, which were hiding somewhere in the wicked
shadows—and tiptoed out the door. Across the hall
from the bedroom was a bathroom with a unicorn
night-light. Bleary-eyed, she stepped in there—and
almost shrieked when she heard a sudden voice.

"Hey, Di." Molly climbed down from the toilet.
Hair tumbling in her face, her feet bare, she stumbled toward her bedroom, dragging a two-foot yellow rabbit in her wake.

She'd disappeared from sight before Diana remembered to breathe. Molly had looked and acted
so sleepy that she might never remember seeing
her...but guilt bells were suddenly clanging in Diana's pulse. This was the exact reason she'd intended to leave earlier, so there was no chance

Molly or Simpson could realize she'd spent the night with Trey. It just wouldn't be right. She yanked on clothes, flew downstairs and grabbed her coat.

Outside, frost rimmed the lawn and dressed the black tree branches with a silvery white coating. The moon had fallen, but the predawn light had a magical moon glow that seemed to put a pearl hush on the whole world. She wanted to savor that precious magic, not charge off like a guilty bandit trying to get away. She still had that magical feeling on the inside from Trey's touch and the emotions he'd shared with her. And yeah, she knew exactly how badly she'd fallen in love with him.

Thick in love. High in love, scary in love. Like she'd rather be with him than eat or sleep. Like she could dance on mountaintops for the sheer joy of it. There'd just never been any other man for her, not like him—and never would be—which Diana figured was about time that she finally faced.

But love didn't make her choices any easier.

She drove home, feeling shaky and edgy, as if every safe mooring she'd always counted on had suddenly turned illusive and uncertain. She hadn't stopped being a romantic dreamer in her youth for nothing. When her mom died, she'd felt ripped apart. Being there for her sister and her dad had held her together. Being needed gave her an identity.

She wasn't afraid of being hurt. But she *did* need to be there for others. And turning into some lunatic wild-eyed dreamer was inexcusable when there was

a child involved—and a man who'd already been
hurt by a troubling relationship. Loving Trey meant
wanting to be the kind of woman he could count on.

But she truly didn't know what he needed in his
life, and that problem was still dominating her mind
Saturday when she kidnapped her sister for lunch at
the Hip-Hop Café in town. Suzanna's baby was due
anytime after Thanksgiving, which meant she was
getting too big to be comfortable doing anything.
Diana figured they both needed a break away from
the ranch and work and real life. She treated her
sister to a manicure and haircut, and then both settled into a booth at the Hip-Hop and ordered heaping
bowls of barley soup.

She'd gotten Suzanna laughing over a steady
round of terrible pregnant-woman jokes when her
sister suddenly stood up, gasping and still chuckling.
"Well, you know where I'm going. Between the
baby and laughing so hard, my kidneys are in real
trouble."

Diana couldn't help but grin as her sis waddled
toward the ladies' room…until her gaze was suddenly drawn to a woman at the back of the café.
There would have been no particular reason to notice her, except that the minute Suzanna disappeared
into the bathroom, the tall, slim older woman stood
up and seemed to be deliberately striding toward
her.

Diana vaguely recognized the face—most faces
were familiar in Whitehorn—but she couldn't im-

mediately place her. Church, she thought. She remembered seeing that patrician profile and swept-up hair and that pricey, snobby look, the woman talking to the minister outside church sometimes…and abruptly her stomach knotted in a fist. She recognized her, all right. It was Molly's grandmother. Regina Kingston.

The Kingstons who'd been fighting Trey for custody of Molly ever since their daughter had died.

Diana's toes suddenly went ice cold with nerves. She couldn't imagine why Mrs. Kingston would be interested in talking to her, yet the older woman kept coming, looking tall, proud, determined…and holding her gloves as she stopped at their booth. "I see your father in church most Sundays, Diana. But I haven't seen you in years now."

The Kingstons had always considered themselves too upper crust to spend much time chatting up the Brennans. Again, Diana felt needles of worry clench in her stomach…but hiding from trouble had never been her way. "Well, I've only been home for a couple months now. And I especially haven't had much time since catching a teaching job on the Laughing Horse Reservation…but I've still been lucky enough to meet your incredibly wonderful granddaughter."

Surprise shone in the older woman's gray eyes, followed by a brief hesitation. "That's why I stopped to talk. For Molly."

"I adore her," Diana said easily, honestly.

Again she appeared to take the older woman aback, but then Mrs. Kingston started meticulously threading her fingers into kid leather gloves. "Yes, well. Molly's mentioned you. More than once. But yesterday she happened to mention that you'd been to a sleepover at her house."

Diana heard the ice cold disapproval in the older woman's voice and felt terror, hotter than fire, lick at her heart. Oh, God. No court would ever take a child away from her natural father unless there were serious grounds. Grounds like immoral conduct. Her smile dropped faster than a lead ball. She just couldn't let it happen, couldn't do nothing, couldn't be part of a problem for Trey and Molly without trying to fix it. Words slipped out before she could think. "Mrs. Kingston," she said seriously, "I want you to know that I love Molly. And I had hoped that word of our engagement wasn't going to get out—even to Molly—until Trey and I had a chance to—"

"Engagement?" One leather glove fell to the floor.

Words kept bubbling out of her mouth like a babbling brook. "We never meant for Molly to realize I was there, of course. In fact, it was strictly for Molly's sake that Trey and I have chosen to be quiet about our relationship. Neither of us want to hurry Molly into—"

"Engagement?" Mrs. Kingston repeated.

"Believe me, Mrs. Kingston, I realize that no one

could ever take the place of your daughter. I would never try. But actually, I hope I can help Molly always remember her real mom…just by being another female adult in her life who really loves and cares for her. And who she can talk to about her mother whenever she wants to.''

When Suzanna emerged from the bathroom, Mrs. Kingston was gone and Diana was so shaken she could barely lift a teacup without spilling.

Her sister noticed immediately. ''Hey, what's wrong? You're all white—''

''Oh, God. I've just done a terrible thing, Suzanna.''

She never lied. It went against her whole grain. And she called Trey the very instant she got home to confess the mortifying fib she'd told, but Molly was right in the room and he couldn't talk. Rather than risk Molly overhearing the conversation, she asked if he might come over to her place later. Trey didn't hesitate. He kept saying that he didn't know what the trouble was, but to quit worrying about it.

But he didn't know what she'd done.

Trey drove toward the Big Sky, his fingers drumming a rhythm of anticipation on the steering wheel. Diana had sounded upset on the phone. Something was wrong—yet ironically, he felt nothing but relief. Hell, he'd known something was wrong from the night they made love, because she'd been skittering away from him ever since. Whatever put this particular bee in her bonnet, Trey was grateful. Few problems were unsolvable if people just talked, but until now, Diana had been so obviously shying away from any serious talk time with him that he'd been worried what was wrong.

The headlights of his black Camry illuminated the Big Sky Ranch sign. Once he turned, the corrals and barn and wagon stable were off to the left. Something was going on tonight in the horse barn, because the doors were open, yellow light spilling out in a rectangular pool. The big house was on the right, white with green shutters, rockers on the wraparound veranda and the yard neatly snugged in with a white picket fence.

Nothing about the Big Sky setup was as fancy as the Derringer spread where he'd worked as a boy, but growing up—even in the years he'd been drawn to money the way only a poor kid could be—he'd been drawn to the Brennans. Everything about their place was built to live in, built to last. His aunt used to say that the Brennans were good people, long-distance runners. That's how Diana's family struck Trey, too, as folks who'd stick it out through the tough times, tend toward common sense, always have a coffeepot going on the kitchen stove and no one minding if you walked in with your boots on.

Diana's place was just beyond the house to the east, a miniature echo of the big house with the same white framing and green shutters. Just seeing the light in her window put a bullet of speed in his pulse. He cut the engine and bolted toward her door, warning himself to slow down, take it easy, give her space, give her time, just keep his hands to himself until he knew what the problem was.

Something sabotaged his good sense, though, because the instant she opened the door, he hauled her close and plastered a soft one on her mouth. It wasn't his fault. Maybe a saint could have resisted her, but not a man as hopelessly, fiercely in love as he was. She looked so damned tempting besides, with a coral cord shirt jammed into jeans, waist cinched tight, all that flaming nervous color in her cheeks and her hair all over as if she'd brushed it with a tornado wind.

And she didn't seem to really mind being hauled up against him. She met his kiss. More than met it. Her eyelashes fluttered down and then her eyes closed and she clutched his arms for ten seconds— a good ten seconds—before suddenly jerking back and getting that hand-wringing-worry look in her eyes again.

"Okay, you. Now what's so terrible?" He shot in, pushed off his coat and boots, looked around when she offered him a drink. He volunteered to take a beer off her hands if she had one, thinking her place was nice. Too small. Barely camp-out room. But the ivories and candles and silk flowers she had around were distinctly Diana, no doodads and clutter, but the scents and textures all distinctly sensual, like her. She emerged from the little kitchen, handing him a wineglass and motioning him toward the couch.

He considered teasing her about the wine he'd never asked for and instead just took it. To test how distracted she was, though, he pulled a pale scrap of coral fluff with lace from his back jeans pocket. "You left something at my place last Tuesday night." He watched her expressions change until she recognized the underpants. First her eyes flashed to his. Then came the flush. Then the hint of a wicked, shared smile—which he loved…but then her gaze darted swiftly away from him.

She sat down on the couch like her heart was carrying lead. "I can't believe I forgot those. And I'd think it was funny, except…except it isn't." She gulped a breath. "Look, Trey. I did something I shouldn't have. I lied. It was wrong. What happened is that I got shook up and I didn't think. I couldn't be more sorry. But the thing is—the thing that matters is—we can make the problem go away. In fact, it never has to be any kind of problem for you. You just have to dump me."

He was expecting trouble. Not a gushed garble of words that made no sense at all. "Huh?"

"I had lunch today. With my sister. And while I was sitting at the restaurant, Regina Kingston stopped at my table. Your mother-in-law—"

At the mention of his late wife's mother's name, he decided maybe he'd have a sip of wine, after all. A patient sip. "Yeah, I know who she is, and she's

Molly's grandma—but she's no relation to me, not any more.''

"Well, she stopped to talk to me when Suze was in the bathroom. The problem, Trey, is that Molly saw me the other morning when I left so early.''

"So?"

"So she told her grandmother that I was there for a sleepover.'' More words gushed out. "That's why she stopped to talk to me. Because she knew I'd spent the night. And it just came out of my mouth— I said we were engaged. God, I'm sorry—''

"Engaged?"

A vigorously guilty nod. "I never meant to do anything to embarrass you. I was just so afraid that the Kingstons would try to make something of that—make out like we'd done something deliberately illicit in front of Molly—when the truth is, Mol would never have known I was there if she hadn't gotten up in the middle of the night to go potty. But the thing is, I just got rattled because I was afraid the Kingstons would try and cause you trouble—''

"So we're engaged, are we?" Trey stroked his chin and tried to look suitably grave. That seemed a more mature response than using her mattress for a trampoline and yahooing at the top of his lungs. Privately, though, he thought, *Who'd have thunk it? Sometimes people really do win the lottery.* He said slowly, "Molly will be thrilled.''

Diana didn't seem to catch that. She yanked a guilty hand through her hair. Again. "It'll all be okay, Trey. You just need to wait a little bit and then kind of let it be known in town that you dumped me. I don't think anyone would judge an engaged couple for spending the night together, and there's no reason the Kingstons ever had to know that wasn't the real circumstance. I'm sorry I made the darn lie up. At the time, all I could think of was trying to protect you both from the Kingstons—''

"What if..." Slowly he stroked his chin again. "What if I like the idea?"

"Pardon?"

"You love my daughter. In fact, you're darn well crazy for my daughter."

A bewildered frown. "Well, of course I am. But—"

Be careful, he warned himself. And he'd already realized that he needed to tread more carefully than a mouse in rattlesnake country with Diana. It was easy to see how fast she leaped to do the responsible thing—one of the things he loved about her—but for some unknown reason, she ducked hard and fast anywhere near the subject of love. Still, there was no way he could have the sun this close without trying his best to reach for it. "You understand Mol better than anyone ever has, Diana."

"Not better than you—"

"In a different way than me. Come on, you have to know how fantastic you are with her."

"It's just that I lost a mother, too, Trey. So we have this kindred spirit thing going—''

"Uh-huh. That's what I'm saying. You *do* have a great relationship going. No one could ever be a better mom for Molly than you. And then there's the two of us."

Shock seemed to stun her to silence. Then she said, "The two of us?"

"Maybe you weren't thinking of marriage. Maybe I wasn't, either, at exactly this moment in time," he lied. "But we've gotten along like a house afire ever since we re-met up. The two of us just keep getting better all the time. I suspect we'd have ended up talking seriously about marriage in a matter of time anyway—"

"Trey, I'm not so sure of that. I can't imagine you would—"

"You seem happy to be back in Whitehorn. You also really seem to love your teaching job on the reservation. And I can't believe you've got any questions about Molly—"

"I don't. About Molly. But—"

He hesitated. Then deliberately let out a worried sigh. "Man, I'm surprised I haven't heard from the Kingstons' lawyers already. It would be just like them to jump on any sign that I was less than a fit parent. They hit their lawyer when I had Mol up until ten o'clock for the county fair last year, did I tell you that?"

"No. Oh, good grief, Trey, they sound so vindictive—"

"Well, I don't want you worried about that. It's

my problem, not yours. But think on it, will you? Marriage?''

"I—"

Before she could try saying anything else, he tugged her close and kissed her. It was the same as before. For some confounded reason, Diana just couldn't seem to believe he really cared about her—no matter what he did, no matter what he said. Yet when he kissed her, everything became mirror clear for both of them.

His heart started chugging. So did hers. Warmth heated her skin. Her lips softened, melted, swelled under his. Her body bowed closer. Fingertips touched his face, shivery, trembly, and then wrapped around his head and pulled him down, pulled him deeper into that nice, wicked, wild kiss.

"Just say yes," he murmured. And kissed her again. And again. "Say yes, love."

"Yes. Yes. Yes."

Right then, he wasn't positive if she were saying yes to his spending the night or to the marriage proposal. But when a man was on a winning streak, he didn't test fate with questions. He just went with it.

Chapter 6

Diana felt as if she were stuck in the middle of a magic spell. Her childhood bedroom had been turned into a dressing room for the wedding, but the last time she'd spent any time in this room, she'd been an adolescent girl who still believed in fairy tales and white knights. Now she was getting married. Only somehow she couldn't exactly remember saying yes. She had no idea how Trey had arranged everything so fast. And something was terribly frightening—because this was exactly how the fairy tale was supposed to end, with the damsel getting the white knight.

And that would be wonderful instead of frightening—except that everyone knew real life never, never worked out that way.

One of the two females in the bedroom, however, was dancing on air.

"We're going to get married today, aren't we?"

"Uh-huh." Diana pinned the last rosebud in Molly's hair. Her sister had raided the famous Derringer greenhouses for the coral roses, because for damn sure there were none locally blooming on Thanksgiving weekend. Outside the wind was howling itself into a fitful blizzard.

"And then I get to call you Mom, right?"

"Now, lovebug, we already talked about this. You can either keep calling me Diana or call me Mom. Whatever you want is great with me." She studied her darling's face, then reached over to the dresser for her blusher. Molly needed rouge like she needed a hole in the head, but she instantly tilted her face with an ecstatic grin for this grown-up treat.

"Put on *lots,* okay? And after we get married, then I get to be your daughter, right?"

"Right."

"And then we get to go on our honeymoon, right? To Disney World? Simpson and I both get to go, for real?"

"I don't know how we could possibly have a honeymoon without both of you," Diana said gravely.

"And I look beautiful, don't I? In fact, I'm pro'bly the most beautiful girl you've ever seen, right?"

"Without question." Because the little one was still hopefully staring at all the makeup pots on the dresser, Diana spritzed her wrists with a little Shalimar.

"Diana?"

"What, darlin'?"

Molly met her eyes in the dressing table mirror. "You look beautiful, Di. Not as beautiful as me, but still really cool. But I have to tell you, if you'd just asked my daddy, I just know he'd have bought you a new dress. You didn't have to wear an old one. You coulda had a new dress just like me."

Diana chuckled. "As hard as this may be for you to believe, I wanted to wear this old one. This wedding dress belonged to our great-great-grandmother Isabelle. My mom wore it went she got married. And then my sister, Suzanna, wore it for her wedding. The thing is, we think of the dress as lucky, Mol. Every woman who's worn the dress so far has had a loving marriage." And man, she needed any luck today that she could beg, borrow or steal. "You're going to go out and find my sister now, okay? You stand with Suzanna and she'll tell you when to go down the aisle."

"With the rose petals. I get to throw all the rose petals."

"Yup. You've got the most important job of anybody," Diana assured her, and kissed her forehead...which resulted in an exuberant two-way hug, which messed both of them up all over again. Still, once Molly pranced downstairs to find her new aunt Suzanna, Diana had a couple minutes alone.

She pressed a hand to her nervous stomach, staring at herself in the dresser mirror. Wearing her great-great-grandmother's dress was not only tradition, but she'd prayed it would give her courage. The gown was so precious, long-sleeved with a demure scooped neck, the Irish lace faded from stark white to an delicate antique ivory. It was the kind of dress that could make a girl believe in magic and white knights and honorable quests and...

Lunacy.

She squeezed her eyes closed, thinking that her dad was downstairs. Family. Friends. It seemed right to have a wedding in the home where she'd grown up, the house where all the Brennan traditions of happy marriages had begun. Yet her stomach was suddenly rolling in waves of panic.

She'd been making nonstop jokes about becoming a lunatic ever since she came home to Whitehorn, but suddenly she wasn't laughing. Coming home had forced her to face up to what really mattered, and the truth was, she'd never wanted to live in a high-rise apartment and teach in Chicago's inner city. She wanted to live where she had roots. She wanted to teach where she had an investment in the kids and the community. She wanted love. The whole-cabana kind of love. The kind her grandmother had, and her mom. Romantic love. The risk-everything-and-don't-look-back kind of love. She wanted to raise children with a hero of a man, wanted to fight and make up and grow old with him, wanted to deepen the soul of what they both were in a place that mattered to them. Only…

Nobody really got it all. Only a lunatic believed in the fairy tale—and that was the whole problem. She believed the whole kit and kaboodle when she was with Trey.

Abruptly she opened her eyes and scowled fiercely at the pink-cheeked bride in the mirror. *He doesn't love you,* she warned herself. Sure, he cared about her. And the chemistry was fabulous. But he needed a mom for his daughter—a stable mom and wife, not a lunatic. She thought, hoped, that if she kept her head screwed on in a practical, responsible fashion, she could work hard at making a good marriage and love would come. For both of them.

With her hand on her heart, she spun around, inhaling the memories from her childhood bedroom. So many nights, she'd dreamed of princesses and castles and knights on white horses in that tall feather bed. So many nights, she'd cried herself to sleep after her mom died. But finally, that pain had lessened and started healing, when she'd turned a corner on growing up and determined to turn herself into a woman that her mom would be proud of. Her mom, her grandma, her great-great-grandma Isabelle—they were all women Diana fiercely respected and was proud of. And somehow she just couldn't imagine any of those good, strong women holding out because of some fierce, loony desire for a truly romantic love. It was past time she gave up those stupid illusions once and for all.

She glanced at the wall clock, swiftly adjusted her veil one last time and was turning toward the door when there was a knock.

"Come on in," she called, expecting Suzanna or Nash or Dad—anyone but a complete stranger. The ceremony was due to start ten minutes from now.

The woman who stepped in was older, wearing the garb of a traditional Cheyenne medicine woman—which made Diana automatically respond with a respectful smile of greeting. Her skin was as wrinkled as a brown raisin, her long gray hair coiled into a loose bun at her nape, her expression hard to read...yet her bark-brown eyes seemed warm and perceptive as they settled on Diana.

"Diana...do you know who I am?"

"I'm sorry, but no. Your face is somehow familiar, but I'm just not sure—"

The older woman nodded. "It's all right. I didn't expect you to recognize me. But I've watched you for weeks now, coming to teach the little ones on the reservation. For me, it has been like watching a circle being completed, seeds planted decades ago finally breaking through the soil to grow. You've come home. Really come home where you belong."

"I..." Diana felt mystified. There seemed to be both caring and affection in the older woman's expression, yet she had no idea what any of this conversation meant.

"Don't be upset. I know you have little time before the wedding ceremony. And it's not a day when you should be concentrating on a stranger's words. I just came to bring you a present. My name is Aiyana, and we are kin. I'm the great-niece of Kyle Running Horse."

"Kyle? As in Kyle and Isabelle?"

"Yes." From a pouch at her waist, Aiyana withdrew a small package wrapped in paper.

When Diana peeled back the crinkly folds, she discovered an oval-shaped amulet of hammered silver. An engraving of two running horses was carved into the top of the locket. "This is gorgeous," Diana said reverently, and stroked the striking carving with a delicate fingertip. "But, Aiyana, I'd feel guilty accepting anything like this. It looks like a valuable heirloom. Surely you have family closer to you than—"

"Blood kin closer, yes. But this amulet belongs specifically to you, Diana. Again, it is like watching the arc of a circle finally come together. The first woman to wear this was your great-great-grandmother Isabelle, and she wore it on her wedding day."

"She did?" Diana's eyes widened.

"She did. And inside the amulet is a herb that the old wise ones have always said would bring love to a marriage. That was why your great-great-grandmother wore it, because she feared she would never know love, never be loved. She felt unworthy.

Afraid to believe. Afraid to reach for what was in her heart.''

Diana frowned, feeling more confused than ever. ''Aiyana, could you have me confused with someone else? Because my sister and I have letters between Isabelle and her Kyle. She was never worried about being loved—they were crazy in love for each other.''

''I know nothing of letters. But I am very sure of the history of Kyle and Isabelle.'' The older woman backed toward the door. ''The women in your family are strong, of good hearts. You take care of others well and you seek to do the right thing. This is all good. But I think you and your great-great-grandmother were kindred spirits, Diana. She feared being unworthy, thought that no one would need her for herself. Wear the amulet and follow your heart. It will give you luck.''

''But I really don't feel that I can accept—'' Before Diana could finish the thought, the Cheyenne woman had backed from the room and closed the door.

She was still standing in stunned confusion in the center of the room when knuckles rapped again on the door. ''Aiyana,'' she started to say. But it was her sister poking her head in.

''Oh, man. You look so beautiful! But you're going to be late if we don't get you downstairs.'' Suzanna walked in, looking beautiful but distinctly ready to pop her baby any second. She set the bride's bouquet of coral roses on the bed and aimed for Diana.

"You goof! You didn't have to climb the stairs— I was coming—"

"Yeah, well, I started to worry when you weren't already down that something could be wrong. And maybe something is." Her sis came over, brushed a strand of hair here, smoothed a fluff of lace there. "You're looking scared."

"I am."

"Yeah, well. That's like saying a rabbi is Jewish or the Pope's Catholic. Brides are supposed to be jittery. It's in the rule book. The question is more, are you sure? Because if you want to call this off, believe me, I'll make sure it happens. We can run off to Poughkeepsie together if we have to. We can—"

Diana started to smile. Her sister made it impossible not to. "I don't think you're going to be *running* anywhere for a little while, Suze. Or that Nash would appreciate my taking off with you."

"Nash loves me. Nash will recover from any darn fool wild hair I come up with, so you can forget Nash. You're the one who matters right now. And you don't have to do anything unless this is what you really want."

Again Diana smiled. She wanted to tell Suzanna all about the mysterious Cheyenne woman and what she'd said—but that would wait. She picked up the bridal bouquet of roses, pausing only long enough to bury her nose in the sweet promising scent for a moment.

"Stop worrying, Suze. I'm sure," she said softly. And she *was* sure that she could be a good mother to Mol. Sure that Trey needed a mother for his daughter. Sure that they'd get along fine when the lights went off, that they liked and respected each other when the lights were on. She was sure that he needed her.

And if she were wildly, painfully in love with him...well, she just wasn't going to worry about whether Trey loved her right now. The old Cheyenne woman seemed to have some family history confused, but Aiyana had still managed to remind her about what really mattered. Her great-great-grandmother's letters had spoken of a passionate love that only grew deeper with time. Isabelle had defied all convention to marry a half-breed in her day, completely ignoring what others believed was important to a good marriage.

Diana could do the same. She would love Trey. They would make a relationship their own way. And maybe in time the kind of love she dreamed of would grow. To give him up—no, there wasn't a chance.

And with that last thought, she clasped the amulet, grabbed her bouquet, hustled Suzanna out and danced down the stairs to find her groom. Guests were congregated in the living room, furniture pushed aside to make room for chairs and create a makeshift aisle. Her dad was waiting at the stair bottom, pacing and staring at his watch. Molly was doing impatient pirouettes that threatened to topple all the rose petals in her basket. Diana saw all of them....

But not really.

She saw the man standing at the fireplace, looking so piratelike and elegant in the black suit and virgin white linen shirt, his dark eyes waiting for her.

He wanted this marriage. She knew from his smile, from the way his hand unconsciously lifted, just the smallest amount, as if automatically wanting to reach for her. They could make anything work, she told herself.

And desperately wanted to believe that.

Chapter 7

Five days later, Trey stood alone on the hotel balcony overlooking a vista of palm trees and aquamarine water and the beginning of a jewel-toned sunset. The magical landscape had no effect on the facts. As honeymoons went, Trey figured theirs qualified for disaster relief funds.

But that was about to change.

He heard the snick of the door lock opening, then a quiet voice. "Trey?"

"I'm here." He turned just in time to see his new bride stumble toward him. Diana had a smile, but no one would guess they'd been in Florida for the last five days. Her face was as pale as if they'd never left Montana's blizzard weather, and her eyes had soft smudges from tiredness. "Oh," she said warily, "you're still dressed for dinner. I'm so sorry, Trey, I couldn't help being so late—"

"I know you couldn't. And I have to believe after this long day that you're too tired to go out to dinner at all, aren't you?"

"I am a little beat," she admitted, "but if you haven't eaten—"

"Not to worry. No reason to change or lift a finger—or go anywhere. I've got a little surprise planned, but all we have to do is walk down one flight."

"A surprise? Well, that sounds like fun."

The words were right, the positive smile was there, but Trey figured Diana was as excited about a surprise as a case of poison ivy. She was trying to be a good sport. The only thing she likely wanted was twelve straight hours in the closest bed—alone. Which he understood. But things couldn't continue the way they had been.

Guiding her toward the door, he asked, "Did you manage to reach your sister?"

"Yes, finally!" No matter how exhausted she was, her face suddenly glowed with enthusiasm. She didn't seem to notice that he was steering her out the door and down the hall. "Oh, Trey, the baby sounds adorable! And they finally settled on the name Travis. Suzanna said both Nash and Dad were just beside themselves—"

"I'll bet."

"Eight pounds, seven ounces, so he's a healthy little slugger already, even if he was a little early. And the labor wasn't so bad. As far as I can tell, all labor is horrible. But at least it only took six hours, which Suzanna was told is really fast for a first baby—"

Trey wondered if that experience was something that ran in families, such that Diana might be more inclined to have a short, not too bad labor if her sister had. But he didn't dare ask. The subject of babies didn't seem to be in their future. Now that they were legal, apparently they were never again going to make love, either.

So far, their marriage seemed headed in a distinctly backward direction. He steered her past Simpson and Mol's suite, past the elevator, down one flight of stairs. It was a measure of how tired Diana was that she never asked where they were going.

Five days ago, he'd innocently believed he had a shot at winning Diana. And yeah, of course, he realized that Di wasn't that positive about being in love with him. It nipped that she thought he needed rescuing from the accusations of his in-laws—as if he couldn't protect and fight for his own daughter without a marriage to hide behind. But at the time Diana said yes, Trey hadn't cared why she'd agreed to the wedding. Gluing that ring on her finger was the only thing on his mind. Making her part of his life. Sealing their vows with time together.

He'd also assumed that loving her—fiercely, strongly, compellingly, night and day—would eventually encourage her to feel the same. One could only fight exposure to an infectious substance for so long before succumbing—he was sure. But then, five days ago, he'd also been sure that getting married was a way of guaranteeing he'd have private time with his bride.

He pushed open an unmarked door on the seventh floor. Diana looked at him with a curious frown. He didn't answer, only gently motioned her through the doorway.

Until this moment, they'd had no private time.

None. Zip. Zero.

The original plan had been to go to Disney World. Maybe it wasn't the most romantic place on the planet, but it happened to be an unbeatable place to keep his daughter busy and happy, and they had a carry-along baby-sitter in the form of Simpson. The disaster began on the afternoon of their wedding, when their flight to Orlando ended up getting plunked down in Denver for an all-nighter in the airport until a raging blizzard cleared.

That was bad enough, but then Simpson got sick when they finally got a Florida flight. Airsickness was unpleasant in itself, but it seemed he had the beginnings of a full-blown flu. Once in the wilds of

Orlando, they stuffed Simpson in a suite with several pounds of medication—Simpson and Molly had separate bedrooms in their own suite down the hall from the newlyweds—and Trey and Diana took Molly off for the next three days to do the Disney World thing. Molly was ecstatic. She also bunked in their suite because the adults didn't want her exposed to Simpson's bug. Mol was ecstatic about sleeping with them, too.

Until she came down with the flu bug herself forty-eight hours ago. His daughter was the most precious, perfect girl a father could have—priceless—she could do no wrong in Trey's eyes. But she was just a *teensy* bit cantankerous when she didn't feel well. She wanted either him or Di constantly.

Her fever had broken that afternoon, and she was on the mend.

Simpson was up and around and feeling hot to party.

It was only the newlyweds who were so exhausted they could barely make it through *Wheel of Fortune* before conking out—and so far they hadn't spent a single night since the wedding without a small body between them either because she didn't feel good or because she was scared from being alone or because his darling daughter was outstanding at conning her two favorite adults.

"Trey? I don't understand where we are." Diana

had wandered through the doorway where he'd motioned her. "Isn't this room part of the motel spa?"

"Yup. In fact, it's the massage therapy room— which is why you see those sheet-covered stretchers. And just through this door—" he opened it "—is one of the motel's indoor pools. The smaller one."

"But no one else is here," Diana said curiously.

"Exactly. I rented this whole area for the next three hours."

"You mean the pool and spa are ours? They're closed to the rest of the motel?"

"Completely. And by the pool, there are drinks and a seafood buffet waiting for us, where you can put your feet up and indulge until you're full. Then, madame, my plan is to treat you to a full body massage. After which, I believe, you'll likely feel like melted Jell-O and will be in no mood to do anything but be poured into bed. So that's the agenda. Food, because we both need it. Then a massage, because you've been running twenty-four hours a day since we got here, and I know you're overtired. And then sleep. Noninterrupted sleep."

"Sleep," she echoed blankly, as if that word was completely unfamiliar to her.

He almost laughed at that carefully bland look in her eyes. She hadn't had a wedding night yet, and God knew, neither had he. If he didn't get his hands on her soon, he just might lose his sanity. This had to be the longest chaste honeymoon on record.

But that wasn't the point. No matter how much they'd shared, he'd had no chance to woo Diana, much less to win her. He hoped to have a lifetime of making love to his wife. First, though, he had the crazy, old-fashioned idea that it might be a better idea to just plain show her...

Love.

"Come on, you," he coaxed. "It's been hours since lunch. No matter how tired you are, you have to be hungry for something."

"Something? Holy moly, Trey." Her mouth dropped when she saw the feast of trays set out buffet-style by the water. In no time, he'd mounded a plate for her, dripping with crab and lobster, strawberries and iced melon, marinated asparagus and chilled pea salad and exotic dips for all types of breads.

He'd brought her bathing suit down earlier—and his. No one was around, including waiters. The doors were all locked. There were times it paid to have money. This was one of them. He'd known she'd be too tired to go out, but he could tell, he could see, this was what she needed. Time with no interruptions. Time when she could stop being on, when no little voice was calling her name and no one needed her.

Once she started diving into the food, the smudges under her eyes seemed to soften, lighten. Relaxed smiles showed up, then laughter, as they sprawled in loungers like decadent sultans, eating a grape here, a bite of succulent white lobster there.

"I didn't even know I was hungry," she said with disbelief when she suddenly realized her plate was empty.

"We haven't touched the desserts yet. They're still covered up, on ice. I was told there's a decadent chocolate mousse and some Napoleons and some key lime pie and—"

"Are you planning on rolling me back to our rooms?"

"If we have to crawl back to our rooms, who's to know? Don't you think we've earned it? This has been a vacation that should get high-risk pay so far."

"It's not exactly the relaxing week we planned, now, is it?" she admitted humorously. "But really, Trey, things just happen. Especially with kids. It's not like we don't have time to be together after this. It's no one's fault the flu bug caught on. And I think Mol would have been scared if she'd woken up sick and you weren't there."

"You know what I think, Mrs. Derringer?"

Her lips curved at the sound of the new name. "What?"

"I think you thrive on being needed." When she leaned forward to set down her plate, he moved behind her, cupped his hands on the curve of her shoulders and started kneading.

Immediately she turned serious, although her eyes closed at the first touch of his hands. "Actually, I do, Trey. I really like doing for others. It's not like I'm so unselfish or anything like that. But I think it stems back from when I lost my mom. Doing for my dad and sister just made me feel good about myself. Sitting around being taken care of would just never be my way. I'd be miserable."

When her voice trailed off, he had to smile. She was succumbing to a simple back rub as if it were a magic spell. The more he rubbed her shoulders and back, the more she turned into putty, liquid, silky, her breath coming hopelessly slower and easier. She really had been up too many nights. Not because Trey wouldn't take care of his daughter himself, for heaven's sake, but because Di kept volunteering. And Molly soaked up attention from her like a sponge.

But over the last few days, Trey had really come to understand exactly how that need thing worked for Diana. She *did* instinctively fire up when she was needed. In fact, he'd come to believe her saying yes to his marriage proposal had that element at the core. She responded one hundred percent to Molly needing her as a mother, to helping him with his in-laws, to wherever her heart understood she was needed.

And that was terrific, Trey considered, since need was sincerely a part of his love for Diana. He *did* need this woman of his heart. Missing, though, had been any chance to show her exactly what kind of need he felt for her...and that this kind of need had nothing to do with dependency and everything to do with choice.

Her head drooped limply. He heard her sigh, heavy and low. And he continued kneading, kneading, kneading.

Eventually her eyelashes lay silent as shadows on her cheeks. Her heart began a slow pattern of respiration that indicated she was out for the count. Absolutely dead to the world. And, after all these days, finally aiming for the restful sleep Trey knew she needed.

A ribbon of shiny yellow sunlight peeked through the curtains. Diana was aware of that first, then aware that she felt rested, the way she hadn't felt in days. And pampered and treasured, the way she'd never felt...ever. She turned her head to find Trey crashed on his stomach next to her.

They'd been sleeping next to each other for the last six nights, of course, being married and all— but sleep had been the only action going on in the midnight hours.

Last night she'd been so positive would be different.

Last night she'd been positive that Trey had been seducing her, with the feast and the privacy and the long, lazy, sexy back rub.

She'd been well aware that his body was aroused and trigger ready. She'd felt him, intimately, when he'd pulled his arms around her. Yet nothing had happened beyond his carrying her to bed and her— apparently—falling into a coma-like sleep.

Absently she remembered something the mysterious old Indian woman said, about her great-great-grandmother Isabelle feeling unworthy, afraid to believe she was loved. The stranger knew nothing about her, couldn't. Yet Diana's heart kept remembering those words, the thought surfacing over and over in her mind like a bubble trapped underwater.

She'd never really felt worthy. Loved. Lovable. Unless she was doing for someone else. And part of what had drawn her to Trey—reassured her into saying yes—was knowing that he needed her.

Yet last night, he hadn't seemed to need her at all. He'd done nothing for himself. Taken nothing for himself. Only arranged everything about the evening specifically for her sake.

Slowly her palm slid under the crisp white sheet, finding warm, bare, bronze skin. Tentative, she offered a feather caress. Just a gentle, exploring touch, meant to be soothing, not arousing. Comforting, not aggressive. Giving. Not taking.

Yet she rubbed and stroked that skin until it heated under her fingertips. Then, quiet as a thief, she ducked her head under the sheet—carefully leaving no drafty air pockets—and pressed her lips along the same wandering path, over ridges and valleys, shoulder blades and the ridge of his spine and the hollow at his nape.

She was busy. Extremely busy. Molding his skin. Learning him. Loving him. Not—honestly—trying to wake him but only to have her loving feelings incorporated into his dreams, into the deepness of his rest.

On that silky, shiny morning, though, she suddenly heard his voice. Something in his husky whisper made her suspicious that he'd been awake for some time. "Are you looking for trouble, ma'am?"

Her fingertips stilled. "Um…I wasn't looking to wake you, if you still need sleep."

"I don't need sleep. In fact, I can't imagine ever wanting to sleep for the next ten years or so. My mind seems to be dominated by other ideas entirely. Did anything in particular bring on this, um, back rub?"

"You love me," she announced.

Abruptly he turned on his back, somehow managing to drag her possessively across his chest at the same time. His gaze pounced on her face as if he would memorize every part of her, eyes, lips, nose, patch of freckles, all savored equally, all loved…the way she never thought anyone would love her. "You're just getting around to figuring that out, Di? Why did you think I asked you to marry me?"

"I don't know. Because you realized how much

I loved Mol. And you and I seem to get on so well. And the way you described your first marriage, it sounded painful and awful, and you surely had to know the two of us could be so much better than…'' She heard herself start chattering and stopped. ''I really didn't know, Trey.''

A long, slow fingertip stroked her jawline. ''Just for the record, my first marriage didn't give me low expectations of what a relationship could be, but the opposite. I was never planning on getting married again. But assuming I was so crazy as to fall, I promised myself I'd never take the risk unless I loved someone, heart and soul. Diana?''

''What?''

''I love you. Heart of my heart, soul of my soul.''

''Oh, Trey.'' She sank into his arms feeling as if she were finally coming home. Really home. ''That's how I felt about you. I was just so afraid of believing in it. It doesn't happen in life, you know? That your first crush turns out to be your first love. That your hero turns out to be…well, your hero.''

''I'm no hero, Di. I've made a lot of mistakes. I make a lot of mistakes. But I do love you, the way I never dreamed I'd find love in my life.''

''And I love you,'' she whispered, and kissed him. A kiss of promise and passion both. For so long she'd doubted that she had the strength of the Brennan women, yet this man she loved had taught her otherwise. Love—the right kind of love—was a woman's source of strength like none other.

As their kiss deepened and darkened and caught fire, she wound her arms around him and hung on. They were not only way overdue a honeymoon night, but the sun-filled morning struck her as an ideal time to start their true life together.

* * * * *

Look out for Jennifer Greene's
YOU BELONG TO ME
in October 2001.
It's the third book of the exciting
MONTANA BRIDES *series.*

ISABELLE

Cheryl St John

ISABELLE

Chapter 1

Chapter 1

Glancing at the nearly deserted train station behind him, Kyle Running Horse Brennan squinted into the afternoon sun and impatiently tugged the brim of his hat lower over his eyes. He scanned the horizon for the train that was now half an hour late. He could have sent one of the hands to meet it, but seeing to Isabelle Cooper had become his responsibility, and he wasn't one to shirk duty—even if that duty was to a silly pampered city female.

She didn't belong here. Ranch life wasn't a society ball. And this ranch in particular, Big Sky, was soon going to be his, anyway.

In the distance, the long, low whistle from what his mother's people called the iron horse broke the stillness. The rails hummed, and the ground beneath his scuffed boots shivered. A covey of quail soared skyward in the distance as the train flushed them out of the tall, dry grass along the metal tracks.

Smoke appeared, then the huge black engine, with dried brush stuck in the cowcatcher. In a hiss of steam and squealing brakes, the shiny monstrosity lurched to a halt beside the station.

At a snail's pace, a black-suited conductor lowered himself to the ground and unfolded a set of metal stairs.

On the grate above, a solitary figure came into view. Kyle had caught only glimpses of her during the four years that he'd worked for her father, and he remembered her as a tall, willowy fifteen-year-old with shining auburn hair.

The exquisite young woman in an elegant dove-gray traveling suit and matching hat who gracefully opened a frilly parasol and descended the stairs with her gloved hand in the conductor's made his heart give a crazy little thump. He recognized Isabelle by her unusual height and the expensive clothing, but the fact that she was a fully grown woman—and that he'd responded—caught him off guard.

He spent as little time around whites as possible—and even less around white women. Being staked in the noon sun over an anthill would probably be less irritating than having to convince the spoiled daughter of his late boss to sell out to him and go back to the city.

She turned, and another portly railroad employee attentively handed down a stack of cylindrical boxes fastened together with gold cord, as well as a dome-shaped object covered by an embroidered cloth. The latter she held aloft, grasping it by a metal ring at the top.

She approached Kyle with her odd parcels, the sun glinting from her shiny golden ear bobs and the jeweled brooch at the base of her slender throat. "Mr. Brennan?"

He removed his hat and didn't miss the fact that her perusal included the sweep of his straight black hair that fell to his shoulders. "Miss."

Beneath the jaunty brim of her useless hat with the unnatural-looking flowers, her wide eyes were a stunning blue-gray. He'd never seen them up close before, and focused intently on his face they made him uncomfortable and hitched his breath momentarily.

The conductor helped her stack the boxes at her feet. At her thanks, the man's neck and ears reddened; he tipped his hat and waddled to the rail car.

"The train was late," Kyle said, grateful for the interruption. "We'd better get going."

From the corner of his eye, he noticed two red-faced porters carrying an enormous securely strapped trunk between them. They lowered it not-too-gently to the battered platform.

He frowned at the cumbersome piece of luggage, then at her. "That yours?"

She nodded.

He tested one end by the leather handle. The thing weighed near as much as his horse! He slid it to the edge of the wooden structure, muscled it onto his back and carried it to the waiting wagon. Catching his breath, he turned.

She stood expectantly at the edge of the platform, the cloth-covered dome securely in her grasp. What did she expect him to do? Carry her, too?

Carefully, she set the object down. "While you get the other one, I'll be just a moment."

The other one? He cut his gaze to where they'd been standing. Sure enough, another steamer trunk had been placed on the wooden landing while he'd wrangled the last. "What the hell have you got in these things?"

Her brow wrinkled. "Why, my clothing, of course. A few necessities."

"A *few?*"

Ignoring his displeasure, she brought the stack of round boxes forward. "I'll be right back."

"Where do you think you're taking off to?"

Her cheeks grew pink, but she straightened and spoke without a qualm. "To use the facilities, Mr. Brennan, since you so rudely insist upon hearing me say it."

He looked away and adjusted his hat. "Be quick about it."

He loaded the other trunk, then the boxes, and grabbed the draped parcel, which was surprisingly light. As he swung it into the back of the wagon, a rapid, fluttering racket burst from beneath the cloth, startling him. He released the ring and flung back the fabric. Tiny feathers scattered in the breeze. Kyle stared at the yellow bird frantically battering itself against the sides of the cage. "A bird."

Isabelle's peg-heeled shoes clicked as she neared.

He turned with a puzzled frown and said again, "A bird!"

She ran down the set of stairs and through the billowing dust. "You've frightened the poor darling! Please, place his cover back over him."

"He's scared because he's trapped," Kyle said. "Has he been hurt? Is that why you've caged him?"

"No, he's not injured, unless he's hurt himself just now." She peered at the bird from beneath her hat brim, concern marring her perfect porcelain-skinned features, then lifted an accusingly haughty brow at Kyle.

"Then you should set him free." He reached for the tiny wire door.

Isabelle yelped and grabbed his wrist. "No!"

He stared at her stark white glove against his sun-weathered skin, and his heart fluttered as if another living thing was caged within his chest.

"It's a domestic creature, Mr. Brennan. Canaries are bred as tame pets. He's never been outside his cage and wouldn't know what to do if you set him free. He'd die of hunger and exposure."

She removed her hand and, able to breathe again,

he lowered his to his side. He blinked at the delicate
bird, still feeling Isabelle's pleading touch on his
skin. Only a city woman would place such impor-
tance on a bird as inappropriately bred for this land
as she herself was. Silly bird wouldn't make a decent meal for one of the barn cats.

Apparently assured that her pet was safe, she
draped its prison. "Please set the cage down on the
floor of the wagon, so that the wind doesn't reach
him."

With his mouth held firmly in an irritated line,
Kyle did her bidding, then turned to raise a brow as
if asking if the placement of the cage met her friv-
olous standards.

Moving to stand beside the wagon and wearing a
calculating expression, she studied the distance between the ground and the footboard, then met his
gaze.

"Want a lift?" he asked.

Obviously lacking a better solution, she nodded.
"Yes, thank you."

He spanned her waist with both hands and lifted
her easily into the wagon. She wasn't a delicately
built woman, but beneath his fingers, her body felt
toned as well as feminine. He shouldn't have noticed. He released her as soon as her feet touched
the wood, painfully uncomfortable with the familiarity.

She caught her balance, adjusted her ridiculous
hat and seated herself. Kyle bounded up in one easy

motion, picked up the reins and released the brake handle. The horses responded to his command and pulled them forward.

A quarter of an hour passed before she spoke again. "The mountains are as beautiful as I remembered."

She was studying the climbing acres of lodgepole pines in the distance, the twin peaks of the snow-capped Crazy Mountains above. An awelike expression lit her black-lashed, smoky eyes.

"How long are you staying?"

She turned her head, and those disturbing eyes focused on him. Something behind them changed. "How long am I staying? Not, 'Please accept my condolences on the loss of your father, Miss Cooper.' Not, 'It's a pleasure to see you. How was your trip?' But, 'How soon will I be rid of you?'"

Her words pricked him with a swift twinge of guilt. "I'm sorry about your father. I did what I could to save him."

"I've no doubt you did." Her voice had become throaty, and she spared him only brief glimpses. Several seconds passed. "I'm planning to stay for good. The Big Sky is going to be my home."

Well, that figured. He should have known dealing with her wasn't going to be easy. He would have to change her mind. He would have to show her she didn't want to stay. Isabelle Cooper was going to have to make different plans.

Isabelle breathed the vibrant air and relished the

wide-open blue sky and the land that stretched and rolled in all directions. Her grief for her father conflicted with her newfound and astounding sense of freedom. The only joyful memories she possessed were those of her too-brief childhood visits to Montana. She thought those memories had been well buried—she'd hidden them to escape the hurt and longing they carried. She'd determinedly made the best of the world her father had insisted she live in and prided herself on becoming a modern young woman.

But now that her father wasn't here to prevent her from staying, she could do as she pleased. She was, after all, the new owner of the Big Sky. Blinking away stinging tears, she remembered how he'd always met her at the station. He'd hugged her, and she'd been deliriously happy to see him—even if he hadn't needed her.

Isabelle cast a furtive glance at the intimidating dark-eyed, copper-skinned man who shared the wagon seat. She'd had only quick looks at him in the past, and he was just as unsmiling and gruff as she recalled. He'd been her father's right-hand man for the past four years. Sam Cooper had trusted him, and she had no choice but to trust him, too.

She didn't know the first thing about running a ranch—but she was going to learn.

The ranch house and buildings came into view, and as always, the sight warmed Isabelle with a safe, secure feeling.

Her attention focused on the enormous house her father had built for her mother after he'd bought this land. After his wife's death, he'd sent Isabelle away and had never allowed this to be her home.

The house stood two stories tall, white with green shutters and pitifully empty planter boxes beneath the upstairs windows. She could picture them overflowing with colorful petunias and verbena, just like when her mother had been alive.

Kyle halted the team before the dooryard, and Isabelle eagerly jumped down without waiting for assistance. Her heels clicked on the stone walk that led to the gate in the white picket fence surrounding the house and separating it from the rest of the ranch buildings.

She stepped through the opening and studied the welcoming etched-oval window that graced the front door. A wide porch stretched across the front and the west sides of the house. Rockers and a swing beckoned for a shady afternoon rest.

Her yearning gaze caressed the house, absorbed it with a sad hollowness that made her chest ache, then she turned and stared toward the wagon shed and the enormous rust-red barn beyond. She would never see her father cross the yard again—never have an evening to sit on the porch with him and ask about the horses. Any chance of gaining his love or getting to know him was gone—except whatever she could learn by being here, by finding out who he'd been and what he'd thought and done all those years they'd been apart.

A small glimmer of hope flickered in Isabelle's heart. The fulfillment of her plans and dreams would eventually crowd the loneliness from her heart, and she would belong. She was home at last.

Chapter 2

Kyle and two of the hands noisily carried the unwieldy trunks up the stairs.

"First room on the left," she called, daintily slipping her gloves from her hands.

Tott, a wrangler barely out of his teens, and Sidestep, the second-best trainer on the ranch, stared at the primly dressed and coifed young woman. Kyle spotted their enamored gaping and urged their attention to the task.

Kyle's aunt had helped him clean the house and launder the curtains and bedding, but he hadn't seen Isabelle's room until he stepped into it with the dusty ranch hands. The three lowered their cumbersome loads.

Sheer white ruffles adorned sparkling windows and draped a canopy above the mahogany bed. The walls had been covered with rose-trellis paper, and the plush, dawn-tinted carpet sank beneath their boots.

Mouth open, Tott swept his hat from his head, then turned and nearly trampled Sidestep in his eagerness to exit.

Sidestep slugged him on the shoulder and thundered down the stairs behind him.

Kyle followed at a slower pace.

"Will one of you gentlemen help me move this table?" Isabelle's cultured voice called from the dining room beyond the enormous tiled foyer.

Tott and Sidestep stopped midstride, glanced at one another and collided shoulders on their way through the door. Kyle shook his head.

"I'd like it over here in front of these windows, if you please. That way Chipper will get the morning sun."

Chipper? Kyle almost snorted, but cleared his throat instead.

At her direction, the two men hauled an oak table from the corner and set it before the lace-curtained windows. Isabelle draped the table with a daintily crocheted cloth, then placed her birdcage atop it. She removed the embroidered cover with a flourish. Wispy feathers floated on a beam of indirect sunlight. Tott and Sidestep stared at the bird huddled on the floor of the cage.

"Thank you, gentlemen."

They mumbled something incoherent and hot-footed it out of the room. The front door opened and closed.

She had removed her hat, and her lustrous hair shone in the afternoon light filtering through the filmy curtains. Her jacket was gone, too, revealing a wrinkled white shirtwaist tucked into the narrow band of her skirt. Kyle forced his attention to one of the china cabinets that flanked the open glass-paned doors leading to the kitchen.

"What time is dinner?" she asked. "I think I'd like to freshen up and rest."

"Harlan rings the bell at the bunkhouse when he has dinner ready." He spared her a glance.

Her expressive eyes widened with a question. "We always had dinner in here when I was home."

"Your father hired someone from town for your visits," he replied honestly. "He ate with the hands the rest of the time."

Her brow furrowed. "Oh. I see."

He couldn't let the woman starve, but her eating alongside the hands was out of the question. "I'll bring you a plate."

"Will you join me?"

She needed to see what ranch life was really like, but she'd just arrived. Maybe she needed one night to rest from her trip. His gaze drifted to the long, empty table where she'd have to eat alone if he didn't join her, and without considering his reasoning, he replied, "Yes."

She folded her hands and gave him a satisfied smile. "Good. I'll see you then."

She picked up her hat and jacket and swept gracefully from the room. He followed slowly, turning to see her gliding along the upstairs hallway toward her room.

Agreeing to join her for supper was all right. He needed to talk to her, anyway. Ambling into the study that had been her father's, he rearranged the papers on the desk and seated himself to finish reading the ledgers he'd left open that morning.

Already her presence was a distraction and a hindrance. He'd wasted his morning and then called hands in from their chores to unload her things. The woman was a nuisance. The sooner he got her out of here, the better.

He'd asked Tott and Sidestep to help him because they were the two he trusted most around women. Even he knew that an unmarried, attractive female shouldn't be alone on a ranch with a dozen men.

What was he going to do about it? The more he thought of her alone here day after day—night after night—the more he knew he had to do something.

He would ask his aunt's advice this afternoon. He only needed a short-term solution. As soon as Isabelle saw how much painstaking work the ranch took, how all the money went into its operation, she'd be on a train bound for finer living.

He'd been working for years to save up enough to offer to buy out her father. Sam hadn't been willing to sell, even though his poor management had brought him to that point. But he had been ready to go into partnership. They'd come to a verbal agreement just before Sam had been killed leading horses from the burning barn.

Sam's death was a tragedy, and Kyle mourned his senseless passing. But his death was also an opportunity—a chance for Kyle to get the land that had been his father's.

Only here on the land where he'd been born did Kyle belong. No prissy city woman was going to keep him from getting what should have been his.

The clang of the dinner bell woke Isabelle, and she sprang from the bed, surprised that she'd napped so soundly. She cleaned her teeth and brushed her hair into order before hurrying down the stairs to set the dining table with a linen cloth and gold-rimmed china that had been her mother's.

The kitchen door closed, and the tall half-breed appeared in the dining room with cloth-covered plates. He stopped and stared at her table setting. "Already have plates here."

He placed them on the table and peeled back the napkins, revealing meat and vegetables in dark gravy. Several biscuits rested on the edge of each plate.

Isabelle removed the china quickly, arranged the

full plates and seated herself in the chair she'd always used. She couldn't help glancing at her father's empty place at the head of the table.

Kyle left that chair empty, took a seat across from her and pulled his meal toward him.

"Did you make coffee?" he asked, picking up the fork.

She unfolded her napkin and placed it across her lap. "No. I can boil water for tea."

"Can you light a fire in the stove?"

She picked up her fork and looked at the food rather than face his scrutiny. He thought she was helpless, and she didn't want to add to his thinking by admitting her lack of ability.

She didn't reply.

"This afternoon there was warm water for you to wash, because I heated it earlier and left the coals banked. I don't do that every morning. I'll have to show you how."

His words registered. "You've been living here—in the house?"

"I've been staying here since Sam died. Someone had to look over the house and the barns," he replied. "I have my own place—my own land to the east."

"Of course."

"I'll be staying here, though."

She met his dark, unreadable eyes.

"You can't stay here alone."

But with him? She couldn't stay in the house alone with him! The thought was scandalous.

"I'm sending a young woman to keep you company so you won't be alone with me. Her name is Pelipa. She'll be here before dark and she'll stay upstairs with you."

"A chaperone?"

"A paid helper."

"Oh."

He ate his meal without further conversation.

Isabelle dug in and found the stew surprisingly tasty and filling.

"You going to eat those?" He gestured to the two remaining biscuits on the edge of her plate.

"No."

He reached across the table and helped himself.

She watched him dunk them in the gravy on his plate and eat them. She'd never eaten a biscuit without preserves or jam, but her father's hired man seemed to think they were a delicacy.

Glancing at the napkin beside his plate, he picked it up and wiped his fingers and mouth and stood. "I'll show you where the wood is. After we make coffee, we have business to discuss."

He handed her a canvas sling, led her out the back door and across the yard where he pointed to a pile of split wood. She loaded the manageable-sized chunks into the sling and carried the heavy bundle. He followed with a few bigger logs.

He opened the door on the cast-iron stove. "Now you build the fire."

Awkwardly, she poked a few logs inside the charred belly of the stove, discovered matches in a tin on the wall and tried ineffectually to light one of the pieces of wood. Frustrated, she avoided looking at him, not wanting to see his criticism.

"Like this." She moved aside, and he showed her how to prop the wood with dry kindling beneath and light the sticks. His movements were sure and methodical, his hands graceful.

Isabelle caught herself glancing from his long-fingered hands to the sleek ebony hair that fell to his broad shoulders. Beneath the fabric of his well-worn flannel shirt, his muscles corded and bunched with each movement.

He glanced up and caught her staring.

Her cheeks warmed, and she dropped her gaze.

"The water," he said, standing. He moved to open the door and showed her the wooden barrel outside. "Fill buckets from here, but keep this barrel filled from the well."

In the past, there'd been a tub carried in for her, but she wouldn't ask him to do that for her. She'd look for it later. As it was, Isabelle had changed from her grimy traveling suit, but she'd barely had enough water to sponge bathe.

He started the coffee boiling himself, then left her alone.

She found the teapot in a china cupboard,

knocked a dead spider from its depths, rinsed the china pot with boiling water and added tea.

While the tea steeped, she searched until she found a tray for the pot and cups, then poured his coffee and found him in her father's study.

The room still smelled faintly of tobacco, and the scent unleashed a flood of memories that immediately saddened her. A fire burned in the enormous stone fireplace that took up the outside wall.

The man sat in the leather chair, and before him on the desk lay an open ledger. From all appearances, it looked as though he belonged there. "Things are not very good."

Not used to a man remaining seated when she entered the room, Isabelle gathered her wits and sat on an upholstered chair. "What do you mean?"

"Your father had been steadily losing money over the past several years."

She blinked. "That's not possible."

He gave her a disgusted look. "Why not?"

"Because he owned land and horses and this house."

"Your father was a good horseman, but a poor businessman. Three years ago when I brought in new breeding stock and got him a contract with the army, things started to turn around. More than half the horses on the Big Sky are mine."

Fear burst in her chest at his words. He could be lying in order to swindle property that belonged to her. "How can I know that for sure?"

A muscle in his lean jaw jumped. Brusquely, he opened a desk drawer, withdrew an accordion-pleated folder and thumbed through a stack of documents before withdrawing several and shoving them across the desktop.

Isabelle took the legal-looking papers and read them, her heart sinking. Her father's signature was unmistakable.

Kyle Running Horse Brennan owned the horses he'd brought to the ranch, as well as half the offspring bred over the past two and a half years. It seemed he already had more stake in this place than she did—and he knew how to run it. As always, she was the outsider.

Chapter 3

"Sam and I came to an agreement," Kyle continued. "I was going to buy half ownership and have my name added to the land deed."

She stared at him. "Why would Father agree to that?"

"He owed me wages. Still does."

"Well, I'll pay you."

"*He* would have paid me if he'd had the cash. He didn't. And since his death, I've covered the pay for the hands as well as building the barn and buying supplies."

An overwhelming, lost sensation wrapped around Isabelle with frightening intensity. But she wouldn't be pushed away again, not for any reason.

"We lost four mares and their foals in the fire," he added. "That sets us back even more."

"Why, that's awful," she said, thinking of the loss of the beautiful animals.

"I'll buy you out."

She blinked, her mind grasping his words on the top of so much dreadful news. "Pardon me?"

"I've saved enough to pay down. I can send you an agreeable amount each quarter. It would be enough for you to live on until—"

"Wait a moment."

"It's sensible," he insisted.

"I don't intend to—"

"You can go back to the city. You'll be getting enough to live on until you find yourself a husband."

A soft roar built to a crescendo in Isabelle's ears. She leaped to her feet and faced him across the desk. She clenched her fists, knowing she was about to break propriety by raising her voice but unable to stop the rush of emotion. "How dare you tell me what to do! I didn't take a husband when my father wanted me to, and I certainly am not going to marry someone just so I'll be out of *your* way!"

"I didn't mean—"

"Oh, I know what you meant. You laid out all the bleak details so I'd see I had no choice but to hand over my house and my land to you and get back on a train. Just who do you think you are, Mr. Brennan, to sit in my house at my father's desk and think you can plan my life so it suits your tidy little scheme?''

He pushed back his chair and moved to stand. ''I know this is upsetting.''

''Upsetting? I haven't even seen my father's grave yet and you have taken over here. Besides which, I've resigned my position at the academy and moved all my possessions across the country with the idea that I would stay. Now I learn that my father's ranch has met reverses and you are trying to undermine my interests.''

He came to his full height and glared at her. It took all her courage not to show that his height and fierce expression intimidated her. ''There's nothing wrong with my suggestion.'' He bit the words out. ''It's best for both of us.''

Anger started her heart thumping, and his proposed exile brought a sting of tears she refused to allow. ''You don't know what suits me. You don't know anything about me.''

She hated the quiver in her voice and clamped her lips closed determinedly.

''I know enough.''

Insult added to injury. Just like her father thought he'd known what was best for her all those years. And just like her father, this man couldn't wait to be shut of her. Well, he didn't have the power to send her away. She was not under his authority.

At the moment she sensed another presence in the room, he glanced over her shoulder. Isabelle spun to see a young Indian girl in a doeskin dress and moccasins.

"This is Pelipa," Kyle said by way of introduction.

"Didn't she knock?" Isabelle whispered, embarrassed at having her unseemly outburst overheard.

"A white custom," he replied so she alone could hear. He spoke to the girl in their language, and Isabelle understood only her name.

The situation and her life seemed to be spinning out of her control, and Isabelle hated the helpless feeling. She hated not knowing what was being said right in front of her. She faced Kyle again. "I'd like you to leave the house, please."

"What?" He scowled.

"I am going to locate a tub and bathe before I retire for the night." She raised her chin a notch. "We will speak again tomorrow, and another solution will have to be found. I am not leaving the Big Sky no matter how many cruel things you say and no matter how bleak the situation appears."

He looked as though he wanted to oppose her statement, but he held his tongue.

"This is going to be my home whether you like it or not. Whether *you* stay or not."

Nothing showed in his expression. He held her gaze unwaveringly.

She turned to leave, and he stopped her. "One more thing."

She turned hesitantly.

He opened a desk drawer and withdrew a deadly looking revolver.

Isabelle's heart leaped. Unconsciously, she raised a hand to her breast.

He turned the weapon abruptly so that the handle faced her and extended it. "Keep this with you at night."

Isabelle's hand remained where she'd flattened it on her chest. Beneath her fingers, her heart raced. "I—I don't know the first thing about guns."

"You're going to have to learn if you're going to stay, aren't you? All you do is aim it and pull the trigger."

She wouldn't be able to shoot at anyone. "I won't need to use it, will I?"

"I hope not."

The weapon he held toward her was a direct challenge. The concept of keeping a gun by her side went against everything she'd ever learned or experienced, and contradicted all that her shielded education had prepared her for. But if she didn't accept it, he wouldn't take her seriously.

Isabelle took a calming breath and reached for the revolver. He released it, and the weight immediately pulled her arm down. She stared at the deadly weapon, shuddered with the anxious sensation that she held a lit stick of dynamite.

"Tomorrow I'll show you how to use it," he said, his voice a shade kinder but no less firm. Then he spoke to Pelipa in Cheyenne.

Their exchange irritated Isabelle, and she hurried from the room.

After locating the copper tub holding potatoes and onions in the pantry, Isabelle transferred the vegetables to burlap bags. Pelipa watched her haul the basin outdoors to scrub it, then drag it to the semi-private pantry.

"Would you mind giving me a hand with this?" Isabelle asked, huffing. The girl merely blinked.

Isabelle pointed to the other end of the tub and then at Pelipa. "You? Lift that end?"

"Pelipa not help," she said, shaking her head. "Pelipa stay with you only."

Isabelle scowled. "Is that what he told you? He told you not to help me? You are being paid to help me, so please lift that end of the tub."

"Pelipa not help."

Isabelle gave her a scathing look and carried buckets of hot water until her arms ached. The girl watched the procedure with mild interest, then wandered away.

Finally climbing into the steaming water and allowing it to soothe her limbs, Isabelle decided the relaxing bath had been worth the work. Behind her in the kitchen, apparently not doing anything useful, Pelipa hummed, and Isabelle's trembling hurt and anger mellowed into a leaden ball of determination in her belly.

Kyle Brennan had done nothing but add misery

to her already heavyhearted homecoming. The ranch's situation was not his fault, she conceded, but his chafing superiority and this…this *rudeness* were inexcusable.

Isabelle had been only six when her mother had fallen from a horse and died and her father had sent her off to boarding school. Sam had insisted through the years that it was for her own good she live in the East and attend school and travel with her mother's despotic aunt.

She had convinced herself that he was right, that she preferred growing up away from this uncivilized country and the dangers it presented. She'd hoped after she graduated from finishing school that Sam would allow her to come back, but he'd insisted she seek a suitable husband.

She'd taken a position at the academy where she'd grown up and had been writing to her father for months, begging his permission for an extended visit. His replies were terse. Her prospects for an appropriate husband were nonexistent in Montana; she was unsuited for the rugged life and treacherous hazards of the untamed land.

Well, that was his fault, she reasoned. She'd become exactly what he'd insisted she be—a well-bred, well-mannered lady. She could play the pianoforte and embroider and set a table. She knew how to behave in polite company and how to dress for a ball, understood the correct manner in which to call on a friend and the proprieties of walking with a gentleman caller.

And even the things she'd learned to do well she'd never been able to show Sam Cooper.

Tears mingled with the drops of water on her cheeks, and she buried her face in a soft cloth. She'd never been wanted or welcomed here when her father was alive, but this was her land and her house now, and no one was going to send her packing.

Kyle helped Sidestep fork down fresh bedding for the yearlings in the barn and changed a herb poultice on the foreleg of a chestnut mare who'd been snake-bitten. Kyle ran his hands soothingly over the horse's neck and flank and spoke softly. Her ears pricked, and she bobbed her regal head in reply.

He brushed her coat, as much for his own peace and harmony as for the mare's. In his mind he saw Isabelle Cooper, her lustrous auburn mane, skin as pure and soft-looking as a rose petal, eyes like a summer storm. Her delicate features and feminine form hid a steely determination and a stubbornness he couldn't help but admire.

He didn't want her here—but he was wise enough to know that nothing he said was going to change her mind. She was right—he had no authority over her. She was the legitimate owner of the ranch. But if Sam Cooper hadn't been able to keep the Big Sky afloat on his own, there was no way this silly girl was going to.

Should he sit back and watch her lose it all? What would that gain him? What would happen to the ranch? He wasn't about to move one foot from the land he believed was rightfully his. Hank Brennan's foolishness had cost Kyle his legacy. Kyle had been seven when his father had run out, and Sam Cooper had acquired the land. Kyle's mother had worked for Sam until her death, and then Kyle had set out on his own.

He'd lived with the Cheyenne for a time, but he didn't fit in among them any more than he did the whites. He learned he had a way with horses and that catching and breeding and breaking them could earn him enough money to buy back the land he wanted.

Kyle had never resented Sam. The man had come by the land fairly enough. He'd earned it and had worked hard, even if he hadn't been good at handling money.

But he did resent Sam's daughter. The girl had done nothing to earn the Big Sky. She was spoiled and unsuited for this life and had a romantic notion of being able to take her father's place.

He patted the mare's rump and hung the curry brush before exiting the stall and blowing out the lanterns.

The moon illuminated the roof of the house; the twinkling stars stretched forever. He studied the other buildings, the corrals and the two-story bunkhouse, where a curl of smoke drifted from the chimney.

A soft light in an upstairs window drew his attention. She meant to stay.

He didn't have to make it easy for her. Nobody got a free ride. Life was hard. Nature could be brutal. A creature was either quick and strong or it was prey for something that was. Same with people. He didn't like what he was doing, but she had to understand the order of things out here. Isabelle would have to learn the hard way.

Chapter 4

Pelipa had taken the room beside hers, but the next morning Isabelle found the tidy space empty when she made her way along the hall toward the stairs.

The icy water in the barrel numbed her hands as she baled a bucketful. The stove wasn't lit, and she fumbled with kindling and a few logs until she had a feeble fire going. It took forever for a pot of water to heat. Her shoulders ached from the buckets she had carried the night before. But, determinedly, she carried water to her room and washed and dressed for breakfast in a traditional flowing morning dress in pale green, a minimum of jewelry, her hair wound in a simple braid.

Isabelle discovered an unappealing plate of cold

biscuits on the table in the kitchen. After peering under the cloth and glancing around the deserted house, she decided to forgo breakfast for the moment. Instead, she exited the back door and made her way across the dooryard and up a rise to the east of the house and the buildings toward an ancient pine that marked the place where her mother and father were buried. Once beneath the shade of the tree, she remembered how her father had sat in this place looking out over the ranch for hours at a time. A neat pile of stones had replaced the wooden cross that had marked her mother's grave. Beside it was another stack, this one with less grass growing at the edges and a slight indentation in the ground where the earth had settled, so she knew the grave to be the newer of the two.

There should be flowers, she thought through the fog of isolation that gripped her. Her mother had loved flowers. But as she knelt, she realized the ground had been well kept and the weeds pulled, so someone had respectfully cared for the graves. Kyle?

Isabelle surveyed the layout of the buildings, the stately house in need of a coat of paint, the tangle of dried vines that used to be roses growing up the corner posts. There was much to be done, inside and out, to restore the place to its former elegance, but she was up to the task.

This was her home, the only home she'd ever wanted, and nothing would discourage her. She knelt in the shade and reflected on the brief times she remembered spending with her mother, as well as her many attempts to develop a relationship with her father. She shook away those thoughts. The disappointment was behind her. She was here to move forward.

Hungry, Isabelle trekked to the kitchen and located a dusty jar of boysenberry preserves in the pantry. She made herself tea, then looked about the empty room, at a loss. Carrying a tray holding her meal onto the porch, she wished she'd brought a shawl down with her. The morning air was chilly in the shade.

She tugged her chair and the table with the tray into the sun along the railing. At school, breakfast had always been a companionably chatty affair, the girls fresh and ready for a new day. As she ate, she thought about all the girls who'd gone back to their families while she'd remained a permanent fixture at the academy, like the bust of Chopin in the upstairs music hall.

She never wanted to feel that way again, heavy with the lonely, unwanted heartache she'd borne since childhood, but it seemed she was destined to live the experience over and over. What was there about her that didn't deserve love and acceptance?

Kyle's tall, dark figure approached from the barn, and Isabelle's heart fluttered nervously. She hated the way she let him fluster her. *It wouldn't happen again today.* The sun glinted from raven black hair caught by the breeze. He climbed the stairs near the back door and approached her. "Ready for your lesson?"

His lack of convention always caught her by surprise. No polite salutation. No small talk. "The gun?" she asked.

He nodded.

She stood and gathered her tray. "I'll take these in and get it."

She returned a few minutes later, wearing her shawl and a straw hat, carrying the gun with her thumb and forefinger, arm extended before her. "Here."

He took the revolver and led the way across the yard. "You can ride?"

"I can ride." She had learned during summer outings with her aunt. Her father had never allowed her to ride here.

"We don't have any fancy saddles."

"Whatever there is will do."

They approached two saddled horses tethered near the equipment stable.

"This bay is gentle," he said, indicating the smaller of the two, a red-brown color with black mane, tail and legs.

"She's pretty." Noting the considerable height of the stirrups, she glanced around.

He pointed to a half barrel placed upside down at the corner of the stable. "Step up from there."

She did so, finding her seat, taking the reins and

adjusting her skirts to cover her legs. His mount was a beautiful combination of leopard pattern—black on white across the middle and hips, the spots larger on the rump—and dark marbled coloring, like frost on red, over the front legs.

"What kind of horse is that?" she asked, once he was in his saddle.

"Appaloosa."

"He's beautiful."

"*She's* beautiful. She's given me three colts, two of them patterned just like her." He turned the animal's head, and the bay followed.

"Where are we going?"

"Out so the shots don't scare the new horses."

Kyle rode as though he were one with the animal, while she tried to keep her teeth from jarring and her hat from flying off. Even so, she loved the clean air and bright sky, and she drank in the rich green vegetation and the abundance of birds and small animals. She'd always dreamed of days like this with her father, the two of them together, riding, sharing, building a life together.

It would never be the way she'd dreamed. She would have to settle for a life here without him.

Reaching a clearing in the midst of a stand of fragrant pines, Kyle jumped to the ground and watched her dismount less gracefully.

She tugged her skirts down in embarrassment.

He drew a rifle from a sheath on his rough-hewn

saddle, grabbed a small box from his saddlebag and gestured for her to follow.

Isabelle was used to a gentleman offering his arm, not beckoning her as though she were a dog. Swallowing her irritation, she followed.

He walked away and lined a series of rocks along a fallen log, returned and handed her the rifle. "These will be in the way." He tugged on her hat until she untied the ribbons at her throat and allowed him to remove it. He pulled her shawl from her shoulders and laid them both on the ground.

"Raise the butt to your right shoulder," he said, turning. "Squint with one eye and get the rock in line with the sight on the end of the barrel. Hold steady and squeeze the trigger."

The rifle was incredibly heavy. Isabelle brought it to her shoulder and worked to hold the barrel parallel to the ground while she peered along its length.

He stepped behind her. "Put this hand here to steady it."

He moved her hand and showed her where to place it; his body enveloped hers, his solid chest and arms circling her shoulders. Silky hair brushed her cheek, and a shiver of alarm passed along her spine. The impropriety of the intimate contact took her breath away.

"Mr. Brennan!" she said when she found air.

"What?"

"It is highly inappropriate for you to stand so close."

"No one's looking."

"Just because something is rendered in private doesn't make it any less shameful."

"You know what would be shameful?" he said near her ear.

"What?"

"For a coyote to attack you or your horse—or a renegade to take a shine to you—and for you to not know how to shoot this Winchester to protect yourself. *That* would be a shame."

A shiver ran across her shoulders—whether at his admonishing words or at his disturbing nearness and his warm breath against her neck, she didn't know.

He cupped her left hand beneath the barrel with his rough fingers. "*Otahe*—pay attention. Line the rock up with the sight. Got it?"

"I think so."

"Squeeze the trigger."

She pulled; it was harder than she'd expected, making her lose her focus on the rock. The rifle fired so loudly and with such a blow to her shoulder that she yelped and stumbled against him. A squawking red-tailed hawk burst from the grass, and tiny kinglets chirped and fluttered in the branches of the nearby trees.

He steadied her.

"Did I hit it?"

"Not quite."

Her ears rang. Her shoulder throbbed.

"Here's how to load a shell," he said, without giving her time to recover.

Isabelle listened to his softly spoken instructions, watched his graceful hands, and each time he stepped behind her, the heat from his body and the brush of his hair distracted her. After three-quarters of an hour, with her shoulder throbbing and her arms trembling, she finally hit a rock.

He proceeded to show her how to load the revolver and went through the same motions of guiding her in each step of the lesson. The revolver was more difficult to aim, but he assured her she wouldn't miss at close range.

He seemed satisfied with her progress by the time her stomach growled. Her face flushed with embarrassment, she realized as she clamped her hand over her stomach that she couldn't possibly lift her arms again.

"That's enough for today. I have to stop by Mother's sister Ma'heona'e's. She'll have something to feed us."

"I—I'm not dressed for calling."

"You're not dressed for riding or working, either."

She ignored his pointed criticism. "How do you say her name?"

"The whites call her Mae."

She tied the ribbons of her hat beneath her chin with as much dignity as she could muster and pulled on her white gloves. "Extend the courtesy of assisting me, please?"

He made a step of his laced fingers for her to reach her saddle, then mounted and led the way. How did he know which direction to turn out here? It all looked the same, sky and trees and waving grass.

Before long, a small, sturdy cabin came into view, smoke curling from the chimney. Kyle called to a woman bending over in a newly planted garden. *"Peveeseeva!"*

Smiling, she turned and raised a hand.

Kyle dismounted and stood beside the bay. "Need help?"

"I can manage." Trying not to tangle her skirts or expose her limbs, she did both and awkwardly slid to her feet without falling in a heap in the dirt. Barely.

She followed him to where the woman stood in the sun, her bare feet planted in the newly turned earth.

Kyle wore a smile when he greeted his aunt. They spoke briefly in their unfamiliar language with the quick stopping sounds between the syllables. Isabelle watched and listened in fascination. "This is Mae," he said, then, "Isabelle Cooper."

"Pleased to meet you," Isabelle said politely.

"Isabelle beautiful *he'e-ka'eskone,*" the tall, dark-haired woman said, coming forward with a

warm smile and touching Isabelle's arm. "Now
beautiful *kasa'eehe.*"

Isabelle glanced at Kyle.

"You were a beautiful child, she says. Now
you're a beautiful young woman. She speaks English, don't let her fool you."

Isabelle flushed at Mae's compliment.

"I got up with the morning star to make your
kasa'eehe a meal," Mae said. "You will eat fried
bread and turnips."

"She's not my *kasa'eehe.*"

"Mr. Brennan told you we were coming?" Isabelle asked.

"Morning star tell me."

"She knows a lot of things without being told,"
Kyle said wryly, and followed his aunt into the
cabin.

Isabelle removed her hat and shawl, tucked her
gloves into her hat and hung them on a set of antlers
near the door.

Mae bustled about the austere one-room structure,
preparing something delicious-smelling. She tore
dough from an enormous chunk, flattened it between
her palms and laid it in a skillet over the flames in
the fireplace.

She served the bread and vegetables on smooth
wooden platters. Isabelle accepted hers and waited
for a utensil.

Finally, she glanced at Kyle.

He said something to his aunt, and she produced a crude three-tonged fork.

"Thank you." Isabelle used the fork to taste her food. "This is delicious."

Mae beamed. She and Kyle ate their food with their fingers, and it took discipline not to stare. "What is this made from?" she asked, nearly finished and studying the fork.

"Bone," Kyle replied. "Antelope or deer, probably."

Isabelle finished the last mouthful with difficulty and set the fork down quickly.

"Miss Cooper likes tea," Kyle informed his aunt, a grin tugging at the corner of his lips.

"Don't go to any trouble," Isabelle insisted.

"Not trouble. Enjoy to serve tea."

"You're very kind."

A few minutes later, Mae placed three tin cups on the small table. Kyle reached for one, but she held his wrist. "That one go for Isabelle. This go for you."

One of his ebony eyebrows shot up, but he took the cup and sipped.

Warily, Isabelle accepted hers and inhaled the peculiar scent of the brew. "What is it?"

"Herbs from my garden."

The tea tasted like none she'd ever drank, but it was hot and quite good, and she finished it.

"I have to get back to work," Kyle said finally.

"You must come visit me next time," Isabelle

said to their hostess. "I will prepare lunch and tea for you."

"I will come." Mae handed Isabelle a tightly rolled packet of cloth. "Tea for you. Make muscles feel better."

Isabelle blinked in surprise. "Thank you."

She accepted Kyle's grudging assistance in climbing on the horse's back, and Mae waved them off.

"Your aunt is lovely."

"Most whites are afraid of her."

"Why?"

"Because she's a medicine woman."

"She knows how to heal people?"

"And other things."

The sun was hot, and Isabelle folded her shawl over the pommel. It had been peculiar how Mae had given Isabelle tea for aching muscles, but the woman's perception didn't frighten her.

When they arrived at the ranch, she slid from the horse gingerly, and Kyle took the bay's reins. "Tonight we talk business."

Isabelle glanced over to see Pelipa waiting for them on the side porch. "Did you tell Pelipa not to help me?"

He turned his hard gaze on her. "Do you need help?"

A confused whirl of humiliation, pride and anger kept her from replying honestly—or at all. She wasn't admitting anything he wanted her to admit.

"We are going to come to an understanding tonight." His steely black eyes held no compromise. The brief pleasantness of their morning ride vanished.

"Perhaps," she replied noncommittally.

"You don't have many choices if you want to stay."

"Oh, I'm staying."

His gaze moved across her face to her mouth and back to her eyes. "Then we're definitely coming to an understanding—tonight."

Chapter 5

If she were going to hold her own against this un-
yielding man, she needed to look her best and feel
confident. Isabelle dressed, then frowned at the darkened burn spot on the puff sleeve of her pale rose
crepe gown. She'd overheated the iron and had forgotten to place a cloth between the fabric and metal.

Once again, Pelipa had been no help, silently
watching as Isabelle built the fire and singed her
dress.

Belatedly, Isabelle wondered if there was going
to be a meal. Kyle hadn't mentioned bringing food.
He may have left her on her own. She would have
to find something in the pantry.

He was standing in the dining room observing the

canary when she and Pelipa arrived. Isabelle breathed a sigh of relief at the sight of three plates on the table.

He took in her attire without expression and remained standing until she and the girl had seated themselves.

He and Pelipa picked up their forks and dug into the plate of—stew.

Isabelle stared at the beef and gravy mixture. "This is the same menu as last night."

"Harlan doesn't have much of an imagination," he replied.

She glanced up to see if he was toying with her, but his expression was unreadable, as always.

"Why do you use your fork when you eat with me and your fingers when you eat with your aunt?"

He looked up. "I honor the customs of both people when I'm in their homes."

"You see eating utensils as a custom?"

"Yes, I do. How do you see them?"

"Well, as—manners. Etiquette."

"And one person's manners are better than another's because—why? Because the person thinks their way is the only way?"

"No, because it's..." Her voice trailed off.

"Civilized?" he asked, his tone underlined with something she sensed was a bone-deep irritation.

Had she been thinking that? Did she see cultural differences in a judgmental light? She'd never had to think about it before. All the people she'd known were from similar backgrounds and held the same beliefs about manners and religion and customs.

This man challenged every axiom she'd believed in until now.

Kyle stared at the lovely white woman, secretly hoping she wasn't as high-minded and prejudiced as he feared, as the rest of her kind had proven themselves to be where the Cheyenne were concerned, and not knowing why he cared. All he cared about was that she come to her senses and sell him the ranch.

He ate the meal, speaking occasionally to Pelipa when she asked him a question. When he'd finished, he made himself a pot of coffee and retreated to the study.

Isabelle didn't show for another hour, and when she did, her fine dress was water-spotted and she carried a tray with the china pot and two cups. She set the tray on the corner of the desk. "Would you care for a cup of tea?"

"No, thanks."

She poured one full, her hand trembling, then lowered herself onto one of the overstuffed chairs, wincing as she sat but quickly masking her pained expression.

She was no doubt sore from the ride and the shooting lesson. He couldn't worry that he was being too hard on her. Rather, he needed to consider if he was being hard enough. Getting her to change her mind was tougher than he'd imagined.

"I don't think you understand the money problem," he said.

"I've considered everything you've told me," she replied. "The most outstanding debts are your wages and the cost of rebuilding the barn. We still need to replace the mares."

"And there is no way you can pay those debts. Have you looked over the books?"

"I have."

That surprised him.

"Can we let any of the men go?" she asked.

"Some good men quit a while back because they weren't getting paid. We're working with as few hands as possible now. Your father handled a big share of the work, but he's gone."

"You don't have to keep reminding me. I'm well aware that he's gone." Her brow furrowed in confusion. "I don't understand something. How could the hands not have been paid? I never saw any change in circumstances."

"Of course you didn't. Sam sent you money he couldn't spare." He eyed the pale pink gown and her jewelry. "Your feminine finery and fancy schools and trips cost the men wages and the ranch repairs. Sam was a fool."

She bristled visibly at the blunt way he'd criticized her father, but she'd needed to know the truth. Recognition and shock slowly replaced the offended expression. She blinked a few times, looked away and swallowed, as though absorbing the distressing information.

"If you take my offer, you can make a nice life for yourself in the city."

Her steady gaze lifted and met his; color rose high in her ivory cheeks. With two deft movements she lifted a hand to each ear, plucked the pearls from her lobes and dropped them on the desk. The brooch from her collar followed. "How many mares can you buy with those?" she asked.

Taken aback, he glanced from the jewelry to her determined expression. "Depends how much they're worth."

"I have more. A whole box full. We can sell them in Whitehorn. Pay the hands."

"That would take care of one problem. And perhaps even part or all of the money due me. But it won't solve getting through the next couple of seasons." And selling her jewelry certainly wasn't the answer he wanted. He looked aside and absently watched flames lick up the side of a log.

He'd been prepared to fall back on an alternate plan, a plan that would assure his name on the land deed, but he'd hoped it wouldn't be necessary. Now it looked like he had no other choice. And this just might be the thing to scare her off. She would either take off running or he would have what he wanted. "If you're determined to stay—"

"I am."

"Then there's one thing that would meet both our needs."

"What's that?"

"If we marry, I can run the ranch on a shoestring. Half the horses are mine, anyway. We would be putting together your land and my horses and know-how. The Big Sky would be ours—together."

She stared at him. "Marry?"

He turned to gauge her expression and nodded.

A thunderstorm swelled in the depths of her eyes. "You'll do anything to get this land, won't you?" she asked.

"Not quite anything."

She raised her chin a notch. "So, I can sleep knowing you wouldn't cut my throat during the night?"

She was goading him, and he rose to her bait. "I don't slit throats. I take scalps."

Those turbulent eyes widened, then she fixed him with a perusing but half-amused stare, the corner of her mouth threatening to tilt.

She got up and walked to the fireplace, where she gazed into the crackling fire. The flames cast a golden glow across her perfect profile.

"Is it just me you hate or all people with white skin?"

The question caught him off guard. Grateful that she wasn't looking at him, he mulled it over. "Not trusting you is more like it."

"What is it I've done to earn this mistrust?"

"How about broken treaties and broken promises?" *How about herding the Cheyenne to a desert in Oklahoma where most starved or died of disease and the rest escaped only to be shot or recaptured?* Even as he thought it, he knew in some corner of his mind that he shouldn't, but long-ingrained beliefs were difficult to mask. *How about destroying a proud, beautiful people?*

Her shoulders straightened slightly and then relaxed. "I read about Dull Knife and Fort Robinson and those horrible times in the papers," she said sadly. "You hold me personally responsible for the mistreatment of the Cheyenne?"

Of course he didn't blame her in particular. He wasn't that ignorant. But he did, in some manner he couldn't help, think she was a product of a society that believed itself above the Plains tribes. He shook his head, even though she wasn't looking.

"What about you?" she asked, as though only now wondering. "Were you among those people sent to Oklahoma?"

"My white name and the deed to my land spared me," he said. "I kept Ma'heona'e and a handful of children with me, too. I lied and told the bureau they were my mother and my children. Pelipa was one of them. Her mother and father were killed trying to return home after the army starved them at Fort Robinson."

"I'm sorry," she said, and he recognized the sincerity.

"I don't hold you responsible," he admitted. "But I can't trust you."

Finally, she turned. "All right. Let's get married."

Her swift acquiescence and the abrupt return to the original subject astounded him. He'd expected her to take offense. He'd expected her to sell and run. She never did as expected. He realigned his thinking. This direction would aid his plan just as well. Once again, she'd accepted his challenge with bravado.

A sense of relief settled over him. The Big Sky would be his at last. "All right," he said. "I wouldn't set my hopes on a church wedding, if I were you."

"Why not?"

"The people in Whitehorn don't think much of the Cheyenne."

She studied his expression. "My father was respected in these parts. We'll go into town and make arrangements."

"Take heed and don't count on the church."

She ignored him. "How soon shall we set the date?"

"As soon as possible."

"Six months?"

"Tomorrow."

She stared in disbelief. "I can't plan a wedding overnight! There are things to do. I'll need a dress. I'll need at least—at least a month."

Hand on hip, she watched him stand and move to the coffeepot hung on a wire beside the fire.

"We don't have a month," he replied. "The sooner the better." He wasn't going to give her a chance to change her mind. His name was going on the land deed without delay.

"At least a week, then. I can't be ready by tomorrow."

"A week, then. No longer."

Her gray eyes looked a little wild, perhaps at the shocking reality of what she'd hastily committed herself to. "Excuse me, please. Good night."

She gave him a preoccupied nod and hurried away.

Escaping to her room, Isabelle tamped down the barrage of chaotic thoughts that questioned her decision. As soon as he'd spoken the words, she'd known marriage was the perfect solution. Combining their interests allowed her to make her home on the Big Sky. End of deliberation. It was all she'd ever wanted, and even though the price was high, her dream was becoming a reality.

But concern took over her confidence and nagged at her sanity until she stopped ignoring it and examined the issue.

Marriage meant more than saying vows and joint ownership in property. Marriage meant intimacy, shared lives and shared beds. A flutter started in her stomach and worked its way to her limbs and her chest. Would Kyle expect them to sleep together? Would he want to consummate this union?

She had vowed to do whatever it took. There was no looking back now. She would deal with the physical aspect when the time came. But wondering certainly cost her sleep.

The following day, their trip to town was as Kyle had predicted. The local minister, though claiming to be sympathetic to their plight, refused to perform the marriage ceremony because of the anticipated reaction of his congregation. He needed his job.

Pausing only briefly outside the church, Isabelle motioned to Kyle. "Take me to the telegraph office. I'll wire my father's friend, Judge Murphy."

She did so, and they waited on separate benches outside the telegraph office for forty-five minutes until the reply came. Judge Murphy would arrive the following Saturday to perform the marriage at the ranch.

That evening, she wrote invitations, and the following day Kyle sent Tott with her to post them.

Apparently now that she was going to be staying, Kyle lifted his order that Pelipa not assist her, because the girl suddenly became helpful, showing Isabelle how to prepare a chicken as well as beef and vegetables from the root cellar. Kyle didn't join them for meals the next few evenings, and Isabelle assumed he was busy.

One morning, she opened her armoire and trunks

and grew concerned over what she would wear for her hasty wedding. Time and again she came back to an elegant white dress she'd purchased in New York, and aside from wondering if one of the hands had been denied wages so that she could purchase it, she considered the possibility of making it presentable as a wedding dress.

Remembering trunks she'd discovered in the attic years ago, she climbed the stairs with Pelipa on her heels.

Isabelle removed protective sheets and opened three trunks that had been buried in the dusty storage space. A forgotten childhood memory sprang to life as she gazed upon the contents. Her father had once discovered her wearing a feathered hat she'd taken from the items and had forbidden her to open them again.

"These were my mother's things," she said to Pelipa. "Aren't they lovely?" She held a gown against her and looked down. "She wasn't as tall as I am. I'd never get into one of them now."

"We use Mother's dress and Isabelle's dress," Pelipa said, holding up one finger on each hand. "Make one dress." She brought the two fingers together.

"That's brilliant!" Isabelle gave her a quick hug. Pelipa had, amazingly, spoken better English since Kyle had given her permission to help. "Which one?"

They sorted through the gowns and shoes and

gloves and finally Isabelle drew out an exquisite lace-trimmed creation with pearl buttons. "If I was a good enough seamstress, I could even use this silk lining," she said wistfully.

Pelipa frowned.

"If I could sew better." She mimed using a needle and thread.

Pelipa held up a hand. "Isabelle walk dress down. Pelipa bring sew better."

Wearing a wide smile, the girl tore down the attic stairs.

Puzzled, Isabelle shrugged and gathered the gown and a few other items and carried them to her room.

Not quite an hour later, Pelipa returned with an older woman in tow. "Pelipa's mother," she said by way of introduction.

The woman knew how to undo the seams of the old garment and carefully press and reuse the material, taking Isabelle's dress apart and lining it, adding the lace trim and buttons and making the gown look as though a French designer had created it.

Isabelle laughed with delight the following day when the project was finished and pressed. She gave Pelipa and her mother each a gold locket for their generous help and time. The old woman proudly wore hers home.

The day of the wedding arrived and brought sunshine. Kyle performed all his normal chores that morning, thinking of the significance of what he was about to do. He didn't take this union lightly. When he pledged to wed himself to Isabelle, he would make the vow with respect and sincerity.

But he was honest with himself. She would never have considered him as a mate if she'd had a better choice in her financial situation. There was no denying his fiery attraction. But she was white and cultured and as citified as they came. He'd be a fool to allow himself any feelings for her or any hollow hopes for a grand love to develop.

Family alliances were common among the Cheyenne, so a marriage like this wasn't unthinkable in either culture. He would take his vows seriously, but he would not kid himself. She would eventually grow bored with the hard life and head out.

As the hour neared, he rode to his cabin, bathed in the creek and dressed in the finest clothing he owned, black trousers and a soft blue doeskin shirt his aunt had made him.

On his way to the ranch, he met Judge Murphy and rode beside the man's carriage until they reached the house.

"I still can't believe Sam's gone," the man said as he stepped to the ground. He had a mane of thick silver hair that hung to his shoulders and a pointed, close-cropped white beard. "Thank you for sending me the wire."

Kyle dismounted. "I tried to let his friends know soon as I could."

"And you're marryin' little Isabelle, eh? I wonder what Sam would have thought of that."

Kyle recognized the friendly grin. "I don't think even bringing him a traditional gift of horses would have won my favor where she was concerned."

"He sure kept her away from here, didn't he?"

Kyle agreed, released his horse into a corral and instructed Tott to see to the judge's horse and those of any other guests who arrived.

Ma'heona'e sat in the shade on the porch, dressed in traditional clothing for the celebration. From her position, she was directing the layout of tables being set up in the yard. His cousins carried out her bidding, and Kyle greeted them, accepting their good-natured ribbing and good wishes.

A handful of guests arrived from Whitehorn, a fraction of the number Isabelle had invited, and soon Pelipa came and gestured for him to enter the house.

The doors to the drawing room had been opened and the furniture moved against the walls, making space for guests to stand.

A fragrant pine-bough wreath adorned the fireplace mantel, a row of lit candles on either side. Judge Murphy stood, Bible in hand, awaiting the prospective couple. He gestured for Kyle to join him.

Kyle took his place.

The resonate notes of a flute floated from the back of the room—one of his aunt's enchanted flutes, he had no doubt. The plaintive notes wafted on the warm afternoon air, a distinctive touch to an already uncommon ceremony. He glanced to see which of his cousins played and caught sight of Isabelle.

She drifted toward him like an ethereal being in a cloud of white lace. Her long-sleeved, scoop-necked dress skimmed the carpeted floor, and her white satin slippers made no sound.

She had prepared her lustrous hair in soft curls and wore a wreath of delicate baby's breath like a crown. As she drew closer, he saw the flush of color on her cheeks and the shine in her lovely storm-cloud eyes. All his thoughts of practicality fled at the sight of his exquisite bride.

Chapter 6

The vows and the legal part of the wedding took only a matter of minutes—minutes Isabelle was later hard-pressed to recall. She didn't think she had drawn a breath the entire time.

She stood on the porch among an unusual assortment of guests and sipped lemonade. It astounded Isabelle that so many of Kyle's family had come, especially after he'd shared his resentment of whites. The Cheyenne women had prepared and arranged an enormous amount of food in wooden bowls and platters on makeshift tables in the yard, and Isabelle marveled over their thoughtfulness.

She walked among the people of all ages dressed in artistically feathered, quilled and fringed buckskin

tunics, shirts and dresses. Thinking of the hardships
they had endured, their admirable talents and pleasant natures impressed her all the more. Men and
women alike wore their hair long and flowing, with
feathers or beads worked into braids. Now she understood why they were referred to as the Beautiful
People.

Isabelle marveled over the soft-looking shirt Kyle
wore. The leather had been dyed a soft blue. Long
fringe hung from the shoulders. Quill and beadwork,
in a striking geometric pattern across the shoulders,
emphasized his height and breadth.

He introduced her to the members of his family.
She couldn't pronounce their names, so he told her
the English meaning of each to make remembering
easier.

A young woman whose name meant Red Star had
a baby in a decorative cradle board on her back.
Isabelle smiled at the baby and touched his shiny
black hair, hair as silky and dark as Kyle's. Her
heart fluttered.

Would she and Kyle have beautiful children like
this together? As much as she'd tried not to concern
herself over the details they had never discussed,
these were important matters, and ignoring them
wouldn't make the situation better.

Buffalo Rib played the lovely sounding flute, and
Isabelle relaxed and enjoyed the enchanting music.
The newlyweds accepted an assortment of gifts,

from shawls, leggings and moccasins to books and candlesticks.

"It was too short notice," she whispered to Kyle. "The others from town probably had plans already."

"I don't think so," he disagreed. "They didn't come because of me. Most in town won't talk to you now."

"Well, they're narrow-minded."

"Just as some on the reservations are narrow-minded. Most of them wouldn't keep company with whites. Twenty years of killing each other does that."

She didn't know what to say, but Judge Murphy approached, and she didn't have a chance to reply. "Best wishes, my dear," he said. "I wish your father could have seen this day."

Isabelle didn't think her father would have *allowed* this day, but she smiled.

He placed his hat over his silver hair and smoothed his pointy beard, a habit she remembered from his visits to her father. "I'll be heading back to Billings before it gets dark."

"I'll hitch your horse," Kyle said, accompanying the man from the porch. A few of the guests called goodbyes before they climbed into their wagons and headed for home.

Kyle's aunt Mae silently moved beside Isabelle. "The tea made muscles better?"

"Yes, it did. Thank you."

"The magical flute was played with song just for you. Now this." She bent her head next to Isabelle's. "You must wear this."

Isabelle opened her hand and accepted the oval-shaped silver locket that Mae pressed into her palm.

"Leaves from my garden will win your husband's heart."

Isabelle touched the hammered silver, her thumbnail tracing the two running horses etched into the metal. Win her husband's heart? What did that mean?

"Put amulet on now," Mae insisted. "Wear day and night."

Not wanting to offend her, Isabelle slipped the quill chain over her head and the amulet's weight lay against her breast.

"Good." Mae's toothy smile revealed her pleasure.

If this was part of their tradition, Isabelle would go along to please Mae. "Thank you."

Mae patted her arm affectionately.

Pelipa said something in Cheyenne. Mae nodded. "Now come," she said.

Mae led Isabelle to where Kyle stood after seeing the judge off. She gestured to Spotted Feathers, and Kyle's cousin handed him a fur robe.

Gently, Mae urged Isabelle forward.

Kyle met her gaze warily. "It's a custom she feels strongly about."

Isabelle glanced at his grinning family members, her curiosity piqued.

"If we had courted, I would have placed my robe around you and we'd have taken a walk."

Isabelle read the imploring look in Mae's shining dark eyes. "Sounds all right to me."

Kyle drew the fur robe around his shoulders and held one arm out in invitation.

Isabelle took her cue and stepped to his side. He drew her close with a rock-hard arm and closed the robe around her, cocooning them in its thickness and combining the warmth of their bodies.

His family members smiled and nodded. Mae said something that sounded like a direct order.

Isabelle was keenly aware of their touching bodies as Kyle led her toward the stable where his Appaloosa and a dozen unfamiliar mounts stood, tails flicking.

Kyle paused beside his horse.

"More of the custom?" she asked.

He nodded.

She accepted his assistance onto his unsaddled horse and experienced a little jolt of shock when he climbed on behind her and reached around her shoulders for the reins.

He tossed the buffalo robe to Spotted Feathers, who rolled it and mounted his speckled horse. His wife, Red Star, waited astride a horse beside him, the baby on her back, and the others were soon mounted, as well.

Kyle turned the Appaloosa's head and urged her into the throng of fancifully dressed riders.

"Were are we going?" Isabelle asked over her shoulder.

"I guess they'll show us. Today you make your formal departure from your family to mine. A Cheyenne woman moves to her husband's lodge."

"But we won't—"

"This is just part of the ceremony," he explained. "Thank you for going along with it."

"I know it's important to your aunt. Besides, it's rather enjoyable."

Her words pleased him immeasurably. But her nearness unsettled him. Beneath the delicate floral wreath, her hair smelled of spring violets. He allowed his cheek to brush the velvety softness. She had relaxed against his chest, and her feminine scent and warmth tormented him through layers of lace and deerskin.

She hadn't seemed ashamed of the presence of his mother's people at her Christian wedding. She'd eaten the traditional feast they'd supplied and had gone along with the robe without a qualm. Was she hiding her distaste for the sake of her good manners?

So far nothing had diminished her obvious pleasure over staying at the ranch...and she'd acknowledged enjoying the ride. Kyle wouldn't admit, even to himself, how much pleasure he took from this closeness.

Walks Last called to Kyle and pointed to a

wooded area on their left. Kyle moved ahead of the others. A primitive shelter made of pine branches and tanned hides came into view.

He led the Appaloosa close, then dismounted and helped Isabelle to the ground. Her lovely gray eyes were wide with questions, but he read no fear or distaste.

Spotted Feathers handed Kyle the robe. Once again Kyle wrapped it around both of them, then he led her toward the flower-festooned bower hidden among the lodgepole pines. The other riders remained on horseback, silent observers. Needles crushed beneath the horses' hooves sent their pungent fragrance into the early evening air.

He'd seen dozens of these honeymoon shelters. A bridegroom prepared it for his wife, provisioned it for their stay and brought flowers for her pleasure. His family had observed the custom for him—probably at Ma'heona'e's direction.

Pulling aside the flap, he guided Isabelle in. She bent to accommodate her height and entered ahead of him. He turned and gave a farewell gesture to the tribe. Returning the hand sign, they turned their mounts and rode away.

With a deep breath, he entered the shaded depths behind her and laid the robe out along one side. The scent of bitterroot blossoms filled the compact and intimate area. Neither of them could stand to their full height, so he sat cross-legged on the blankets that had been spread, and she followed his example.

His bride observed the pots and bundles lining the hide walls. "What is all this?"

"Food to last several days."

"Several days!" Her eyes widened.

"It's—"

"The custom," she finished for him, with a wry grin.

"We won't stay," he added quickly. "One night should be enough to satisfy Ma'heona'e."

This time her expression did look a little fearful. "Spend the night? But I don't have anything with me."

"I'm sure all you need is here. Pelipa must have been in on this plan."

"But there's no—" Two bright pink spots appeared on her fine, high cheeks. "No facility."

"There's the whole woods," he said with a sweep of his arm.

She refused to meet his eyes.

Mindful of her maidenly blush, Kyle's heart beat too rapidly. *His bride.* The crown of tiny white blooms lent her face a sweet and completely feminine softness. The dress bared her throat and delicate collarbones. The intriguing hollow at the base of her throat pulsed rapidly, and he imagined tasting her skin there, feeling the beat of her heart against his lips.

This was dangerous thinking, and he knew better than to allow it. She might be enjoying the uniqueness of the situation for the moment, but if her upbringing and the color of her skin, as well as the fact that she was a lady, had anything to do with it, she'd soon tire of the primitive life. Her worry over the natural functions of her body proved that.

She moved across the blankets to the stacks of baskets and began a search. Holding up a porcupine's tail sewn to a strong stick with ornamental beadwork over the seams, she asked, ''What's this?''

''A hairbrush.''

She studied it, her expression perplexed, then went back to her exploration. In a leather bag, she found several smooth, brightly colored stones.

''A game,'' he said, enlightening her, before she had a chance to ask.

''Will you show me how to play tonight?''

He nodded. She examined and tasted dried fruits and berries, asking about each one. Her fascination with the cooking equipment had him showing her how the pouches and bowls and bones were used.

''Well,'' she said after her study was complete and everything had been neatly returned to its place. ''I guess it's time I...'' She scooted toward the opening. ''I'll just take a brief walk.'' She stopped. ''You don't think anyone's out there watching us, do you?''

''There's probably a guard, but he wouldn't be near enough to see you...walk.''

She nodded, gathered her lace hem and disappeared.

He would have to find out who to thank for the coffeepot, he thought as he exited the shelter and built a fire from the nearby stack of sticks and logs. He filled the pot with water and added grounds. The tribe hadn't forgotten anything. They believed newlyweds should have nothing to think about but each other.

Right now he'd be grateful for some distractions.

As a guilty afterthought, he placed a pan of water over the fire for Isabelle's tea. He was used to keeping company with cowhands and Ma'heona'e, not helpless city women. Maybe getting fired up over her muleheadedness would get him through the evening.

Twigs snapped and leaves crackled as she returned. "Something is out there!" she said, out of breath. She wore a becoming flush. "An enormous animal!"

He stood. "What kind of animal?"

"I'm not sure. Nearly as big as a horse! His eyes were so pretty and he looked right at me."

"Probably a moose."

"Yes, a moose! I saw a picture of one once. But this one was so big!"

"Might have been a bull. I have some water ready for your tea."

"That's very thoughtful of you. I'll get the tea." She started to turn, but stopped. Her gaze drifted to the fire, to his boots, then over his shoulder. "I'd like to change out of this dress and into something more comfortable. The doeskin dress I saw in one of those bundles looked so soft.''

He settled beside the fire. ''I'll wait right here.''

''Well, I—um—I can't get out of this dress alone.''

''What?''

''The entire back is buttons. I can't reach them.''

''That's foolish. How did you get it on?''

She rolled her eyes. ''With *help*.''

Muttering under his breath about the vain stupidity of white women, he got up and stalked toward her. ''Turn around.''

''Here?'' Her voice came out as a squeak.

''Where would you have me unbutton your dress, my lady?''

''Well, we're standing right out in the open!'' She glanced around wildly, and her hands came up to her midriff defensively.

''Nobody's going to see except me, and I'll see whether we're out here or in there.''

''Yes, but—''

''Get inside.''

She ducked under the flap, and he followed.

The light had waned, and the interior had grown dim. The heavy floral scent and the extreme intimacy closed in around them.

Chapter 7

She presented her back.

Kyle raised his hand to the top of the row of buttons.

Even over the pervading bitterroot, he detected the stimulating scent of her hair, her skin—unfamiliar, exotic, arousing. For a spellbound moment, he imagined that this desirable woman loved him and that he would be making love to her this night. Here in this romantic bower, away from both their worlds, they would come together in a place with no boundaries or restrictions or prejudice.

His body reacted with a bold surge, and he had sudden difficulty breathing. The earthy vision lasted until he noted his dark hand against the snowy white lace and satin that enveloped her. A reminder that he was half Cheyenne and she was one hundred percent white. His clumsy fingers felt like tree stumps on the minute buttons. He had the dress unfastened to the middle of her back, and one side of the fabric slid to reveal her ivory skin and a lacy undergarment.

Kyle swallowed hard and continued his task. "Only a white would fashion a dress so utterly impractical."

"There's nothing practical about those beads across your shoulders, or the fringe. They're an expression of art."

"I can pull the shirt off over my head by myself."

He thought about doing just that. And pressing his heated bare skin against her revealed back, molding himself to her feminine contours, like when they'd been riding. He imagined how her body would feel and react and where he'd like to taste and touch her. Maybe she thought about it, too, because she shivered. Gooseflesh rose on her slender shoulders.

He applied himself to fumbling with the pearl buttons until the dress was completely open down the back, then with great control, he dropped his hands and ducked out of the shelter.

Isabelle clutched two fistfuls of Irish lace with trembling fingers. He was gone, but she could still feel his calluses brush her skin, his warm breath on her shoulder. If he'd been planning to consummate their marriage, it would have been right then, wouldn't it?

They'd never discussed the subject, but she'd assumed they would take on all the aspects of husband and wife. She hadn't known how she felt about that until this moment. Shamefully, she felt somewhat disappointed—and yet relieved. She barely knew the man.

But it would have to happen. Sometime. Someday.

She shrugged her arms from the sleeves, let the top of the dress fold over and stepped from the skirt. Stooping in her silk chemise and drawers, she looked for somewhere to hang the garment. Not wanting to snag it on the branches that formed the ceiling beams, she settled for spreading the dress out on one of the blankets.

Isabelle ran a palm over the lace, smoothing the silky fabric, feeling a tangible connection to her mother. She had come to Montana from Illinois, a woman out of her familiar environment among the rugged men and the extreme elements of this wild, unforgiving country.

Isabelle removed the baby's breath wreath, unpinned her hair and used the quill brush. It took some getting used to, to figure out how to hold it and run the quills through, but it did the job quite cleverly. She made a braid and tied the end with a strip of leather that had been fastening a bundle.

She removed the silver amulet, studied it curiously in the dim light for a moment, then placed it with her other things. Mae had said it would win Kyle's heart. He had a heart; it was plain by the way he interacted with his aunt and the rest of his family. But she didn't think his heart could be softened toward her. He didn't bother to hide his obvious disdain for her and her kind. And who could blame him? With what little she knew, she believed the Cheyenne had been treated abominably—and he knew far better than she.

But his parents had defied convention and put aside their differences to marry, hadn't they? She wished she knew something about them.

And what of her own parents? Had they loved each other? Her elusive memories of them as a family were of her mother laughing and her father lavishing attention. When he'd sent Isabelle away after her mother's death, she hadn't understood. Maybe she reminded him of his wife, and the sight of her had been too painful.

Maybe he'd been irrationally afraid for her wellbeing and couldn't bear to lose her, too. However, they could have comforted each other. She'd certainly needed comfort...and love.

Isabelle gave the dress a last fond look. Perhaps someday a daughter of hers would wear it. But that was far in the future, and she still had tonight to worry about. Her stomach quivered with growing concern. What was to happen between them this night? Unfolding the doeskin dress, she slipped it on over her head. Long fringe brushed her arms and her ankles.

He was still a stranger. But she didn't want to displease him. And neither did she want to deny herself anything good that might come of this marriage. Plenty of marriages got started this way. Her situation was not unique—except to her.

Her silk slippers looked foolish with the costume, she realized, gazing down, so she removed her stockings and garters and slipped her feet into the smaller of the two pairs of moccasins.

This marriage had never been in her plans, but then her plans had never been definite—except that she'd wanted to come back to Montana. But then Kyle's plans hadn't included her as a wife, either. Did he resent her?

A horrible thought struck her, and she stood glued to the blanket. What had this hasty arrangement done to Kyle's plans? Had there been a woman he'd wanted to marry? If so, he would resent Isabelle's interference.

When she stepped through the flap and straightened, Kyle stared from his seat beside the fire. Her cheeks flamed. "Do I look foolish?" she asked.

"Do you think Cheyenne clothing is foolish?"

"No, I—I just feel strange."

"Tomorrow you'll be home and you can wear your own clothes."

She took several hesitant steps closer to the fire.

"What kind of clothing did you picture your wife wearing on your wedding day?"

"I never thought about it."

She settled down a few feet from him. "Did you plan to marry a Cheyenne woman?"

His dark gaze studied her without expression. "Why would I?"

"Well, because you think white women are silly and useless and wear foolish clothing."

He picked up a stick and rearranged the burning embers. "Even if I had a mind to, I'm not exactly a sought-after brave."

The fact was hard to believe. He was hardworking...and handsome. She couldn't imagine the Cheyenne women not falling all over him. "Why not?"

"I'm not a brave warrior. I didn't count coup with the others. I traded with the Cheyenne and Blackfeet and Sioux, but I sold horses to the army. I wasn't sent to the reservation with them. I'm too white."

"But you saved some of their children from that awful experience. You did what you could. Surely they respect that."

"They tolerate me."

"Those there today do more than tolerate you, I believe."

He shrugged.

Isabelle could understand his refusal to participate in the wars. The blood of both nations ran in his veins, and choosing a side would be difficult—or impossible. "Tell me about your parents."

She wasn't sure if he'd answer, but he spoke almost immediately. "My mother was Ameohne'e, Walking Woman. My father was a trapper, sold beaver and wolf pelts to the whites, traded with the tribes. Hank Brennan was his name. My mother found a young raccoon caught in one of his traps. He ran across her nursing the trapped animal, crying over its suffering. He freed the raccoon and helped her care for its wounds.

"My mother sought Ma'heona'e's help," he continued. "Ma'heona'e says their father didn't want my mother to marry Hank, but it was what Ameohne'e wanted. Land was cheap back then, and Hank bought good sections and started a ranch so my mother would be close to her family."

"He loved her."

Kyle shrugged. "He had wandering feet. I was small, but I remember him being gone for long periods of time. I thought he was working. Talk later was that he had another wife in Colorado."

Isabelle's surprise must have shown on her face.

"That would have been acceptable if he'd brought her here to help my mother," he said. "Cheyenne women often suggest that their husband take another, younger wife to share the workload."

She stared at him. "I wouldn't share my husband even if I had to work like a stevedore! You don't plan to take another wife, do you?"

A grin inched up one side of his mouth, catching her by surprise.

"We had a Christian wedding," she told him firmly. Maybe he did have another woman! "Surely you don't think—"

He laughed out loud then, the outburst startling a small creature in the nearby brush that scampered across the clearing in the dusk.

Isabelle started and instinctively moved closer to Kyle, even though he was laughing at her.

"You don't want to share me?" he asked, his voice seductively low.

She looked away from the devastating smile that made her stomach flip-flop. She had no intentions of sharing him as a husband! That was—well, it was *unacceptable*. "It wouldn't be proper. Or legal."

"Depends on who you ask."

She met his unfathomable dark gaze. Once again he made her feel that everything she knew and believed in was questionable. "So where was this ranch of your father's?"

"Right here."

She glanced around the clearing. "Next to the Big Sky?"

"It *was* the Big Sky. This section is all that was left after my father sold out to yours. He left my mother and me enough land to live on and then he took off. Never saw him again after I was seven."

Finally Isabelle understood. No wonder he had

such possessive feelings. Just as she did, he felt a kinship with the land.

"I want to learn everything I can about the ranch," she said, pulling her knees up and wrapping her arms around them. She rested her chin on her forearm. "I want to learn about the horses and go over the ledgers. I'm going to be an active partner."

"As long as you don't get in the way of anyone's job."

She'd be working herself—how could that be interference? His insinuation was insulting.

"And don't place yourself in unnecessary danger. Always let me know where you'll be and I'll have someone with you."

"I don't need a nursemaid."

He leaned forward and poured himself a cup of coffee from the dented pot. "I can't spare a nursemaid."

"You find me the most trivial creature alive, don't you?" she asked, once again irked. "I'm not valuable because I don't know as much about life out here as you do. I'm in the way and I'm a nuisance. I know you'd rather I'd never come back. You've made that very plain. My father never wanted me here, either. I was never important to him, either."

She stopped when she realized the burn of tears was threatening to fracture her dignity. She blinked and looked into the darkening woods.

The fire crackled. An animal howled in the distance, and a shiver ran up her spine.

"Your father protected you like a she-bear with a cub," he said finally. "He'd already lost your mother."

The fire warmed her skin. "I might have believed that if he'd ever visited me. Or tolerated my visits. If he'd ever done anything but send money."

"Maybe that's how he showed…"

She turned to look at him. "His love?"

He nodded.

She shrugged. "I'd have rather had a home."

With those revealing words, Kyle's perception of this woman altered so dramatically that he almost reached over and touched her to offer comfort. Had his impression of her as spoiled and pampered and greedy been based on lack of knowledge? If so, he'd done her a great injustice.

But even if he'd known her true character, he'd still have wanted the ranch…and she still wouldn't have wanted to give it up. At least he understood her desperation in a clearer light. And he didn't hold her insistence against her.

And, strangely enough, he couldn't resent her any longer, either.

But she couldn't help who and what she was. She still couldn't be trusted to stay or to be responsible. Promises and treaties and vows were like dry leaves in a brisk wind to whites.

"What more do you expect of me, besides not getting in the way?" she asked.

He studied her haughty profile in the firelight. "What do you mean?"

"Will we be—" she swallowed "—intimate?"

The word, her voice, the *idea*—hit him like a punch in the chest. What was she willing to trade— no, *sacrifice*—to make herself a home? Did she think he would treat her so callously as to hold her at arm's length and yet take her body for his own selfish pleasure? Her opinion of his character angered him—and shamed him.

"It's too soon," he replied, hoping to relieve her worry and end the discussion. "That's not the purpose of our agreement."

She didn't look at him. "But it's part of marriage."

"When and if the time is right," he insisted.

She nodded. Agreement? Understanding? He wasn't sure which.

"You know either partner can annul a marriage if it's not consummated," she said.

"I don't know what that means."

"Cancel. Either of us could cancel our marriage if we haven't been…intimate."

"I'll never do that. That would have to be your choice."

"I never will, either."

He was sure she meant it *now*. But someday… "I'll sleep out here," he said. "You stay inside."

She glanced around their darkened campsite. "I guess you've slept outside before."

"Many times."

"Do you still want to show me the game with the rocks?"

"Another night."

She stood, unconsciously smoothing the doeskin across her thighs in a sensual manner that shouldn't have affected him, but did. Especially with the question—the suggestion of intimacy freshly painted in his mind and the woods hiding them from the world.

Had she felt his hunger inside? Had she sensed the fire that raced through his veins as he stood behind her and smelled her skin and hair and saw her sleek ivory flesh? Had she expected him to do something about it then? Had she prepared herself for the possibility?

He didn't want a woman who offered herself as a sacrifice—or a trade.

He watched her disappear inside the shelter. He'd been so single-mindedly focused on obtaining the ranch that he hadn't wasted time wishing or wanting things that were out of his grasp. Today he had married Isabelle Cooper, a beautiful, intelligent, willful and utterly charming woman, united in a marriage he would never have dreamed for himself.

The untouchable young girl Sam Cooper had protected so zealously was now Kyle's mature and incredibly desirable wife.

And now, he had to ask himself…what *did* he want?

Chapter 8

Each successive day proved that Isabelle was a quick and eager student, her bookkeeping and mathematical skills far surpassing Kyle's. Every evening he joined her for dinner, and afterward they retired to the study where she showed him what she'd gone over that day and made suggestions and recommendations.

Her grasp of the business end of ranching surprised him. He would have more time to devote to the horses if she could be trusted with this work, but undoubtedly it would all fall back on him eventually.

"I've spent enough days inside," she informed him one evening. "I've been arranging things to my liking and cleaning the attic and the corners, but I'll be out to join you tomorrow morning.''

He wanted to smile at the bossy way she pointed the ink pen at him, but he knew better than to let her see his amusement. If he didn't challenge her, she'd discover on her own the difficulty of the outdoor work and be able to save face.

She sat straighter, and one slim eyebrow rose, an expression he'd learned meant a defense was brewing.

He said nothing.

Isabelle rubbed at an inkstain on her finger and directed her gaze away from Kyle's. His dark, unreadable expressions wore on her nerves until she wanted to throw something at him. No one was always that stern and inscrutable. Annoying him pleased her, because then she at least got to see him react.

He'd been more distant than ever since the night of their wedding, when he'd assured her that a physical aspect to their marriage was something he was not considering. She'd felt almost foolish for being the one to voice it—to think it—to wonder in the first place.

And she'd wondered again…and again, numerous times in those days that followed. Perhaps there was something wrong with her to anticipate it. Perhaps he saw something wrong with her, and that's why he didn't initiate it.

Perhaps she'd better direct her thoughts elsewhere.

Remembering his criticism of her clothing, she dressed as sensibly as she could the following morning, and after eating sausage and biscuits with Pelipa, she made her way to the barn, where the sounds of activity drew her.

As she entered the cool interior, the potent scent of horse and hay and grain met her nostrils. She walked the center aisle, glancing at the parallel rows of facing stalls to her right, and continued toward the sound of men's voices.

In an open room on the left, Kyle and several of the hands stood or sat on kegs and sawhorses. An enormous stone forge sat cold on this day. Kyle held several tools, which he'd just taken from a bench that ran along a wall opposite an exterior doorway.

The comfortable dialogue stopped abruptly as she stepped into view. There were six of them all together, counting Kyle, Sidestep and Tott. The other three, whom she'd seen only from a distance, whipped their hats from their heads and straightened to attention as if she were a commanding officer.

"Miss Cooper," came the self-conscious murmurs.

"Mr. Tott, Mr. Sidestep," she said cordially. Their faces reddened. "I'm afraid I haven't had the pleasure of making the acquaintance of the rest of you gentlemen."

Kyle introduced the others.

''I appreciate you men remaining in spite of the fact that your wages were in arrears. I find loyalty a commendable trait.''

The men glanced uncertainly at Kyle.

''She thanks you for staying on without pay,'' he translated, with a droll cock of one eyebrow.

Isabelle nodded. ''And I want you all to go about your work just as you normally would. Nothing should change just because I'm here to help.''

The men glanced at one another, over at Kyle, and took their cue to get to work.

''What's on the agenda for today?'' she asked Kyle after most of them had replaced their hats and exited.

''The hands are bringing a herd in from the south pasture to the corrals this morning. Tott and I are going to be checking the animals over. We're starting with feet out here.'' He led the way toward the stalls.

''Feet?'' she asked, hurrying to keep up.

''Check for thrush and scratches and trim hooves.''

''Oh, well, you show me what to do, and I'll do it.''

Tott had moved down the corridor and led a horse into the center, where he bent over beside the animal, a hoof held firmly between his knees.

''Like that,'' Kyle said. ''Approach the horse calmly and deliberately to gain his confidence. You don't want to spook 'im. Slip his halter on and lead him out here.'' He demonstrated with a spotted mare.

Isabelle slid the bolt on a stall gate and found a halter on a nail. ''What's this one's name?''

''No name.''

''Why not?''

''Too many horses pass through here to keep track of their names,'' he replied.

She slipped the halter on and adjusted it. ''Then how do you know what to say to them?''

''It's not what you say, it's how you say it. Now lead her out here. There. Now stand facing her rear beside her front leg. They have to be trained to let you do this. You can't just try this on one of the broncs.

''Touch her shoulder and run your hand down so she knows you're going to handle her leg. Now move your hand down to grip her foot and press her shoulder with your other hand so she shifts her weight to her other leg.''

She pressed, but the enormous animal didn't budge. ''She's—uh—not going anywhere.''

''Lean against her and put your weight into it. When her weight shifts, lift the foot up off the ground and place it between your legs, just above your knee. Flex your knees, turn your toes in—''

His instructions were lost as Isabelle fought with her skirts to get the hoof between her knees. Finally she had to reach between her spread feet, grasp the back hem of her skirt, pull it up and tuck in into her waistband. The remedy bared the tops of her shoes and her calves, but she had little choice if she planned to proceed with this task. Finally she got a hoof between her knees.

"What *is* this?" she asked, her nose crinkling at the foul smell and the ghastly smear on the freshly pressed fabric of her skirt.

"Manure."

"Oh, my—" She turned her face aside and tried not to gag.

"Here, clean it off with this so you can see the bottom of her foot." He handed her an iron tool. "Run the pick gently from heel to toe, and be careful not to poke or bruise the tender spot here. If she jerks away, don't accidentally poke her."

"Clean this stuff out?" she asked. He couldn't be serious!

"I'll take over if you'd rather find something else to do."

She looked up and caught the unguarded amusement in his expression. "This is truly an important job?" she asked, not trusting him.

"Not doing it can cause disease or leg problems, sometimes faulty gaits."

Isabelle glanced over her shoulder to see Tott diligently working at the same task. She ran the pick carefully across the horse's foot as Kyle had told her.

He'd given her the most docile animals in the barn, she realized sometime later, after she'd checked three horses and he'd inspected her work. He'd finished with six or seven in the same amount of time.

Though he gave a running verbal lesson while he worked, watching Kyle was the best teacher. The horses seemed to listen, too. With his voice and his gentle, confident movements, he had earned their trust. He ran his hands over their necks and shoulders, scratched their massive foreheads and made an odd clicking sound in his throat to which they responded with perked ears.

Isabelle could have watched him forever.

Her back ached from bending over in the unnatural position, and she arched it as she observed him leading a reddish mare into her stall. The bell clanged, and the sound of horses reining in outside caught her attention.

"Dinner," Kyle said with a gesture indicating she should follow.

She let her hem down, massaged the small of her back and trudged toward the bunkhouse beside him.

The interior of the men's quarters was amazingly clean and orderly, with a large open room for cooking and dining, scarred tables and assorted benches. A few rockers and footstools were set before the fireplace at the northeast end of the room. A checkerboard sat in wait on a small, sturdy table. Open stairs led to the sleeping area above.

"This is Harlan."

She glanced at the man who wore denims and a

faded flannel shirt just like everyone else. The only sign that he was the cook was the flour dusting his scraggly gray beard.

Isabelle accepted a tin plate of beans and a bent fork and seated herself on a bench. Tins of biscuits had been placed on the tables. The men kept their distance, taking places at the opposite end from their female newcomer.

Kyle sat across from her, and his presence made her feel less like an interloper. She offered him a grateful smile.

He spared her one acknowledging nod and dug into his food.

She ate a few bites and glanced around. "Are they usually this quiet?"

"They're hungry."

She'd washed at the pump, but the odious smell remained on her skirts or in her nose and killed her appetite. She forced herself to eat the pile of salty beans and bacon so as not to offend Harlan. Kyle had been right about the man's lack of imagination, however. And she was *paying* him to supply these meals. Perhaps they could go over some menus.

One or two at a time, the hands stood and stacked their plates in a bucket beside the door.

She met Kyle's obsidian gaze.

He expected her to beg off. The thought appealed. She could come up with an excuse to change out of her smelly clothes and bathe. "What now?" she asked instead.

"I'm going to cut a few horses to break. Watch and learn."

She fell into step behind the others. "All right."

Tott and Ward had mounted horses and worked to cut a horse from the big corral and urge him through a gate into the round corral on the north end of the barn. A gleaming black horse with a gray mane broke into the space and galloped in a circle.

Isabelle took a place along the fence with the others and watched all afternoon as Kyle worked.

She'd seen her father breaking horses once, and he'd been bucked clear over the beast's head. But he hadn't taken nearly the time or the patience that Kyle showed in getting the creatures used to being handled and touched.

A tender place warmed in Isabelle's chest at the gentleness and care Kyle afforded his animals— *their* animals, she reminded herself. All this was half hers. Watching him, doubt about her ability to contribute as much to the ranch as Kyle did awakened in her mind. She lulled the discomfiting thoughts back to sleep by telling herself that none of this would be his anyway if she hadn't agreed to his proposal.

Okay, except a good share of the horses.

Horse after horse fell under Kyle's gentle submission. The last, a nervous spotted gray, fought the ropes and shied from Kyle's hands until he and Sidestep tied his feet, laid him on his side and worked the halter over his head while he fought.

This one Kyle didn't try to saddle or mount. Once he was bound and haltered, they let him stand. His eyes rolled wildly, and Isabelle could sense his fear and distress. Kyle spoke to him, touched him, rubbed him with a blanket until he calmed. Then they let him out into the big corral, where he galloped to the far side.

"Why didn't you saddle him?" she asked when Kyle approached the fence where she stood.

Kyle noted the sunburn across her nose and wished he'd thought to find her a decent hat. "Someone has tried to break him before."

"How do you know?"

"Scrapes on his shins. That scared look."

"What will you do?"

"Let him get used to me slowly. Your nose is red."

Isabelle touched her nose with one finger. "Pelipa is fixing her fried bread and vegetables for supper."

"I think I'll eat with the men," he said. "I want to stay with the chestnut mare tonight."

"The one who's close to foaling?"

He nodded.

"Why don't you let me bring you supper? Then you won't have to eat stew."

Not even stew. He remembered the beans he'd seen soaking that noon, and he wasn't about to refuse her offer. "If you wouldn't mind."

"I don't." She glanced away nervously before she said, "What would you think of me making a shopping list and having one of the hands ride into Whitehorn with me?''

That wasn't out of the ordinary. Why would she ask?

''And then,'' she went on, ''I would like to go over a few menus with Harlan, make a few suggestions.'' She glanced up as though waiting for his response.

''You're asking my *opinion?*'' Now *that* was out of the ordinary.

''I need to know if you think he would be offended. I truly believe the men deserve variety and good nutrition.''

''You can ask the workers to do things the way you want them done,'' he said with a shrug. ''You're the boss, too.''

''And what about offending him?'' she asked.

''If you make him mad, you can hire a new cook, I guess. But remember, there are worse ones.'' He turned and strode toward the barn.

Later Isabelle dipped hot water and sponge bathed in her room. She carried her smelly skirts to the back porch, not looking forward to having to wash them—or any of her clothing, for that matter. Another task she had to learn.

While she and Pelipa ate, the girl hinted that she'd like to visit the reservation. ''You go see your friends,'' Isabelle encouraged her. ''I don't mind an evening alone. Is it safe for you to go by yourself?''

"Pelipa know the way. Not afraid. Long Knife ride back together with Pelipa."

"Long Knife?"

The girl nodded.

"Is Long Knife your beau?"

"What is beau?"

"Gentleman caller. Sweetheart." Isabelle didn't know words to convey the idea, so she pressed her hand over her heart, fluttered her eyelashes and sighed. "Are you fond of each other?"

Pelipa giggled. "Long Knife wear many years on his face. He not a beau."

Isabelle stacked the dishes. "Oh. Well, I thought perhaps you had someone special at the reservation. You're a lovely young woman."

"Someone special is rancher son," she confided. "But he white and Kyle say not for Pelipa."

Isabelle studied the lovely girl's disillusioned expression. "I'm sorry," she said simply, understanding Kyle's feelings and yet wishing things could be different. "What's his name?"

A shy smile crept across Pelipa's face, and her bright black eyes twinkled. "William."

How sad that Kyle had discouraged her from a relationship with a white. How sad that he saw the need. Would Isabelle ever find a way past his resentment?

Scraping soap into the heated water, she paused and reflected. How surprising that she suddenly realized wanting to work her way into his trust wasn't only for reasons of their working relationship.

She'd begun to care what he thought of her…and she wanted him to care, too.

Chapter 9

The sun was setting when Isabelle carried a tray toward the barn. The long days and backbreaking work involved in keeping the ranch running had become real to her. Her contribution to the day's tasks gave her a new sense of accomplishment, and even though her body ached and her palms had blistered, she was happier than she'd ever been all those years studying and teaching in the city.

She found Kyle and the mare in one of the large stalls on the left side of the barn. He sat perched on a nail keg, a tangle of harnesses and bridles at his feet, oiling the leather with a rag, and glanced up at her arrival.

"How's she doing?" she asked.

"She's fine. I'm the nervous one."

She smiled and placed the tray on another keg.
"I kept this hot for you."

"I'll wash off outside and be right back."

She offered the horse a few pieces of dried apple
she'd brought and rubbed the animal's head.

"She likes you," Kyle said when he returned and
sat to eat. He'd removed his hat and tied his black
hair at the back of his neck. A damp lock fell across
his forehead.

"I bribed her," she said.

Of course he didn't smile. He ate his meal in silence.

Isabelle rubbed the mare's shoulder and ran her
palm over her distended side. "You touch them all
over when you're working them. Why is that?"

He sipped coffee from the tin cup and studied her.
"Getting them used to being handled."

"Her sides are sticking out so far. Does it hurt
her?"

"I don't think so." He got up and came to stand
beside her. "Reach under her belly. Sometimes you
can feel the colt moving."

"Really?" She ran her hand along the animal's
hide.

"Like this." He took her wrist firmly and
stretched her left arm far beneath the horse, pressing
her entire arm against the belly. "Now wait."

Kyle and Isabelle bent beneath the horse, their
sides and hips touching, and after a moment, the

animal's hide rippled and rolled, and she felt the muscular sensation along her limb. "I felt it! Oh, my goodness!"

She became aware of Kyle's solid, warm body where it touched hers through her clothing along her side. His strong rough hand was clamped over the back of hers, holding it to the mare's belly.

As though he, too, had become acutely aware of their closeness, Kyle's touch on her hand changed. No longer was he holding her hand in place, but he seemed to stroke her skin in nebulous discovery. Her hand trembled under the gentle caress.

As one, they straightened and stood facing each other. Kyle let her hand slide as their bodies straightened, but kept it firmly in his enormous palm. His dark gaze lowered to her fingers, pale in his dark-skinned grasp, and her attention followed. Her heart chugged like a train engine on an incline, and she experienced a quickening desire for their sweet, tentative connection to deepen.

While he studied their joined hands, she looked up and found his black lashes hiding those unreadable eyes. His features were an intriguing blend of stern angles and dramatic symmetry, his lips classically sculptured and full.

An emotion she couldn't name fluttered in her chest just looking at him, the same unidentifiable yearning she'd felt watching him with the horses, a longing utterly sweet and forlorn at the same time.

She raised her right hand and opened her palm

along the side of his face. His skin was warm and smooth, and touching him sent a tingle up her arm.

His dark gaze shot to hers, his eyes examining, weighing, boring into hers. His attention dropped to her mouth.

Isabelle's lips parted on a shaky breath.

She slid the hand against his jaw behind his neck, silky hair brushing her fingers, and raised her face expectantly.

He didn't disappoint her. Kyle lowered his head and touched those perfect lips to hers in a warm, ardent press of satiny flesh and a mingling of breaths.

He tasted like coffee…and energy. He released her hand and cupped her face, aligning, burning, drawing, tempting, until she lost herself in the feelings, wrapped her arms around his torso and pressed in closer for the deep-drawn pleasure.

One of his hands slid from her face down her neck, and his fingers brushed the sensitive skin, slid inside her collar and drew circles against her flesh.

Isabelle's weak knees left her pressed to his hard frame, her breasts crushed against his chest where his heart pounded.

He cupped her face again, more roughly this time, and held her head while he separated their mouths long enough to kiss her chin, her jaw, her neck, her ear. A shiver coursed through her body. She gripped his back less for support than to avail herself of the sensual onslaught.

His mouth returned to hers, pausing for a divine moment of expectancy as unsettling as the actual contact. Then he reclaimed her lips, and her world changed.

Tears smarted behind her eyelids; her throat constricted. She wanted to melt into him, against him, around him. She wanted to become him. She wanted...

Something subtle changed between them. Something powerful and frightening.

Almost as one they drew back, and their hooded gazes locked.

Kyle released her, then, when she swayed, had to steady her with a hand on her shoulder.

"Kyle, I—"

"Go back to the house." He withdrew his touch.

She tried to read emotion in his eyes, in his granite-hard expression, but he kept his reactions shuttered, as always.

"What's wrong?" she asked, the question burning from her aching heart. He seemed almost angry.

"Go back to the house, Isabelle." His voice was a deep rasp.

"Did I do something wrong?"

"No, I did something wrong. Now go." He picked up the tray and shoved it into her trembling hands.

Ashamed, she tore her gaze from his hard black eyes to the dirty dishes. She could still taste him, could still feel his touch on her neck, his body against hers. She still harbored the same disquieting yearning she had a minute ago.

In her mind, she went over that disorienting encounter and tried to understand what had gone wrong. Had it all been one-sided? Had she only dreamed he could feel the same way about her?

She turned her back. Rejection was something Isabelle was accustomed to. She'd been turned aside and sent away her whole life. She should have developed a thick skin for being shown she was unwanted. But this hurt as much as any of her father's rebuffs. Maybe more, because she had tried as hard as she knew how to be useful, to become the kind of wife a rancher needed.

She wanted to hold her back straight and her chin high, but her usual brave facade failed her, and she turned and exited the stall and the barn as fast as she could, striding into the darkening night before he saw the hurt. Damn him, anyway!

Why had she gone and done that? Why had she risked her heart when she knew better? Halfway to the house, the fresh injury turned to anger, and she flung the tray as hard as she could. It landed with an unsatisfactory thump in the dirt, and the tin plates clanked together. Isabelle ran forward and attacked them with the toe of her boot, sending plates and cup and silverware flying.

Kyle might not want her, damn his hide, but he couldn't send her away. The ranch was hers, and it was all she had. He might not need her, just as her father had never needed her, but there was still one thing that needed her—the ranch.

She would pour her soul into the ranch, and never again would her heart be lacerated. Isabelle ran into the house and up the stairs, not pausing for water or to say good-night to Pelipa. She closed herself in her room and nursed her humiliation and pride.

A long, sleepless time later, she pulled back a frilly curtain and gazed at the moonlit barn. Lighting a lamp, she changed her rumpled clothing, removed the pearl combs from her hair and placed them in her jewelry box.

The twinkle of silver caught her attention, and she picked up the chain and dangled the engraved amulet before the lamp.

Leaves from my garden will win your husband's heart. Mae had spoken cryptically on their wedding day. Isabelle scoffed again at the foolish hope of someone loving her. She was obviously unlovable, and a few weeds wouldn't change that.

But something bigger than her wounded self-esteem and her skeptical outlook wouldn't let her return the necklace to the velvet-lined box. She spread the quill chain wide and slipped it over her head. The amulet nestled between her breasts, almost warm against her skin.

She smiled at the fanciful girlish fantasy, and soon an indescribable peace settled over her. She was tired, and the day and her emotions had caught up with her.

She blew out the lantern, climbed into bed and fell into dream-filled slumber.

Kissing her had gone against every rational cell in his brain. He watched the light from her window disappear and admitted he could only take so much temptation.

For weeks he'd had to tamp down his reactions to her long-limbed form in her feminine clothing, ignore the sweep of her dark lashes against her pale skin and resist the enticement of the heart-kicking bow of her lips—those innocent yet seductive smiles and touches she couldn't know were eating his soul alive.

Once again entering the stall, he spread a wool blanket on a pile of straw in the corner and stretched out to chase some rest.

That kiss had sent him into a spiral of passion and confusion. She was so soft and her kiss so dizzying, it had taken an eternity for him to come to his senses. He wanted nothing more than to hold her, to enfold her and possess her.

But he couldn't allow himself to weaken. She didn't belong to him. She belonged to a glamorous life-style and a society of which he would never have any part—of which he never wanted any part. But she would. Once she came to reason and stopped playing games here, she would.

Kyle closed his eyes, though he didn't have much hope for rest. Her image had been branded on the inside of his eyelids. Her voice had become a melody that played inside his head. The smells of her skin and her hair were burned into his memory, and now that he'd tasted her, held her, he knew an aching hunger that had spread from his body to his head.

Why did it have to be her? Why did he have to want this woman when he'd never felt strongly about another in his life? Why had he fallen in love with one who wouldn't be staying? Because it would take a far stronger man than him to resist Isabelle Cooper, he admitted ruefully. And because life wasn't fair.

Chapter 10

At first he was dumbfounded by the realization that he loved a white woman. Against the mandates of his head and his beliefs, his heart had betrayed him.

At noon a couple of days later, Kyle entered the bunkhouse with the men, and his mouth watered at the savory aromas.

The table had been set properly with stoneware dishes and pitchers of milk. Two glazed hams had been sliced and placed on platters beside bowls of fluffy mashed potatoes and creamed vegetables. Loaves of crusty thick-sliced bread sat at either end of the feast.

"Whee doggie!" Tott shouted, and plunked himself down on a bench. The others quickly joined him, platters were passed and silverware clinked.

Kyle savored the delicious meal, listened to the men's profuse compliments.

Isabelle and Harlan accepted the praise, but Isabelle didn't appear as excited as Kyle had thought she should be over seeing her plans carried out. She sat in the corner chair that had become hers and ate her food without joining the men's banter.

The changes he'd seen in her these past days disturbed him. She put in as many hours as any of the hands—as Kyle himself—keeping occupied nearly round the clock. But the childlike joy he had once sensed had turned to grim determination. He felt responsible, as though he'd pulled her dreams out from under her. There hadn't been a choice, really. She would be better off once she admitted to herself that she couldn't be happy here.

He'd be better off, too. The longer she stayed, the more difficult her leaving would be. And he'd begun to dread that inevitable hour—and all the hours that would follow.

The men finished eating, noisily stacked their plates and lumbered out of the bunkhouse.

Kyle sipped his coffee. He missed her company these days—missed the optimistic twist she placed on everything. Glancing at her from the corner of his eye, he asked, "Did you go see the new foal?"

Shaking her head, she said, "I've been busy. Sidestep said he's a beauty."

"I thought you'd want to have a look at him."

"I'll look in on him when I'm over that way."

He'd been keeping an eye on her activities. She'd been clearing flower beds and the garden area all morning. The previous afternoon she'd scraped and painted the front and back doors. He'd set out to make her feel unwelcome, and he'd done his best to discourage her participation in all areas, so her sudden lack of enthusiasm about the horses shouldn't bother him. "Want to see him now?"

She got up and stacked her plate with the others at the end of the table. "Thank you, Harlan. You did an excellent job on the hams." Then to Kyle, she said, "I'd better help Harlan with the supper menu."

"You kin read me the chicken recipe later if'n you want to head out," the cook said.

"What about the dishes?"

"Washed 'em alone before you got here," he replied. "Reckon I kin still do it." He plucked stacked cups from her hand and waved her off.

She stepped outside behind Kyle. He settled his hat on his head, and they walked across the yard in uncomfortable silence.

The double-wide back doors of the barn stood open. Kyle headed in that direction. "Might as well come see him. They don't stay small long."

Obviously reluctant, she joined him in the shady barn.

Kyle opened the stall gate.

The spindly chestnut colt lay curled on the straw, the mare placidly munching oats beside him.

"You can touch him," Kyle said, noting her hesitation.

She touched the mare first, showing her hands and greeting her, then knelt close to the colt. "He's darling. He's not the same color as his mother."

She was a natural around the animals. He'd noticed from the first. "She and the sire are both quarter horses, just different coloring. I chose the sire for his muscled legs and thighs and wide hips. This year's foals will be good cow ponies."

The colt butted Isabelle's hand and nibbled at her fingers. She stroked his coat, and when he lurched to his feet, she stood back and laughed. He nuzzled his mother.

Kyle studied Isabelle's features as she watched the mother and baby. She glanced at him and dropped her gaze.

Was she remembering what had taken place here a few nights ago? Kyle had thought of little else. Or did she wonder what he'd do next to steal the smile from her lips? This one faded slowly, and it seemed as though a cloud had passed over.

Isabelle sensed the tension emanating from Kyle's body. The tangible disquiet was only tension and obviously not the attraction she'd once perceived this disquieting spark between them to mean. It was easier to stay away—easier to thwart her wild imagination when she kept her distance. She hadn't come to see the new horse until now because she was still reeling over being ordered from the barn.

She didn't want Kyle to think she would throw herself at him again. One rebuff had been enough. But neither did she want him to believe she was going to roll over and play dead. She had doubled her efforts to make herself useful. The ranch was showing improvement already.

Kyle picked up a pitchfork, scraped soiled straw to the side and spread fresh. She contemplated him while he was absorbed with the task. He didn't need the hat to mask his expressions—his granite-like facade was enough. But the hat did an even better job of preventing her from reading anything on his face. He set the fork outside the stall and rambled after a fresh bucket of water.

He'd rolled his sleeves to his elbows, and his corded arms flexed with each movement. She'd never taken so much interest in watching a man's every move, but when she was around this one she couldn't help herself. His masculine grace and efficiency appealed to her in a wholly disturbing manner.

The mare chose that moment to raise her head and press a nose against Kyle's shirtfront. Kyle paused to rake his knuckles over her forehead. Bobbing her head again, the horse knocked his hat into the straw.

One side of his mouth inched up. "Good thing for you I just cleaned that floor."

He glanced over and caught her watching him. His smile faded, and a heated awareness arced between them. Isabelle didn't understand him at all, and she hated this weakness of character, but she was drawn to him against all her self-preserving precautions.

He retrieved his hat.

Heart thudding, she rubbed her damp palms against her skirt.

He settled the hat on his head and studied her from beneath its brim.

She met his gaze, drawn to the stern but sensual set of his mouth. She would give anything for him to cross the few feet that separated them and gather her in his arms again. She was weak and foolish and would regret it later, but this artless need had a mind of its own.

Never should she have come in here with him. More than anything, she wanted him to feel something for her in return. She wanted him to accept her. Once again, she was ready to forfeit pride for a few scraps of affection and attention. Garnering her purpose, she turned and hurried from the stall.

"Isabelle!" he called behind her.

Chest aching, she kept walking.

She didn't show up at the bunkhouse for supper. But then she never used to, either. He'd assumed one reason was the food, but Harlan had prepared a savory chicken and stuffing dish that was obviously her doing. Her lack of familiarity with the men might have been a factor originally, but the hands had begun to accept her, and she seemed comfortable around them.

"Miss Cooper'll be back in an hour or so," Harlan said.

Had Kyle's face given away his thoughts? "Where did she go?"

"Didn't say. Just said she'd be gone for supper."

"The brown bay and a saddle are gone," Tott added.

Concern destroyed Kyle's appetite. The western sky had been dark with storm clouds when he'd completed his chores. Hastily, he finished the meal and pushed away from the table. Stupid woman had no idea how to take care of herself. What did she think she was doing, riding out alone? She'd been a bother since the day she'd arrived.

He hurried to the barn and a sweet melody caught his attention. He paused. From the house floated the trill of a bird, a bright, energetic warbling that carried across the landscape. Giving the house a quick once-over, he noticed the open dining room window and the cage that sat inside. That such a tiny bird could sing so loudly was remarkable—that and the fact that it seemed perfectly content in its imprisonment.

Darting for the corral, he summoned the Appaloosa and saddled it. He grabbed his rifle and a slicker and mounted, studying the ground until he found Isabelle's tracks leading east. Following them, he imagined every danger that could arise. The bay could spook and throw her. Snakes and coyotes were common, and even if she'd thought to bring the Colt, she'd never hit one. Another hour and it would be dark, and it got cold at night. Thunder rolled overhead.

Almost a half hour later, he spotted the bay standing on a grassy slope that led down to Bear Tooth Creek. The Appaloosa hadn't stopped when Kyle's boots hit the ground. He ran toward the bank.

Isabelle, sitting on her shawl on the ground, turned and leveled the barrel of the Colt on him, her eyes as wide and gray and fierce as the Montana sky.

"Kyle!" she squawked, and her shoulders sagged with relief. She lowered the gun. "You nearly frightened me to death."

"What are you doing out here?" He strode over to where she sat and glared.

"Sitting. Thinking."

"It's getting late and it's going to rain."

"I was just getting ready to head back."

"Do you know how to get back?"

"I was hoping so."

"This wasn't very smart. Something could have happened to you. You could have been lost—or hurt."

"Well, it didn't and I'm not. You're not my father, and I won't be treated like you are. There's danger everywhere. I could have been struck by a carriage in the city, too, but I wasn't."

She got to her feet, and he stared at her, rolling that twisted logic around in his head. "You have to take precautions out here."

She raised the gun.

He glanced at it and back to her stubborn face. She was the loveliest thing he'd ever seen and the most irritating person he'd ever met, though he saw her differently than when she'd first arrived. Now he understood that she was the result of the life her father had forced on her. Once she'd seen the opportunity to change and to grow, she'd done so with a determination and a spirit that he'd had to admire.

She wanted to make a place for herself here and had done all she knew how to see it happen. After seeing the determination and hard work and loyalty she'd poured into the Big Sky, he couldn't help but wonder what she would give to a man who loved her.

Perhaps she'd been willing to do just that before he built a wall between them.

Now she didn't trust him. And he understood mistrust. He took the revolver from her and tucked it in his belt. Lightning streaked, and thunder split the air. Spattering raindrops sounded on his hat and glistened on Isabelle's nose and cheeks.

He grabbed the slicker from his saddle. "Get up," he said, pointing to his horse. Taking a step from his bent knee, she arranged herself on the horse with a flurry of skirts and white petticoats.

Kyle caught her horse's reins and mounted behind

her, wrapping the slicker around them both and leading the bay.

She was as soft and erotic-smelling as he remembered, the reality better than the memory. He nudged the Appaloosa into a gallop and headed for shelter.

Isabelle would have liked to lean back into the warmth and protection of his arms, but their pace didn't afford time to relax. Her hair grew wet, and her teeth chattered by the time he drew up in front of a cabin and leaped down.

"What's this place?" she asked.

"My home." He wrapped the slicker around her. "Go in while I put the horses in the lean-to."

Obediently, she ran through the deluge to the door and entered the dark cabin.

Shivering, she stood inside until he returned and found a lantern. A golden glow illuminated the sharp angles of his tight jaw and carved brow. His glistening ebony hair dripped on the wet shirt molded to his chest.

Isabelle removed the slicker and hung it on a peg inside the door. She turned back, and Kyle was coming toward her with a stack of folded burlap toweling. "Dry your hair," he said.

"Yours is wet, too."

"I'm used to the weather."

"You're dripping all over."

He kept a length for himself, dried his hair and slipped out of his shirt. He moved to the stone fireplace, and arranged a stack of wood and lit kindling beneath. Isabelle watched the play of muscle beneath his smooth bronze skin as he performed the chore.

She hung her shawl over a wooden chair back, then scampered near the fire and waited impatiently for the flames to engulf the sticks and send heat. Careful not to stare at him, she studied the room.

A sturdy, rough-hewn table and benches sat on one side, a small cupboard and a few crates the only storage space.

The other side held a bed, its low frame fashioned from joined logs. The furs and blankets covering the mattress looked warm and comfortable. Beside the bed, a shelf held an assortment of books. Other items were stored in stacked baskets.

Two furs covered the rough plank floor before the fireplace. Like the man himself, the room was an interesting and elementary blend of cultures.

Her gaze flitted to the cabin's owner. She found him watching her. "Want dry clothes?" he asked.

She glanced at her sodden hem and spattered skirts. Her damp bodice clung uncomfortably to her skin. She raised a brow. "You have a spare gown lying about?"

"I have tunics and leggings. You can adjust them with a drawstring."

"Where would I change?"

"I'll be a gentleman and make coffee and keep my back turned." He rose, drew a bundle from beneath his bed and handed it to her. Opening the door, he darted out long enough to draw a bucket of water from the corner of the cabin.

Isabelle glanced from the clothing to his back and slowly unbuttoned her shirtwaist.

Chapter 11

Her skirt came off next, followed by her petticoats. Her chemise and drawers were dry, thank goodness, so she would leave them on beneath his soft clothing.

The leather smelled like him. She raised the tunic to her nose, and the scent created a nervous flutter in her belly.

"Let me brush your hair."

The nearness of his voice startled her. She turned her head and found him behind her. Surprisingly, she wasn't frightened or embarrassed. "You said you'd keep your back turned."

"I'm not a gentleman."

She let the clothing fall from her fingers, reached and pulled the combs and pins loose.

His palm appeared in her vision, and she placed the items within, her fingers grazing his calloused skin. He set the hair accessories on the table that held his books and picked up a quill brush, which he raised and drew through the ends of her hair. Of course, having long hair himself, he would know to start at the ends. She smiled.

He worked his way along the tresses to her scalp, and Isabelle let her head fall back in sensual pleasure.

"I remembered your hair," he said near her ear.

"What do you mean?" she asked through the seductive haze of indulgence.

"I remembered it from a time when you were here to visit your father. I saw you in the yard one afternoon, and I never forgot the way your hair shone like the fiery ball of the sun at sunset in midsummer."

That revelation took her aback. Poetic words. Revealing words. But the message behind them came into focus. He'd noticed and remembered her.

He buried his face in her hair and made a throaty sound. He lifted the tresses, and his warm breath caressed her neck as he nuzzled her skin around the quill chain. Shivers spread across her shoulders and tightened her breasts. He nipped her flesh, and her knees weakened.

As if sensing her loss of stability, he wrapped an arm across her chest and drew her against him where he easily supported her weight with his arm and his solid body.

With his other hand, he held her damp hair away from her face so he could kiss her temple, her cheek, her jaw.

"I remember you, too," she said on a shallow breath. "You were so stern-looking, so unsmiling and…" She turned in his embrace, and he didn't loosen his hold, just pressed her ardently against his body. She raised a hand to his cheek.

His black eyes smoldered. His lips parted. She'd wanted to shake him up to see him react just once, but she'd never thought to do it this way. His usually severe mask had been fractured, and desire plainly softened his features.

Isabelle smiled and drew her thumb across his lower lip.

The heat from the fire spread though the room, danced on their skin and delved through muscle and tissue to create a tremulous heat that fused them.

The nagging memory of his hurtful reaction to the kiss they'd shared in the barn stole into her thoughts, but the desire to have more of him banished the worry. Her heart and her body begged for his sweet touch, and she wouldn't be ashamed of her need. She loved him.

His fingers threaded into her hair, and her arm stole around his neck. She was tall enough to meet his kiss aggressively, and she did so with singular determination.

He banded her with an arm across her back; his other hand gripped her bottom and pulled her hips against him.

White-hot fire licked through her veins at the rush of sensation and pleasure. His tongue sought entrance, and she tasted a new and immeasurably sweet passion. Her body trembled against his.

His touch on her bottom changed to a caress, and she held her breath. Their lips parted, and as one they sighed, a mingling of breath and wonderment.

Never had anything felt so right or so perfect before. Isabelle ran her palms over his smooth shoulders, across his chest, testing and discovering and delighting.

His black eyes raked her face and dropped to the thin cotton barrier that separated them. He brought his hands up her sides and drew his thumbs across the aching crests beneath the fabric. She let her eyes drift shut to savor the achingly sweet sensation.

"I don't want to do this," he said, his voice low and gruff.

She forced her eyes open.

"If you'll regret it afterward—if you'll be ashamed for wanting me."

She shook her head to clear it. Why would she be ashamed? Did he plan to humiliate her again?

"This is where I come from," he said, and one hand left her breast to indicate the cabin. "You've met my family, and I've never claimed to be anything except what I am."

Understanding dawned slowly. "What are you that would be shameful for me to want?" she asked.

He held her gaze. "A half-breed."

Was that hard for him to say? "Is that a slur?" She raised her palm to his face and cupped his jaw. "I know you as an honest, hardworking man. A man I want to know better. The man I married. Period. Don't let other people's attitudes affect the way you see me, and I'll do the same."

"I was wrong about you," he said. He let their bodies part in order to take her hand and lead her to his bed. She sat on the edge tentatively, but he wouldn't allow shyness.

He'd been wrong about so many things, and thankfully he'd straightened his thinking before it was too late. She wasn't like his father. She wasn't even like her father. He'd seen her with his family, with Pelipa, and her heart was genuine and good.

He had resented her, along with every other white, simply because of her birth and her upbringing— just as people judged him without knowing him. By her example, she'd shown him how to let the hurts of the past go and embrace the present.

He wasn't going to waste another minute that could be spent with her, loving her. Her silky, warm skin set him on fire. He stroked her arms and untied the flimsy garment that teased him by revealing the clear outline of her nipples.

He kissed her to keep the tension high, and her burning response assured him of her excitement.

He kissed the ivory skin that was revealed as together they peeled away the last of her clothing. The amulet hung between her breasts. He touched it once, leaned to place his nose in that valley and inhale her unique scent as well as the curious fragrance of the herbs.

He kissed her breast and straightened to fill his eyes. She was more beautiful than he'd ever dreamed. And she was his wife.

He kissed her lips, and she clung to him.

He touched her body, and she opened to him.

He loved her, heart and soul, and she responded with heat and sighs and silken tremors.

When at last they joined, she cried out, and he soothed her with kisses and tender words. She drew him closer then, and he made it up to her slowly, steadily, gently, until they lay boneless and sated, his fingers still whispering across her skin in lazy circles.

It took several minutes for the hiss of steam and the smell of coffee boiling over into the flames to get his attention. Kyle rose and used a towel to remove the pot.

He poured a mug and carried it to her, amused at the blush staining her cheeks. "Not much left."

She grinned and set the cup on the floor beside the bed. "We'll share."

He stretched out beside her, curling his body around hers and dangling the amulet over her chin

playfully. "Now you can't have our marriage can-
celed," he teased.

She went still and silent, a terrible, deafening silence he could hear.

His heart forgot to beat, and he neglected to
breathe. Had she forgotten her goal in a moment of
passion? Had she been planning to leave, after all?

She sat up so suddenly, her shoulder connected
with his jaw and slammed his teeth together. She
scooted toward the end of the bed and pulled a blanket up to cover her breasts. "Is that what this was
all about?"

Kyle leaned on one elbow, rubbed his jaw and
tried to detect her meaning. "What *what* was
about?"

Threading one side of her tousled hair back, she
glared at him, a frightening mixture of hurt and betrayal on her gentle features. Her lips were red and
puffy from their kisses; he still tasted her passion.

"This!" She jabbed a finger at the bed, at his
nakedness, but her attention stayed riveted on his
face, as if it hurt to read betrayal there, as if she
strained to read truth, hope. "You just made certain
that I couldn't go have our marriage annulled." Her
voice trembled on the words. "The Big Sky is yours
by all rights now."

Tears glimmered on her lashes.

He almost allowed anger to push rational thought
away. So this was how she trusted him. This was
what she thought of him. Her mistrust cut deep.

With his next heartbeat, he remembered how he hadn't trusted her until this very night. She had every reason to question his honor and intent, especially after the way he'd bullied and provoked her. Self-preservation was a strong instinct, and no one knew that better than he did.

Inside this beautiful woman, seeking acceptance, was the insecure child that her father had created.

"I can't say I'm sorry," he admitted. "We're legally bound now."

One silvery tear slid down her cheek and pierced his heart.

"I've made you my wife. For good."

Her transparent gray eyes revealed a touch of wonder and a cloud of disbelief. The fingers she brought to her lips trembled.

"I want you, Isabelle," he said, not remembering if he'd ever spoken her name aloud before and sorry if he hadn't. He loved the sound. If he lived to be an old man, he'd never tire of saying it. "I want you to stay with me. I need you to stay with me. I was afraid I'd lose you, so I tried not to love you."

"Kyle," she said with a shaky exhale.

"What's between us here is not about the ranch. It's about us." He leaned forward and took her hand away from her mouth. He looked at his big, rough hand holding her fragile one and felt something so pure and intense, it took a moment to form words. "*Nemehotatse*. I love you," he said at last.

Tears welled in her eyes, but a hopeful smile raised the corners of her lovely mouth. "Truly?"

How could he tell her so she would understand? So she would believe? So she would know in her heart? He brought her fingers to his lips and tasted the backs with a kiss. "I could live without the ranch," he said. "I could take the horses somewhere else and start over."

He took her other hand in his and caressed them both with his thumbs.

"But I couldn't go on without you. You are...like the rain that fills the rivers and the sun that makes things grow. That's what you are to me."

"Oh, Kyle!" She threw herself against him, and he caught her, rocked her as she sobbed against his neck. He let her cry out her relief and joy while newfound assurance blossomed in both their hearts. He understood her deep-seeded need for love and acceptance. He had lived too many years without. But no more.

The blanket had worked its way down until the only thing between them was the hard knot of the silver amulet. Isabelle had grown calm, and her fingers stroked the hair at his neck.

He cupped her shoulders and held her slightly away so he could see her. She gave him a watery smile.

They talked into the night, sharing their hopes and dreams, not only for the Big Sky, but dreams for them, and for a family. She restored his faith in people, in himself.

"I'd like you to take over the bookkeeping," he said at last.

She raised a brow.

"You're better at it than I am."

"All right, I'm convinced that you love me and trust me," she said.

The first real joy he could remember feeling welled in his chest.

"You're smiling!" She touched his cheek reverently. "I love you."

The words rang through him, filling him with emotion. This time, it was he who had tears in his eyes. Tears of happiness. Of love.

Epilogue

My Beloved Husband,

Each day grows longer and each night darker without you here to experience it with me.

This is not the way I wanted to tell you this, but I shall burst if I do not share this most blessed and joyful news. The gladness and fulfillment that our love yields is unceasing! Next spring, when the mountain streams flow and the countryside bursts with new life, we will bring a new life of our own into the world. We are going to have a baby.

I think of the day we were married, and how skeptical I was about how things would turn out, and it seems like a miracle that we've reached this beautiful turn of events. The only future I could see was to keep the ranch, and you were the answer to that. You turned out to be the answer to many things—things I knew deep inside I needed and wanted, but was too afraid to dream for. How grateful I am that your determination was as great as mine, how thankful that you suggested we combine resources to keep the ranch.

If someone had told me that day as I walked toward you, wearing my mother's Irish lace and quivering with trepidation, that I would love you as much as I do this day, I would have not believed it possible. Sometimes I wonder if Mac's amulet actually had anything to do with our love, but then I think that's foolish, too, so who can really know? All that matters is that our arrangement turned out to be so much more…and now we have made a child with whom to share our love.

I shall pray for your safe travel and ex-pedient journey home so that we may celebrate this new and exciting chapter to our lives in the proper manner.

. I remain as always,

              Your Devoted Wife, Isabelle

P.S. Your Aunt Mae says it's a son.

* * * * *

Look out for Cheryl St John's
THE MAGNIFICENT SEVEN
in February 2002.
It is the tenth book in our exciting
MONTANA BRIDES *series.*

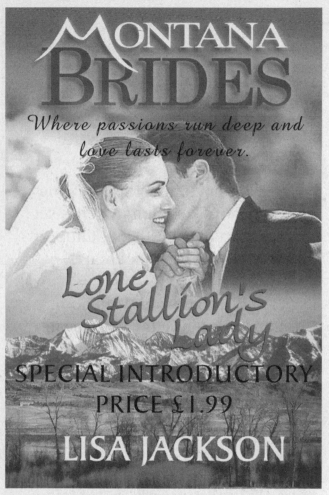

17th August 2001
Lone Stallion's Lady   By Lisa Jackson

21st September 2001
His Forever Bride   By Laurie Paige

You Belong To Me   By Jennifer Greene

19th October 2001
The Marriage Bargain   By Victoria Pade

Honourable Intentions   By Marilyn Pappano

16th November 2001
The Baby Quest   By Pat Warren

One Wedding Night   By Karen Hughes

21st December 2001
The Birth Mother   By Pamela Toth

Rich, Rugged…Ruthless   By Jennifer Mikels

18th January 2002
The Magnificent Seven   By Cheryl St. John

Outlaw Marriage   By Laurie Paige

15th February 2002
Nighthawk's Child   By Linda Turner

MONTANA BRIDES